You Are Mine

Detective Stella Carrigan Book 1

Lisa Kent

Lisa Kent

ISBN: 9798533670166

Author's note: This is a work of fiction. Some of the names and geographical locations in this book are products of the author's imagination, and do not necessarily correspond with reality.

"No tears in the writer, no tears in the reader. No surprise in the writer, no surprise in the reader."
— **Robert Frost**

TABLE OF CONTENTS

Chapter 1

The choking sound of the cappuccino maker snapped Henry out of his daydream. He managed to get his favorite seat at the window in the coffee shop and had drifted away in his mind as the people of Chicago passed by on their way to work or breakfast or the cash machine or wherever. It was a special day for Henry. Without anyone noticing he checked his appearance in his reflection in the window. For today's special occasion he'd bought a new shirt, just a simple gray Polo, and wore his favorite khakis that fit perfectly. Although he didn't need it, he wore his hiking boots as they made him just a pinch taller than his usual five-eleven. His coffee was lukewarm at best but still, he took a sip as he watched out the window. When he looked at his watch his heart skipped. Any minute now he was going to see her. Without thinking he smoothed his black hair back.

The coffeeshop was getting more and more crowded. The baristas shouted back and forth trying to be witty. They really just came across as annoying. People chatted loudly on their cell phones to make sure everyone knew their business, no matter how intimate. Coworkers flocked in together and laughed about the new temp in accounting or how working from home was a total possibility even in retail. Henry shook his head. Had he not been in such a good mood today he might have made a scene. He imagined himself in the center of the coffee shop taking one long deep breath and shouting at the top of his lungs for everyone to *shut the fuck up!* The thought made him chuckle.

Finally, there she was. Suddenly, all of Henry's lines, all the words he wanted to say, all the scenarios he'd rehearsed flew out of his head like pigeons scattering off the sidewalk. Still, he wasn't going to let that stop him. How many times had she walked past and all he did was watch?

"You've got this, Henry. She's been waiting for you," he muttered as he stood. In an almost panic he pushed his way roughly through the crowd of people and caught one last look at himself in the mirror by the door. He was looking good and felt invincible. If this was what the mere sight of her did for him, he could only imagine what he'd feel like when they were together.

Of course, you're going to have to dodge the guy with her. The voice. Henry knew it wasn't going to be quiet. Henry knew all about her friend. They walked together every day. They worked together for Pete's sake. That fellow was no threat at all. He was at least a couple inches shorter than Henry and although they had a similar build, Henry wasn't scared. Anyone can have a fit physique. But not everyone had the fire in their belly that Henry had. That had given, and would always give Henry the edge.

With his confidence renewed, Henry took off in pursuit. There were half a dozen people between himself and her. She looked so lovely. Today she was wearing those tight black slacks for work. Wasn't it funny that in his dreams when they finally talked, she was always wearing those? They weren't the slutty spandex pants that so many women wear. These were classy. She had on a gray sweater. It was a few shades lighter than his shirt. He took that as a sign. Today was the day.

Carefully, Henry stretched his legs to gain on her and her companion. He didn't want to suddenly appear behind her like some kind of weirdo. He wanted to slowly ease up to her like a luxury yacht inching into the dock. It was luck and Divine intervention that brought them together at a red light.

Henry's heart was pounding. In his mind, he knew that once she saw him, she'd feel the same thing for him that he felt for her. All he had to do was speak to her. The DON'T WALK sign was exactly what he needed to steel his nerves and interrupt her conversation with the man walking with her. Normally, Henry didn't care about him. But at the moment he was as annoying as a swarm of gnats at a picnic.

Just pretend he isn't there. This doesn't concern him, anyway.

Henry pushed his way through the people gathering at the corner waiting for the light to change and heard her beautiful voice.

"I know, Ben. But this guy thinks it's just fine I'm a cop. It's just ducky that I bust pervs and slime-balls for a living. It's totally cool that I sleep with my gun on the nightstand," she said.

"So, what is the problem, Stella? He sounds like a keeper," Ben replied.

"Something is the problem," Stella replied.

Henry felt like he'd been punched in the gut. What was she talking about? A guy? There had to be some kind of mistake. Stella wasn't supposed to be going out with any guy. She was supposed to be searching for him, even if she didn't know it yet. She was supposed to feel an emptiness, a longing late at night for the prince who she'd dreamed about as a young girl.

"Yeah, I know what it is," Ben replied cheerfully. "*You* are the problem.

"Come on," Stella huffed.

"It's true. Look, do you think it was easy for Rochelle and me to get together? I didn't know what I could tell her or couldn't tell her about my job. Being a cop is hard enough. Being a detective in our line of work is even harder. But she's still around, we have our new baby, and we're doing great," Ben said.

"I don't know, Ben," Stella shook her head. "Rochelle is special. I knew that the first time I met her. Especially if she can put up with you on a regular basis. Let alone when you're on a tough case."

"Very funny," Ben replied.

"But this guy is eager to hear about my job. Don't you find that strange?" Stella asked.

Henry clenched and unclenched his jaw. His hands were in tight fists as he listened to their conversation. This was an obstacle he hadn't planned on. How could she even consider going out with anyone else? Slowly, he inched up closer to her. He was close enough to run his hands through her black hair. If she would turn around Henry would gaze intently into her icy blue eyes and she would recognize him... maybe not immediately, but she would feel the pull from deep inside and would have no way of denying it.

"I've been looking for you," Henry imagined saying. She'd smile. She'd nod her head and say she knew that he'd find her eventually. They would talk playfully, dance around their mutual attraction until they could be behind closed doors. Then, Henry would take her, and she would respond with groans and screams of his name, holding him tightly in her arms while they made love, promising to never leave his side again.

"Oh, Stella. You didn't say the guy was eager to hear about your job," Ben replied while shaking his head. "Gosh, that can only mean one thing. That he wants to get to know you. Yikes. Run, girl. Run in the opposite direction."

"You are no help, Ben. None at all," Stella snapped.

Small black clouds of exhaust kicked out the tailpipe of a bus that lumbered slowly past followed by two cabs that hit the gas as the light turned yellow, honking to let any slow cars or fast pedestrians know they were not stopping. The click-click-click of a bicycle messenger also zoomed by. Henry could smell Stella's perfume. He was sure it was her that smelled like vanilla and a natural musk that only he recognized. It was intoxicating.

"Excuse me. Excuse me!" a bossy blonde man who stood about five-feet-tall pushed past Henry in an effort to cross the street. The light had changed. Stella and her partner had already reached the other side of the street. She was smirking as she talked and looked over her shoulder quickly in his direction.

Did she know he was there? Of course, she did. She could

sense him. He knew she could. This wasn't the end. This wasn't some kind of rejection. On the contrary, this was part of her game. She couldn't just throw herself at him. That would be what a whore did. No, Stella would never behave that way. She was a good girl. That was why she was having trouble going on a date. She didn't want to admit that she was waiting for Henry to return to her. Even if she wasn't completely aware of it. He would rescue her again. He would wait and see her again soon. And then he would reveal himself completely to her. She'd be so grateful, maybe she'd even cry with relief and desire as he took her.

Once she realized all he'd done for her she'd be unable to not return those three words, *I love you*. Henry watched as she continued on her way to work. She flipped her hair and he knew it was a signal to him, letting him know that she was aware he was still there watching her. After a couple of deep breaths, Henry unclenched his hands and smiled. Sometimes he was surprised at how playful she was. Of course, he was slightly disappointed that Stella had postponed their reunion but it was only so it would be more intense later. It was because she loved him that she toyed with him this way. It wasn't malicious. It couldn't be. Not her. She was probably as nervous as he was. He chuckled. He would have so much fun with her once they were united.

Chapter 2

Stella Carrigan took a sip of her margarita and tasted plenty of the fruity mix and very little tequila. That was what she needed to calm her nerves. She hadn't been this tense since she was a newbie at the police academy taking her psychological exam with the department head-shrinker. She was sure the doctor was going to find something wrong that he'd zero in on. Then she'd have no choice but to go ballistic, call him some choice names, and storm out to cry in private. That never happened. The exam went without a hitch.

Now, Stella looked across the table at her date, Cole Morris, who smiled and winked at her. It made her chuckle.

"Thanks for meeting me. You seemed a little nervous when I asked you. I was afraid I might get stood up," Cole said.

"I'm not nervous," Stella lied. "I bust up child sex rings and arrest wife beaters. As long as you don't have anything to do with that, I think we'll get along just fine." She took another sip, desperate for a little more alcohol. She didn't know what made her spill out such a crude description of her job. But, in a nutshell, it was what she did. Part of her wanted to see if her comment shocked Cole. So far, he was a very nice, polite man. There was no denying he was more than easy on the eyes with a jaw so chiseled it could slice a single piece of paper and a broad chest that would be perfect for resting her head on. But she couldn't turn the 'cop' inside her off, even for a second. She studied his face waiting to see him look nervously to the side. When he looked at her confidently, she counted how long he gazed into her eyes to see if he were trying to dominate her. It was like trying to read a book while at the same time an action movie was blaring from the television set. She couldn't concentrate on one or the other.

Stop it, Stella. The guy is nice. He was punctual. He's told you about his family. He's a veterinarian. If anything can tip you off if a guy can be trusted, it's how animals act around him. Obviously, he's good with animals. Stella blinked her eyes and refocused on what Cole was saying. It was something about the restaurant.

"I'm glad you like Mexican food. This is one of my favorite places. And not just for the margaritas," Cole raised his glass and took a sip.

Stella didn't want to admit to Cole that back at the Boss Bar on Lake Street, just a hop-skip-and-jump from the police station, she'd closed the place down drinking straight tequila after her first big bust. Sure, she paid for it with interest the next day but if he thought these margaritas were strong, she might be carrying him home after the date.

"It's very nice," Stella said as she looked around. Everything was decorated with the red, white, and green colors of the Mexican flag. It wasn't a fancy place but rather a hole in the wall tucked between a currency exchange and a beauty supply store. The smell of Mexican spices hit her from the sidewalk when she found the place and her stomach growled with approval... Until that moment she had been considering walking right by and going home. When she thought of that and looked at Cole, she was sure he read her thoughts.

"Okay. Let's clear the air a little," he leaned forward. Stella got a faint whiff of his cologne: a wonderfully spicy scent. He didn't smell like a criminal.

"Clear the air?"

"What's on your mind right now? Because something is in the way of you having a good time and if it's me, well, we can just have a nice meal and..." Cole sat back.

"No! No, it isn't you at all. It's me, for sure," Stella said quickly. "I haven't been on a date in a while. That's all. I don't even know what I'm supposed to do. I think the last time I went on a date the boy picked me up at my foster parent's house and took me to the movies and McDonalds."

"Well, I think I can top that," Cole chuckled.

"Funny. I work. I work all the time and sometimes I have a hard time shutting it off. That's not your fault," Stella said feeling her cheeks burn with embarrassment. "I'm sorry."

"Don't be sorry. I understand. Look, let's order some food and another round of drinks and just relax. No pressure," Cole said and waved to the waitress.

"I *am* starving," Stella said as she looked at the menu. When the waitress arrived, a short girl with dark skin and long, jet black hair braided to the middle of her back, Stella forgot her nerves and let her appetite take over. Pork and green chili verde sauce with a side of chicken tamales was enough to get her to sit through even the worst, most boring date.

"No beans," she added.

"That's very thoughtful of you," Cole teased, making Stella blush, shake her head, and chuckle. He ordered the same and refrained from beans as well.

"What are you, twelve?" Stella asked.

"I'm just trying to make you laugh a little. You have a pretty smile," Cole replied. "And I like your dress. No one would ever guess you bust child sex rings and wife beaters for a living."

You have a pretty everything, Stella thought but said nothing and instead took another sip of her margarita that was now nothing more than melting ice. Thankfully, the waitress was quick with the next round of drinks.

"Thank you for the compliment. The truth is I don't like beans. I don't know if it's an allergic reaction or what but ever since I can remember just the thought of them makes me ill. So, let's not pursue this conversation. Tell me more about my pretty smile or what you like about my dress," Stella said after a sip of her second margarita. This one definitely had more of a kick.

Cole laughed. He had a nice laugh and it definitely broke the ice. From there it became easier for Stella to relax. Cole came from a big family and ever since he was a kid he wanted to work with animals. He saved and studied and went to veterinary school. He worked with an old fellow who had been in Chicago for years and someday might retire.

"Every time I think he's going to pass the torch he tells me he's not ready yet. Gotta put a granddaughter through college or buy a piece of property in Florida," Cole shrugged. "But there are worse things in life."

"That's for sure," Stella replied.

"What about you? Why did you decide to join the Thin Blue Line?" Cole asked.

"I don't like people who hurt kids," she said as if she were telling Cole the weather. "I get off on roughing them up and dragging them to jail. Watching them cry when they realize what's going to happen once they are behind bars. I'm not trying to be gross or scare you. It's just the most honest answer I could give."

"I appreciate that. And I don't think you're gross or scary. Tough, yes. But not scary," Cole said just as their food arrived.

"This looks good—" Stella was interrupted by her cell phone. "I'm sorry."

"Justice never sleeps," Cole teased before taking a big bite of food.

"It's my partner," Stella said after seeing the familiar number. "I better take this."

"Of course," Cole said as he stood and gently pulled the table back for Stella to get up from her seat. He was very polite, and he was funny and he got better looking by the minute. But this was work and as soon as Stella turned from the table she was no longer on a date as Stella Carrigan. She was *Detective* Carrigan.

In the hallway near the ladies room was a small corridor with no foot traffic. Stella pressed a few buttons and speed-dialed her partner. It wasn't that she was glad he called but a short break from the date was exactly what she needed to focus and make sure neither the tequila nor Cole's deep, dark eyes altered her perception of the evening.

"How is your date going?" Detective Ben Carey asked. In the background, she heard some shouting, some papers rustling, and a whole lot of action.

"Fine. What's going on over there?" Stella asked.

"Nothing. A small altercation between a couple of junkies. *Just fine?*" Ben asked.

"Yeah. I mean, no. It's going...pretty well. Is that what you called for?" Stella flipped her hair over her shoulder as she was ready to give Ben a serious scolding for checking up on her like a big brother.

"No. That isn't why I called. We've got a new one. Just got the file on my desk," Ben said with a big sigh.

"What is it?"
"Homicide," Ben replied.

"How old?" Stella always braced herself for this detail. Since she primarily worked on cases that dealt with kids, she had learned early on that the more she knew upfront the easier it would be to get mad and not be overwhelmed with pity and depression.

"Female. Thirty-four years old. Found in a motel in

Vandalia, Illinois where she..."

"Vandalia? Why is she being given to us? Don't they have cops down there?" Stella grumbled. An adult in her thirties was probably going to turn out as some love triangle gone wrong as if they ever go right, or a case of being in the wrong place at the wrong time.

"I'm sure they do. But she has a home address here in Chicago. Our jurisdiction." Ben replied.

"She's a long way from home. That's about five hours away, isn't it?"
"Yeah. And we are expected there first thing in the morning," Ben added.

"Of course, we are."
"Since we'll have a long drive ahead of us, I'm hoping we can hit the road before the rooster crows. That's the only reason I called. There isn't anything we can do at this point. Go on and finish your date. You've kept him waiting long enough," Ben said.

"Yeah. I'll meet you at the station around four. You driving?" Stella asked.

"Yes, I'm driving. Let you take me to southern Illinois in that beat-up old jalopy you call a car? It doesn't even have a radio," Ben teased.

"What do we need a radio for when we've got stimulating conversation to whittle away the hours? Don't you have some new book on Babylonian architecture or the history of French cookware to share?" Stella replied.

"You're a riot. Hope your date likes sarcasm," Ben teased.

Stella had almost forgotten Cole was still sitting at the table waiting for her. She shook her head and flipped her hair behind her again. When she finally hung up with Ben, she wasn't sure what she should do. As much as she was pleasantly surprised by

Cole's behavior and the fact that the man did get better looking by the minute, a new case was like a siren's song. How was she supposed to concentrate? And what if things went *really* well and she had to get up early to meet Ben at the station? That was the oldest line in the book. Sorry, I've got a meeting early tomorrow so thanks for the roll in the hay but...to go box

Wait. Was she really thinking of a roll in the hay with Cole? Already? She could barely remember his last name. In fact, she didn't even think she knew his last name.

Stop beating yourself up. He's a good-looking guy. And he's obviously into you. Stay. Finish your meal and then tell him you have to go because you are leaving for Vandalia tomorrow. No harm ever came from making a man wait. That little voice inside was making a lot of sense. As she wove her way through the tables of patrons, Cole stood up and made room for her again.

"Is everything all right?" he asked.

"A new case just crossed my desk. My partner and I have got to go to Vandalia tomorrow," Stella said as she took her seat again.

"Vandalia? That's outside the Neutral Zone. How come you have to handle it?" Cole asked as he took his seat again.

"The Neutral Zone? That's funny," Stella smiled. "The victim was from Chicago."

"Was?" Cole asked.

"Yes. It's a homicide," Stella said as she looked at her food. Suddenly, her appetite for Mexican food was no longer there. Instead, she was desperate to know what the meat and potatoes of this new case were going to be.

"Do you need to go?" Cole asked before Stella could make up an excuse. As if a dead woman wasn't a good enough excuse.

"I think I better. I'm not going to be very good company with this on my mind," she said.

"I don't know about that," Cole winked again making Stella smirk as she blushed. He waved for the waitress again and apologized that something had come up and could they get a couple of to-go boxes. "You may as well take this with you to work. I don't think you'll get much done on an empty stomach."

"That's sweet," Stella replied. Those were the last words she'd expected to come out of her mouth on this date. She was so ready to dislike Cole. She was sure he'd have some kind of annoying tic, maybe a psycho girlfriend he couldn't stop talking about, or perhaps sometime during the course of the evening, he'd grow fangs and a tail. But he didn't. The jerk was not a jerk at all.

Chapter 3

Even though she told him not to, Cole insisted on walking Stella to her car. He carried the to-go boxes and before she slipped into behind the wheel, he put her on the spot and asked the worst question imaginable.

"I'd like to see you again," he said. "Maybe we could finish this date on another night? I'm free just about every evening, barring any unforeseen emergencies from my patients."

"Oh, I'm sure you've got a few admirers who will keep you busy," Stella wasn't sure why she said that and instantly regretted it but didn't apologize.

"Not really. I'm very particular," Cole replied and stepped closer to her. She inhaled the sweet smell of his cologne and had she been able to toss back one more tequila she would have fallen willingly into his arms. But unfortunately, she had her wits about her and extended her hand to shake.

"I had a really nice time," she said.

"Did you? Or are you just trying to let me down easy?" Cole asked. His hand was firm, and Stella was sure she felt a callous on his palm. She always thought a man with callouses on his hands was sexy. It meant he worked hard.

"I had a really nice time," Stella squeezed his hand. Before she could do anything, Cole leaned in and kissed her on the cheek. She inhaled the scent of his skin, felt the soft whisper of his breath next to her ear, and suddenly wished Ben hadn't called her. But he had. And there was a dead woman in Vandalia.

"I'll call you in a couple days?" Cole asked.

"Okay," Stella replied then got into her car that Ben called an old jalopy, started the engine, and slowly pulled out into the street with a wave good-bye.

After a couple of blocks, while waiting at a stoplight Stella looked in the rearview mirror at herself.

"There is something really wrong with you," she scolded before hitting the gas and speeding to the station.

When she stepped into the 18th Precinct on Chicago's southside the only thing that indicated she had been on a date was the fact she was wearing a dress. It was too late for her to change her clothes. She was instantly spotted at the front desk by Officers Meeks and Taylor. They looked her up and down, smiling as they buzzed her into the internal workings of the station. As soon as she stepped into the bullpen, she felt like she was under a spotlight. This part of the station was where the detectives had their desks and offices and there was never a shortage of uniformed cops milling around before they got their assignments or after they escorted some of Chicago's finest citizens to booking. As Stella walked through the catcalls commenced.

"Who's the lucky guy?" asked one of the uniformed officers on Stella's shift.

"None of your business, Jake," Stella snapped back.

"Did you bust him afterward?" another uniformed officer asked.

"Very funny, Rudy."

Just then Ben appeared from the office he shared with Stella. "What the hell are you doing here?"

"What do you mean?" Stella said innocently, batting her long black lashes that looked even longer with mascara on.

"Don't tell me you dumped your poor date to come here. I

told you we couldn't move on anything until early tomorrow," Ben said, rubbing his head in disbelief.

"It's okay. It wasn't that great of a date," Stella shrugged.

"I'll show you a good time, Detective," A big, burly cop named Hicks said as he passed by. It got him a punch in the arm before Stella disappeared into her office with Ben behind her.

"You said you were having a good time," Ben said once they were out of view of the entire night shift.

"I was but this is more important," Stella replied. "What have we got?" She took a seat behind her desk and looked for the new file. Ben picked up a flimsy folder and tossed it in front of her. She flipped it open. Inside was just the preliminary write up. The woman's name was Regina Phelps.

"I can't believe you left your date for this. There isn't a damn thing that can be done. In fact, it's so flimsy right now that I'm answering emails and returning phone calls. That's how uninteresting this new case is at this point."

Stella said nothing but pouted as she read the description of what had happened to the woman. It had been violent.

"This is a rage killing," Stella replied. Stabbed with something that may not be a knife? Sexual component to it, too. Plus, she was found nude. Any word if she was assaulted?"

"You know forensics. That will be about two days. She's at the coroner's office as we speak. Won't have anything until tomorrow. I'll bet if you call him your date will be happy to meet you again," Ben suggested.

"You've got to be kidding," Stella muttered.

"Okay. No use wasting that nice dress. You look great. Go out there and let a few guys fight over buying you a couple drinks," Ben shook his head.

"What is your obsession with me going out and getting drunk?" Stella said. "If I remember right, I'm the senior detective on this case, I outrank you. Maybe not by much but I do."

"You might outrank me in the office, but I outrank you in life. I'm the one who is married, remember? I found someone who understands me," Ben picked up the picture of his wife, Rochelle, holding the new baby they had adopted. "You don't get this if you don't take a couple of risks."

"I'm not looking to get married, Ben."

"Who said anything about getting married? You need to get laid," Ben huffed. "I never met a person more wound up than you. You are so uptight that you left a date to come and sit in this small office and study three pages of a new murder case."

"That's how I get them solved. I'm not like these other shlubs, Ben. I solve cases. I don't let them collect dust. No cold cases. That's my rule," Stella clicked her tongue as if Ben should have known this by now. They'd been partners for two years. Stella couldn't think of a better partner to have. No one in the 18th was more qualified or more decent to work with. In fact, the catcalls and comments made by the other officers was the most any of them had said to her in months.

Stella wasn't very sociable. She did get drunk with her team when she made her first bust. But when she continued to make bust after bust there wasn't as much of that camaraderie that she'd first experienced. It was okay to have beginner's luck. But to make a habit of showing up the seasoned detectives, well, that wasn't so kindly received. Often celebrating a bust meant going home with some take-out and enjoying a bottle of wine alone.

Stella's partner before Ben was a salty old geezer by the name of Gavin Halloway. He had been just two years away from retirement and had told Stella he wasn't taking any unnecessary risks to help her get her name in the papers. Stella learned what she could from him, but it was her own instincts, her own gut reactions that put her on the fast track to detective. Gavin didn't like it and he didn't like her. When he retired she didn't go to the party. She wasn't invited. Then, the same day she became detective news spread through the 18th that Gavin Halloway was dead. He got drunk and fell down a flight of stairs at a cabin he rented every summer where he went fishing. Her promotion was overshadowed by the stupidity of some old copper who couldn't maneuver the wooden steps of a cabin he went to for the past thirty years.

Stella had a small group of friends in her corner. Ben was the most outspoken one. He didn't care what anyone said about her using her looks to get where she was or that she'd slept her way to the position of Detective. That didn't explain her almost scary way of getting to the heart of cases and rooting out the bad guys like a honey-badger does beehives. She certainly sustained a number of stings over it.

"You don't have to tell me, Stella. I'm on your side, remember. But one thing I do know is that a cop who doesn't get away from it, even for just a couple hours, is eventually going to crash and burn," Ben replied as he took a seat at his desk and replacing the picture of his wife and son. They were quiet for a few minutes before Stella spoke again.

"You hungry? Cole got the food to go. Mexican," she held up the carry-out bag.

Ben's eyes lit up. "You're not hungry?"

"I might have a taste," she replied.

Ben pulled out a couple of paper plates and plastic forks from his desk. It was almost a ritual that they ate like this at least twice a week. They split the leftovers as they worked quietly completing paperwork that never seemed to end, answering emails and returning calls. Both of them had stacks of folders on their desks of files that were closed, files that needed signatures, files that hadn't been looked at yet. Those piles, like the other bits of paperwork, never seemed to go down either.

"This is some damn good Mexican. Where did you go?" Ben asked.

"I don't know. Some hole-in-the-wall on Wells Street. Under the "L"," Stella replied with a mouthful.

"Did you taste this before you left? Damn. You would have had to drag me out of there," Ben said before wiping his lips with a napkin.

"I'll tell Cole next time to take you," Stella joked. "Any idea why our victim was in Vandalia?"
"What victim?" Ben asked.

"Come on, Carey. Get your head in the game," Stella said as she waved the new file.

"Are you kidding? The body hasn't even cooled yet, Carrington. Give it a rest until tomorrow. You need to relax."

"I'm relaxed," she snapped.

"Have you tried those hypnosis CDs I gave you?" Ben threw his paper plate in the garbage after eating every morsel, wiped his mouth again, and then stared at his partner.

"No. I did not. But it is on my list of things to do after a fun trip to the dentist and standing a couple hours in line at the DMV," she replied without looking up.

"Stella, do you ever stop to think that your mental well-being is just as important to me as it is to you? If my partner isn't operating at her full mental capacity due to stress or sexual frustration it could have a negative impact on her judgment as well as her reflexes. Do you want me to die, Stella? Is that it?" Ben folded his arms across his chest. He was fit but not as brawny as Cole was.

"At the moment...?" she stared at him.

"That's it. I'll put in for my transfer," Ben whined.

"You've been saying that for two years. If you can find another detective that wants you as partner go for it," Stella replied making Ben chuckle. She liked to see him laugh. And she certainly didn't want him to ever think she was in such a bad way as to put his life in jeopardy. "I'll listen to your hypnosis CDs. I promise."

"Promise?" Ben pushed.

"Cross my heart. I promise," Stella replied.

Ben let out a deep sigh and stood from his desk. "You won't be sorry. I'm not saying they'll help your dating life. I don't think there's anything that will do that. But it clears your head. Helps you sleep."

"Got it," Stella smiled.

Once Ben left for the rest of the night, Stella closed her office door and began researching her victim. The woman's name was Regina Phelps. There were seven of them listed on social media but only one in Chicago. There was nothing out of the ordinary on her Facebook page. She didn't come across as one of those people who posted every bowel movement or hangnail they ever had for all the world to see. There was very little real activity. Most of her page consisted of other people tagging her with their bowel movements and hangnails. Nothing controversial or threatening. No cryptic messages or strange followers that she could see. And nothing that would indicate why Regina was going so far south.

When she looked at her watch, it was almost ten o'clock. If she was going to be worth anything tomorrow Stella had to call it a night. Luckily, her apartment was less than ten minutes away.

She didn't live in the greatest part of town. Her address on

North Winthrop was known for cheap rent and frequent turnaround of tenants. But it wasn't the worst part of town, either. When she got through the front glass door then the second locked glass door and to the elevator that required a key, and finally to her apartment that required several keys to get in, she felt safe and sound.

Her apartment was a good size for just one person. Two bedrooms and a big kitchen made it more than enough space for just her. She slept on a full-sized bed. Her furniture was mostly second hand either from the Good Will or found in an alley somewhere. Nothing matched but since she rarely entertained, she didn't care. Ben had come to her apartment once when she was out sick with walking pneumonia. His wife had made her some chicken soup and he delivered it along with a couple of files she requested from work. He commented on her reading material.

"Do you know something I don't?" he asked holding up a copy of her favorite magazine, *Preppers*. It was a survivalist magazine that gave excellent tips for surviving the Big Bad if and when it happened. Stella couldn't help it. Something about living in the city had hardened her to the elements around her. It wasn't surviving the concrete jungle that made her nervous. It was surviving out in the woods, in nature, that gave her the jitters. Of course, in her eyes, the key to any survival technique was superior firepower and she had that. She also read *American Survivalist, Off the Grid,* and *Bug Out.*

Just as she slapped all of the door locks in place Stella heard scratching on her front room window. The fire escape was just on the other side of the thin pane of glass. And although Stella had her weapon and was sure the ladder was high enough off the sidewalk to prevent anyone from climbing up, she took no chances. Even on the cool evenings like this one, her window would stay closed when she slept. But the scratching persisted and was all too familiar.

With the lights still off Stella went and pulled the curtains open. There, sitting pretty on the milk crate Stella used as a seat was Cleopatra.

"Cleo, I just got home," Stella said as she unlocked the latch and removed the thick dowel that braced the window shut. The black cat meowed her disapproval through the glass. As soon as Stella opened the window the cat slinked inside nearly pushing her out of the way. It was a cool night in the city. The sound of honking horns and the elevated train going by was like a comforting symphony. The gritty feel of the fire escape railing was cold on her hands as Stella pulled herself out and took a seat on the milk crate. There was nothing exciting going on in any of her neighboring apartments across the alley. Down below an occasional car drove through but right now it was empty.

"You kidnapped my cat again didn't you, Stella?" came the voice of her neighbor through his open window.

"No, Mr. Zarowny. Cleo was waiting for me. I told you if you didn't want her visiting you shouldn't leave your window open." Stella replied.

"Oh, I'm just fine. Thanks for asking. I'm only blind and in a wheelchair! Your manners are impeccable," Mr. Zarowny snapped back making Stella chuckle.

"Are you still whining about that? You'd think you would have gotten over it by now." Stella replied. She could hear Mr. Zarowny giggling inside his house. He really was in a wheelchair and was as blind as a bat. But he was anything but helpless. With a pistol under his hemorrhoid cushion and a canister of florescent orange pepper spray at his side plus a row of no less than eight locks on his front door, no one was going to have an easy time trying to rob the old man. Having a cop next door was also a perk.

"Did I tell you that I donated to the Fraternal Order of Police last month?" Mr. Zarowny shouted.

"You didn't. Thank you, Mr. Zarowny."

"Maybe now you'll give me my cat back!" he shouted.

"I'm not keeping her here. She probably just wants to be around a pleasant person for a change," Stella laughed.

"Cleo!" Mr. Zarowny called. Like the Pied Piper of cats, Cleopatra emerged from the bathroom at the sound of his voice. Effortlessly and silently she hopped up on the windowsill. Stella stroked the cat, feeling her motor running as she purred contentedly.

"Mr. Zarowny, do you need anything from the store? I've got a new case. I might be hard to get hold of for the next couple of days," Stella asked as she leaned closer to Mr. Zarowny's window.

"No, Stella. I'm good. The last time you went you bought enough food for Coxy's Army," Mr. Zarowny replied.

"Whose army?"
"Oh, dear. Didn't they teach you anything at the Police Academy? You can't just get by on your looks, Stella," Mr. Zarowny needled.

"Yeah, they taught me how to protect myself from grouchy old men. Sorry," Stella clicked her tongue and shook her head.

"Next time you come visit I'll tell you about Coxy's Army," he replied. "Cle-o!"

"It's a date."
"Speaking of dates, didn't you say you had a date coming up?" Mr. Zarowny asked.

"Yeah, that was tonight," Stella sighed.

"It didn't go well? You scared another one away, huh?" Mr. Zarowny replied.

"No, smart guy! I got called to work." It wasn't a total lie. Just a little white one.

"Oh. Well. Better luck next time," Mr. Zarowny soothed.

Finally, the black cat daintily stepped from the fire escape platform to Mr. Zarowny's windowsill. She let out a big meow to let him know she was there.

"Good night, Mr. Zarowny. Don't stay up too late," Stella called.

"Good night, Stella," Mr. Zarowny replied.

Stella sat for a few moments just letting the residue of the day fall off. She had looked forward to her date with Cole, even if she didn't tell anyone she did. Part of her wished that she had stayed to see how things turned out. But if she had found out about the case and having to leave early tomorrow after she'd had a few more drinks it would have really ruined the evening. What if she were having a really fun time with Cole? What if things took a romantic turn and...what if Regina Phelps had been found an hour earlier. Stella wouldn't have made even part of her date. The funny thing was that she would have liked to sit and daydream about Cole and seeing him again. But a switch had been thrown and now she knew about going to Vandalia she couldn't, wouldn't focus on anything else.

She snapped off the lamp and got undressed in the dark. A shower was the only plan she had and once underneath the hot running water, she was able to force Cole to the back of her mind and concentrate on Regina Phelps. Ben was right that there wasn't much to go on. This was going to be a fun one. If any of her murder investigations could be called fun. At this stage she was almost positive she'd be dealing with a love triangle gone wrong (as if they ever go right).

With her hair still wet after her shower, she slipped into baggy shorts and a t-shirt and climbed into bed. Her sheets were crisp and white and smelled of the spring-scented detergent she used. She loved fresh linens. Ever since she could remember, the thought of having dirty sheets and pillowcases made her cringe. After making love for the first time when she was seventeen, she asked her high school lover if they needed to wash the bed linens right away. He told her no and she was okay with that. But the next time they met for a tryst and Stella saw the same sheets on his single bed with a tan-colored bedspread she insisted he change the sheets first. A guy will do just about anything for a roll in the hay.

She snuggled into her sheets and within minutes was asleep. Before the sun came up her eyes popped open. It was three-thirty in the morning. Time to get up.

Chapter 4

Vandalia, Illinois looked like a town plucked out of an old episode of *The Andy Griffith Show*. There was a row of life in the middle of town with a twenty-four-hour laundromat, a gas station/convenience store was also twenty-four-hours so no one would be deprived of late-night beer or toilet paper. On the higher end of things, there were several antique shops surrounding a bank, a women's clothing boutique, and a nail salon. Then there was a greasy spoon called Blueberry's and several bars in a row.

"At least we know where to get a drink," Ben said as Stella just started to wake up. "Thanks for sleeping the whole trip. I could have used a little conversation."

"I can't help it. Driving in your wife's car is like being lulled to sleep. It has butt warmers, Ben. That's luxury at its finest," Stella said before she stretched and yawned. "Besides, since when do I need to be awake for you to talk?"

"You're a riot. Okay, I'm looking for Locust Street. There's supposed to be a motel there," Ben said. They drove a short way past the center of town and several rows of country houses that might not have been ready for the cover of *Better Homes & Gardens* but were lovely none-the-less.

They drove over a railroad crossing that supported several forlorn and graffitied cars that appeared to have rusted to the track. A couple of grain silos could be seen in the distance.

"It's almost like another planet," Stella muttered.

"I could get used to this," Ben said.

"Really? Do tell," Stella said as she shifted in her seat.

"Country living? That's where it's at. Fresh air. Simple folks. Everyone knows everyone. The worst I'd have to deal with is a local drunk or two, maybe some kids vandalizing the high school. My kid could play in the front yard without worrying about anyone shooting or speeding by. I'd cut the grass every Saturday. Rochelle would hang the laundry on a clothesline in the summer," Ben mused.

"You make it sound pretty good. Just throw in a murder every ten to fifteen years to keep it exciting," Stella smirked making Ben smile and nod his head.

"See? You get it,"

"Aha. Locust Street," Stella pointed. They turned right. Within minutes they were in front of the Open Plaines Motel. The vacancy light was bright even in the daytime. She'd heard what Ben was saying and at first, it might sound nice. But she worked in the city. She lived in the city. There was always someone around. Even though she enjoyed her solitude, Stella would feel claustrophobic in a town like Vandalia if she had to reside here for any real length of time. Too many vacant spots and wide, open spaces. Of course, that was in direct contradiction to her doomsday prepping hobby. She wasn't exactly prepping. But she loved to read about those who did. She rubbed elbows with a couple of people who lived the life. At the gun range, all Stella had to do was throw a stone and she'd clunk a prepper. Still, the idea of planting stakes in a place like Vandalia didn't sit well. She was still too comfortable in the bustle of the city.

She and Ben got rooms next to each other at the motel. Stella's room had a strong smell of lemon cleaner. She opened the curtains. The windows were clean aside from a couple of dead flies on the sill. The bedspread was a simple navy-blue quilt. The carpet was dark brown. The sheets were white and clean as were the towels in the bathroom. There were a few rust stains around the sink and tub faucet but nothing she didn't have in her own apartment back home. Instead of bottles of shampoo and wrapped bars of soap, there were bright blue packets labeled LessWet. Stella picked one up and read the description.

"Get clean with less water. Smell great. Conserve water. Save the planet." She rolled her eyes. When she stepped out of the bathroom Stella thought the room was nice. If she'd come in this room armed with luminol and a black light she'd probably be blinded by the glow of trace elements from various samples of DNA. But, thankfully, she wasn't a germaphobe.

She dropped her overnight bag on the bed and decided she'd unpack later. She wanted to get started. As if he was reading her mind, Ben knocked on the door.

"Should we go to the police station?" he held up his cell phone.

"Yes," Stella replied before she grabbed her key and stuffed it in the back pocket of her pants. She let Ben drive and took in the scenery of the little town in southern Illinois. There were no apparent closed-circuit television cameras on any corners or outside any businesses. Even the bank was just sitting there. It made Stella wonder if the residents of this pretty little town even locked their doors at night.

Even the police station was without a watchful eye. The stark white building looked more like a church than a police station. Stella could see why they requested the help of two Chicago detectives. The building had lovely manicured shrubs. Cute black shutters flanked each window. The police car parked in front of the building was spotless.

"Jeez, is that a *new* cop car? It looks like it's never been driven," Ben said.

"This is the cleanest police department I've ever seen," Stella replied. "I think I'm underdressed."

The Chicago detectives parked and walked up the sidewalk. The birds were tweeting. Bees were buzzing. The sun was shining.

It was a pleasant day except that they were there to discuss the murder of a young woman.

An older woman with bright red hair and bright blue eyeshadow looked up from behind the big counter that was her desk. There was no bulletproof glass or plexiglass between her and anyone who would enter the building. Behind her was a door with a keycode lock on it. A window showed a couple of desks, a folding table with a coffee machine, and Styrofoam cups stacked along the side of it. There was no other movement inside the building. It was obvious by the way she looked at Stella and Ben, taking note that Stella wore black slacks and a matching jacket and Ben a thin suit with a loose tie that she wasn't used to seeing strangers.

"Good morning," she chirped. "Can I help you?"

"I'm Detective Stella Carrigan. This is Detective Ben Carey. We're here to talk to Sheriff Darlow." Stella watched the woman as she picked up the black phone on her desk.

"May I tell him what this is regarding?" the receptionist asked without looking at Stella.

"The murder victim in your cooler," Stella replied.

Instead of repeating what Stella said, the receptionist told her and Ben to have a seat. In a hushed voice, she called the sheriff. With a matter of seconds, he came through the door with the key code lock on it looking jittery. He nervously shook their hands and after quick introductions and small talk about the drive from Chicago, he led them to the back of the station. There was one uniformed officer sitting at his desk reading the paper. The other two desks were empty. A young man in plain clothes was in a small cubby hole lined with file cabinets slipping manila folders inside.

"I'm not even sure where to start with all this," Sheriff Darlow said. He wore blue jeans and a brown shirt with his badge and name tag attached over the right breast pocket. Stella thought he looked like any guy who might be shopping at a Lowes or Menards for stuff to kill the weeds in his yard or a ceiling fan he might install in his kitchen. A simple gold band was around his left ring finger.

"How about at the beginning? Can you tell us how she was found and by who?" Stella asked. She watched Darlow's eyes bounce from her to Ben as if she wasn't supposed to be doing all the talking. Stella picked up on it and cleared her throat. Some things didn't change. The longer she was on the force the more Stella realized that.

"Sally Greene works at the Washington Motel and has been there for as long as I can remember. She's the housekeeper. There are only twelve units to the place. We went to high school together," Sheriff Darlow nodded his head as he took a seat behind a plain metal desk. Ben walked over to the window and looked out. Stella took a seat in front of the sheriff's desk, took out a small, leather-bound journal and began to take notes.

"They don't get too much action at that place. Not many visitors in Vandalia looking for a room to stay in. Strangers in town are usually here to stay with family." The sheriff cleared his throat. "Anyway, she was making her usual rounds to the rooms and noticed one of them had been occupied when no one had checked in."

"Sheriff, how many motels are in this town?" Stella asked.

"Two. Not the one you are staying in. Why?" Sheriff Darlow asked.
"How do you know where we're staying?" Stella asked without flinching.

"Word of new people in town spreads fast," Sheriff Darlow smirked.

"Not fast enough or someone would have spotted our perpetrator and victim before they were either one, right?" Stella snapped back without thinking.

Sheriff Darlow's smirk quickly fell off his face. He cleared his throat. "The Open Plaines Motel is the only regular pay-by-the-day place. The Washington Motel is the only place in town that charges by the hour, day, week, or month. Forgive me but I didn't think you guys would be bed and breakfast types," Sheriff Darlow shrugged. Stella thought it was a good observation but said nothing more and only nodded for him to continue.

"Well, at first she thought that there were just some kids pulling a prank. Sometimes they play hooky from school and sneak into a room at the Washington Motel to smoke pot or screw around. When Sally looked into the room, she thought there was a mannequin in the bed."

Stella wrote in her notebook and hated to admit how many times she'd heard a person say they thought they were looking at a mannequin when it turned out to be a real person. The eyes aren't supposed to see things like that, a dead body, usually nude, in an unnatural setting like an alley or a field or in a cheap motel. That's why the mind says no at first. It has to be a mannequin in an equally unnatural setting. Then reality hits.

"Well, she left her cleaning supplies outside the door to get a closer look. According to her she almost peed in her pants when she saw it was a real person. The wounds she couldn't even describe. She shut the door without touching anything. Then ran to the office where she told the guy on duty what she found. She stayed there until Deputy Winger showed up." The sheriff scratched his cheek like he was thinking. "We haven't had a murder in this town in over thirty years," he mused.

"Really? And what was that about?" Ben asked. Stella could tell by the sound of his voice that he was concerned this might be the return of a killer who had been here before.

"A woman playing both sides of the coin. She left an abusive boyfriend for another man. When the boyfriend found out where she was and who she was with he went to "talk" to her." The sheriff used air quotes and Stella and Ben understood those were probably the words the killer used when he confessed.

"Let me guess. Things got out of hand and the next thing they realized one of them was dead," Stella said.

"You got it. The woman was shot five times at close range with two bullets in the back of her head. The boyfriend confessed after he was found hiding under an overpass three towns over. The whole thing was wrapped up in less than a week. I don't see that happening with this case," Sheriff Darlow said.

"Can we see the body of our victim?" Stella asked.

"Yes. It's at the coroner's office. That's just across the parking lot. Do you mind a walk?" Sheriff Darlow asked.

"Not at all," Stella stood and straightened her slacks while flipping her hair behind her shoulders. She closed her notebook and tucked it under her arm as she noted some of the things in the sheriff's office. He had a picture on his desk of a woman and three young boys she assumed was his family. On a slightly crooked shelf, she saw two awards for outstanding work with the sheriff's name on them. His desk wasn't cluttered with files and scraps of paper scribbled on with notes that only made sense to their author. His inbox was empty. His outbox had only two pieces of thin paper in it. There was a ledger with numbers in it that Stella assumed was some kind of record of petty cash. Next to the door was a corkboard with a couple of newspaper clippings from the local paper tacked to it. If Stella hadn't known she was at the police department she could have mistaken the office for a high school principal's.

The sheriff held the door open for Stella and Ben and pointed across the parking lot to a simple, square, red brick building with no visible windows. They walked across the parking lot that was dark black asphalt with sharp yellow lines for the police cruisers to park between. In addition to the car in front of the building, there was room for six more police cars. A civilian's automobile was parked in one space and Stella was willing to guess that was the receptionist's car. The other spaces were empty. The whole force was out on the street.

They cut through some grass and instead of going in through the front door Sheriff Darlow pounded on a heavy metal back door. Within seconds it opened.

"Trying to wake the dead, Sheriff?" a woman about five feet tall with blue rubber gloves on her hands opened the door.

"Christine Lustyk, this is Detective Carrigan and Detective Carey," the sheriff said as he once again held the door open.

Christine pulled off one glove and offered her hand. "Come to see our newest guest?"

"Something like that," Stella replied.

"Follow me," Christine said before turning back into the dark hallway. It smelled not unlike the motel room Stella was staying in. Very sterile and clean but no hint of lemon. Just the intense cleaning product smell—The kind of strong chemicals that would give a person a headache if they were exposed to them too long.

The building was even smaller on the inside than it was on the outside. It looked like a doctor's office. Stella half expected there to be a few people sitting in the waiting area reading old magazines or watching some crappy talk show on a television mounted to the wall.

Just then a man dressed similarly to Sheriff Darlow emerged from behind a red door that read Authorized Personnel Only. He was about ten years younger than Sheriff Darlow putting him closer to Stella's age. He wasted no time making an impression.

"So, you're the cops from the city?" He looked Stella and

Ben up and down.

"Detective Carrigan. Detective Carey. This is Deputy Clarence Winger," the sheriff said sounding as if he were tired of saying those words.

Stella stretched out her hand but got nothing but a chuckle from the deputy in return. Stella wasted no more time on the deputy.

"Ms. Lustyk. Can we see the body?" Stella asked politely.

"This way, Detective," Christine said when she pushed past the deputy and held the red door for Stella and Ben. The room was crowded with everyone in it, so the sheriff hung back. Stella saw through the small window he was speaking firmly with the deputy.

Without giving it another thought, she turned and looked at the body covered with a sheet on the long silver table. It looked like all the other bodies Stella had ever seen. Stella looked around the room and thought it looked like an oversized janitor's closet. There was an old sink in the corner. A tall ugly olive-colored locker that was slightly open and revealed white towels, cotton balls, tongue depressors, metal bowls, and plastic bags. A long counter no different from one at a diner lined the far wall, empty except for a spread of sharp tools on a light blue piece of sterile paper. They were all covered with drying blood from the victim.

"I've never seen anything like this," Christine said. "There hasn't been a member of the community come through my office who hadn't died of natural causes in a long while. I've been lucky. A car accident, maybe three in the past five years. One child who died of an allergic reaction to peanuts. That was hard but I understood what happened. This I can't understand."

She pulled the sheet back to reveal the blue, naked body of Regina Phelps. She had a lovely figure. A braid tattoo around her right ankle. Manicured nails. Hair dyed blonde, but the roots were dark. Then there were the wounds. Stella lost track of the stab wounds after she counted thirteen including the one to her left eye. Her face was bruised. She'd also been beaten about the head, probably in an attempt to subdue her.

"She was stabbed about twenty-two times. It's hard for me to have an exact number as it seemed her assailant stabbed her more than once in the same spots. There was a fight, but it didn't seem to last very long as there aren't enough defensive wounds. The wound to her face punctured her brain. That was the one that killed her," Christine said.

"Can we see the file?" Ben asked.

"The deputy was the last to have it," Christine said almost apologetically.

Before Stella could say anything, Ben put his hand up, nodded his head, and left the room to ask the deputy for the file.

"How long do you think she was dead before she was found?" Stella asked as she looked at the body.

"Based on the pooling of the blood I'd guess she was left there about six hours. Whoever did this would have been covered with blood," Christine said. "Our victim was soaked. So it's my amateur guess that whoever did this left quickly afterward before the sun came up. I took her temp. She was below room temperature which also made me think she was in a colder place before she was finally brought here. I was told the heat wasn't turned on in the rooms until someone checks in. So, that is probably the cause of a low temp."

"May I?" Stella pointed to a box of rubber gloves.

"Help yourself," Christine replied.

Stella snapped on the blue latex gloves and leaned over the body to inspect the wounds. "These are strange puncture wounds. They are kind of ragged. What do you think made these marks?"

"I thought that too. These thin punctures were definitely made by the blade of a knife. But for these others, I think the assailant used a crowbar. See this wound?" Christine pointed to a mark on Regina's arm. It was more of a scratch but there was a "v" marking in the middle like the thin space in the flat end of a crowbar. Stella concurred. There was nothing else that she could think of that made such a mark. There were a lot of scratches like Regina had been rocking or moving back and forth not allowing her assailant to get a good lick in until he'd had enough and struck her through the eye.

"Whoever got hold of her tried to strangle her. She's got ligature marks on her throat, but she died due to...well, you can see her eye is missing," Christine pointed to Regina's throat and Stella saw the rope burns on the cold, gray skin.

"Any sexual assault?" Stella had to ask.

"No," Christine replied with relief.

"A killing like this with an object like a knife, or in this case a crowbar, is very personal. Intimate, even. In the mind of the killer he's right on top of her and has total control," Stella said. "He probably can't function normally. This is as close as he'll get to real sex with a woman."

"There was also this," Christine turned and pulled a baggy marked as evidence from the silver table behind her. "It was around her face."

Stella took the plastic bag and looked at the contents. It was a black piece of cloth. Stella pouted but had no thought about it at the moment. In fact, her mind had paused.

"Around her face?" Stella stared at the evidence feeling a rush of shivers run up her arms from it. "Bondage? Some kinky game gone wrong? People get aroused by the strangest things."

Christine shook her head. "Look, I don't know what the sheriff has told you, but we aren't equipped to handle something like this. I, for one, am glad you guys are here. We're simple country folk here. Not dumb. Don't get me wrong. But we live here to avoid things like this. I don't think there's a person in town who will be able to wrap their head around what has happened."

"Except the person who did it," Stella said as she looked at the body. She liked Christine. There was a down to earth quality about her that made Stella feel she might be a kindred spirit in some ways. Being a woman coroner in a small town like Vandalia was probably not much different in its challenges as a woman detective thrown into the mix at the 18th precinct in Chicago.

Just then Ben came back in holding Regina Phelps file and shaking his head.

"Everything okay?" Stella asked.

"Yeah. Just a little local po-po drama. You know how it can be. Big city coppers infringing on the local lawman's authority," Ben replied before he looked at Christine. "Pardon me. I know you all probably went to school together all your lives.

"Was it Sheriff Darlow?" Stella asked.

"No. Deputy Dog," Ben muttered as he read the file and got most of what Christine had said to Stella as well as the photos of the body and where it was found.

"Deputy Winger was born with a burr in his side," Christine said. "He doesn't like anyone, and the feeling is pretty much mutual. Don't let him get under your skin."

"Christine, can you excuse us for a few minutes?" Stella asked as she carefully took the file from Ben.

"Of course, detective. Take your time," Christine replied pleasantly and walked out to join the sheriff and deputy and to get herself a cup of coffee.

Ben looked over the body as Stella read the file and looked

at the pictures of the crime scene. Regina didn't even look like the body on the table. Her hair was matted by the amount of blood. Her face had been a pretty one. But this was distorted and swollen from the beating and ultimately being stabbed. Stella was sure the body was placed in this position to get someone's attention. That was a bad sign. Murdering attention whores were the worst. Just as she was about to hand the file back to Ben, Stella saw something in the pictures that made her stop and hold her breath. She didn't even realize she was holding her breath until she went to speak.

"We've got something here," she said staring at the glossy image before it slipped to the floor. When she picked it up and looked at it, she froze.

"What is it?" Ben asked. "Stella?"

She swallowed hard as she looked at the picture. There was something there like she was looking at the image of a UFO and was trying to find the strings or the telltale airplane landing lights or the cutout line that proved it was a fake. But they weren't there. Something was familiar about this picture, but Stella couldn't put her finger on it. No. She wouldn't put her finger on it because if she did it might open up a casket she wouldn't be able to shut again.

"Here. Sit down," Ben said as he grabbed a metal stool tucked underneath the counter. Stella took a seat but shook off Ben's concern.

"I didn't have anything to eat this morning. Not even coffee. Sometimes I'm just stupid and forget my body needs fuel. Let's get some breakfast after this. We'll stop in that diner. Maybe find out a thing or two," Stella said, honestly believing her own line that she was just hungry, even though her gut knew that wasn't true. There was something about the black cloth around the victim's eyes that was too familiar.

Chapter 5

They drove to the Washington Motel and when they both walked into the office the young man behind the counter looked at them suspiciously. Both Stella and Ben produced their badges causing the man to suddenly shed his attitude and become more accommodating as they introduced themselves.

"What's your name, son?" Ben asked.

"Latham Green. I'm not the owner. He's in the back. I'll get him," Latham said. He was twitchy and his Adam's apple bobbed wildly when he swallowed. Stella thought he looked like he could use a cheeseburger or maybe a steak to put a little meat on his bones. A strong wind could blow him over and Stella didn't know why an owner would put such a guy at the front desk. He looked scared of his own shadow.

Meanwhile, the actual owner of the place was a man as wide as he was tall with a black comb-over and stubble. "Let me guess. You are here about the body?"

"You are the owner?" Stella stepped up and asked the man. She saw a United States Marine Corps tattoo on his forearm.

"Ed Nepal." His dark eyes studied the detectives as much as they were studying him. After quick introductions, Stella took out the picture of Regina Phelps that was a copy of her driver's license, and held it up to Ed and Latham.

"This is the woman found in your motel. Regina Phelps. Do you recall seeing her here anytime during the past couple of days or at any time before?" Stella asked and watched as both men looked at the picture.

"Nope. She doesn't look familiar," said Ed Nepal. "No one new checked in yesterday."

"You're sure? You don't need to look at your register or anything?" Ben asked.

"Look, I deal in cash only. Some people pay for the week. Others pay by the hour if you catch my meaning." Ed replied. "This ain't the Four Seasons."

"I didn't think it was. But this woman had to check in here. One of you saw her or does someone else handle check-ins?" Ben asked as Stella looked around the office. It was a typical cheap motel office. Shag carpet dating back to the Carter Era covered the floor and held the smell of cigarette smoke from the days smoking indoors wasn't a crime. The walls were wood-paneled. There was one painting of a landscape of mountains and a lake that Stella was pretty sure was not located in Vandalia. There was no computer to check-in. No credit card swiper. But there was a camera pointing to the counter.

"You've got cameras. Mind if we take a look at the tapes?"

Ed shook his head slowly. "They are just for show. They don't work. It would cost a lot of money to have surveillance videos running all the time. I'd do better to collect insurance if something happened," Ed sniffled and looked at Stella then Ben as if he were some kind of economic genius. "I don't know if you are aware of this but people who come to the Washington usually don't want anyone to know they are spending a few hours here. The regulars slip their payments under the door and it's all cash."

"We might need to talk to some of them. Can you give us the names and room numbers of folks that are your permanent residents?" Stella asked.

Ed nodded and grabbed a piece of paper and a pen. He didn't seem all that concerned that a woman was found dead in his motel and proceeded to write from memory the regulars in his facility.

"I understand that it was your regular cleaning lady who found the body. Is she here?" Stella asked.

"She'll be back. She went to the store to get some more cleaning supplies," Ed said.

Ben tapped Stella on the arm and jerked his head toward the door. "This place only has twelve units. I'd like to get a look at the room, too. The Sheriff said it was secured."

"We'll need the key to the room Regina was found in," Ben called to Ed. As if he was asked to pull out all receipts from the year 1990 through today, Ed looked at Ben, rolled his eyes, and muttered something in his native language that no one understood yet everyone got the gist of. He pulled the key off a shelf where it had been sitting by itself and handed it to Ben. He and Stella walked out into the parking lot and the smell of asphalt and someone burning leaves somewhere relieved them from the stale smell of the lobby.

The motel room where Regina Phelps was found was across the almost empty parking lot at the very end of the row. Room number twelve. Ben took the key and sliced through the sticker that marked the door as a crime scene and warned trespassers it was a felony to tamper with the door in any way. Aside from the taped notice the door was barely closed. It was warped and barely fit into the jam leaving it vulnerable to a strong push or a hard kick.

When they opened up the door the light cut through the dark room. It smelled bad. The mattress and the linens were gone having been confiscated by the police for evidence. Half a dozen squares of carpet had been cut from the floor for the same purpose. Pins in the wall marked tiny droplets of blood that had reached the ceiling. Nothing but the skeletal frame of the bed was there.

Stella crouched down to inspect the door. It didn't look like it had been tampered with. Ben walked inside and went to the bathroom.

"Stella. Take a look at this," he called. When Stella walked into the bathroom, she saw the window was open about an inch. There were smudges in the dust around the sill. The towels were still neatly stacked but there were no soap bottles.

"Take a picture of that windowsill," Stella ordered. "I'm going to walk around the building and see if there is anything of interest the sheriff's men might have missed."
Just as she reached the door Stella's path was cut off by a garbage can on wheels with a supply caddy attached to it. A woman with wide eyes and gray smoker's skin peeked in the room.

"Are you the cops?" the woman asked with a voice graveled by a lifetime of smoking.

"We are." Stella quickly introduced herself.

"I'm Sally Greene. I found the body." Sally said the words as if she said them three times a week. There was very little shock or even interest in the situation at hand which perked up Stella's interest. She stepped outside the room, took out her notebook, and asked Sally to start at the beginning.

"Well, I've been working at this place for about six years now. I don't have any trouble. Ed pays me in cash, I hope I'm not ruining anything by telling you that." Stella shook her head and nodded for Sally to continue. "I like the job. I'm left alone and as long as I get the job done there are no problems. Sure, we have some unsavories that take up a room every once in a while. I'll find needles on the floor or half a dozen condoms. It happens. But all in all, I got no real complaints. People don't bother me, and I don't bother them. If they've paid for a room, I don't care what they do behind closed doors. But what does bother me is when people try to stay here for free. See, we don't have the greatest security," Sally said.

"I noticed that when I looked around," Stella replied as she watched Sally pull a pack of cigarettes and a lighter from her apron. She pulled out a single cowboy killer, Marlboro Reds and after lighting it took a deep drag sucking up almost half the cigarette with one puff.

"This room is continually broken into. It's at the end of the line so it's easier to go unnoticed. I've been telling Ed to fix the door but he doesn't seem to be all that concerned about it. Maybe this will get him to buy a new door." Sally took another drag and sniffled, wiping her nose on the back of her hand.

"You've caught people sneaking in before?" Stella asked.

"Sometimes kids jimmy the door, or some bums will climb in through the bathroom window. Oh, I'm sorry. I mean, homeless people. We aren't allowed to call them bums anymore. Like I said, nothing really locks all that well here. This room especially. So, I check the rooms once in the morning when I first start around ten and then once at night before I call it quits."

"What time do you leave work?" Stella asked.

"I don't stay a minute past six o'clock. If I did Ed would find a dozen other things for me to do and he does not pay overtime," Sally took another puff before dropping the spent cigarette to the ground and crushing it beneath her foot.

"So, there wasn't anything unusual going on last night when you were getting ready to leave. You didn't see anyone acting strange?" Stella asked as Ben appeared behind her.

"I'm sorry, Detective. I don't mean to be rude. But have you seen the people that stay here? We aren't talking about monuments to society. Mr. Rogers, who stays in room seven, has arguments every night. With himself. Taleea and Roscoe, who have been staying on and off in room four, sit outside their room on two metal chairs and drink from a paper bag all day every day. I've got a couple of people who have been having affairs meeting here for all the years I've been working here. This isn't the Four Seasons," Sally chuckled.

"I get that. I think you guys should consider that your slogan," Stella replied.

"I don't usually check the rooms where no one had checked in. But because we sometimes have squatters, I'll do a random search. Sort of like they used to do to kids' lockers at school. Remember those days?"

"I do," Ben replied.

"Yeah, well, that's how I stumbled across the woman. I've seen some crazy things in my life especially in the six years I've worked here. But I never saw anything so sad in my life," Sally swallowed hard. "I walked in because I didn't think I was seeing what I was seeing."

"Did you touch anything?" Stella asked.

"Are you kidding? I thought I was looking at a sex doll for starters. Then I saw she was beaten up and stabbed and blue and thought what kind of a sicko wanted a doll that looked like this. It wasn't until I saw the blood... I'll admit, Detective, I stood and stared for a while. I don't mean like half an hour or anything. But I was sort of in shock. I couldn't really believe what I was seeing. I had to make sure it was real, I guess. I don't know. All I do know is once it sunk in, I ran out of the room and called the sheriff."

Stella had been writing down everything Sally had been saying. Sally didn't seem to be the kind of woman who rattled easy. But as Stella watched her pull out another cigarette, she couldn't help but notice her hands were shaking slightly.

"Are you all right, Mrs. Greene?"

"I have a daughter. She's almost thirty-five years old now. I haven't seen her in a while. I talked to her on the phone at Christmas time," she took her usual long first drag. "I don't know why I'm thinking about her right now. I'm sure she's not thinking about me."

Stella remained stoic. There wasn't anything she could say or do in regard to Sally Greene's strained relationship with her daughter. It wasn't like Stella had any real-life experiences with her own mother or even a mother-like figure she could pull a reference from. So, she remained quiet.

"Mrs. Greene, we'll be in town staying at the Open Plaines for a few more days," Ben interrupted.

"That's a much nicer motel. Smart choice," Sally replied.

"Is there a number where we can reach you if we need to?" Ben asked.

"The sheriff has all my information. I'm not leaving town any time soon. Although I do plan on striking oil someday. Can't say I'll stick around after that happens," She chuckled at her own lame joke. Then Sally shook their hands and left Stella and Ben to go about her rounds of cleaning the recently vacated rooms. That was when Stella noticed the curtain of room number eleven fall back into place.

"I think we had an audience," she whispered to Ben who looked where Stella nodded her head. He walked up to the door and knocked. At first, no one answered but when Ben pressed his ear against the door, he was positive he heard breathing on the other side. He knocked again.

"That's Vietnam Victor. He's a resident here," Sally said, "and he'd been told to get rid of his fucking cats but he doesn't seem to think Ed is serious. He'll be looking for a new place if he doesn't."

"He lives in this unit? Next to the crime scene?" Stella asked. Sally nodded her head.

"Good luck getting an answer from him. He claims PTSD

but I don't think he spent a minute in the military," Sally shook her head. "Good luck, detectives."

Chapter 6

Ben knocked on the door again.

"Yes?" a weak voice came from inside.

"Police. Open the door," Ben ordered. After a few seconds, they heard the chain fall from the slot and the doorknob jiggle a few times before the door was yanked open about three inches.

"Yes?" the voice was no stronger with the door open and neither Stella nor Ben could see the individual very clearly due to the lights being out and the curtains drawn. It was like they were looking into a black and white movie.

The smell coming from the room was clove cigarettes. And both detectives heard a distinct meow come from inside. After Ben made introductions, he asked the man if he'd heard what happened to the woman in the room next door.

"Yeah. They sneak around like shadows," the man said.

"Who does?" Ben asked as Stella tried to get a good look at the man as she made notes in her notebook.

"Look, I don't have time to explain everything to you. The cops around here won't do anything anyway," he snapped.

"Sir, would you mind stepping out here with us?" Ben asked.

"What for?"

"So, we can talk. I'd like to know more about who has been sneaking around," Ben replied.

There was a sigh of frustration from the man. He pulled the door open wider, stepped out, and quickly pulled the door closed behind him.

"What is your name?" Ben asked.

"Private First Class Victor Gaines," the man said. He was a couple inches shorter than Ben. Victor had a potbelly and his arms dangling from his baggy t-shirt were thin without much muscle tone. It looked as if he hadn't seen the sun in quite some time as his skin was pale and his eyes were rimmed with red. He saluted Ben.

"You don't have to salute me, Mr. Gaines," Ben said patiently.

"Right. I don't have to." Victor huffed as if Ben was lying to him.

"There was a murder in the room next door last night between six o'clock in the evening and ten in the morning. By any chance did you hear anything?" Ben asked.

Victor rubbed the graying stubble on his chin then scratched under his arm. Stella studied him as his eyes darted around like he was waiting for someone. He was wearing wrinkled khakis that didn't look dirty, but they hadn't been ironed. His feet were bare and looked like normal feet. He hadn't been traipsing through the graveyard or walking over hot coals as far as Stella could see.

"I didn't hear anything," he grumbled staring straight ahead without looking at Ben.

"Are you sure? A woman was stabbed multiple times. Her face was bruised. Are you sure you didn't hear anything?" Ben asked.

Victor clenched his teeth, his nose twitching as he clenched his fists. "No. I didn't hear anything. Not a thing. Not a peep. Just like it was on the nights in Vietnam. It was quiet like a tomb. That was when they killed the most. But I got wise. You wouldn't understand."

Ben looked at Stella who gave a very subtle shrug.

"Victor, did you hear a woman cry out last night when it was quiet?" Ben tried.

"I told you I didn't hear anything. And I'm not saying another word," Victor replied reaching behind him to place his hand on the doorknob.

"Okay, Victor. That's all right. Victor, if you think of anything that might help us, would you give us a call?" Ben took a business card out of his pocket and handed it to the man who took it between yellow fingers.

Victor took it, studied it, sniffed it, and then smiled. "That smells like a very good year."

Ben looked at Stella who had been watching Victor with her sidearm at the ready. He reminded her of a jack-in-the-box. Even if you wound him slowly, carefully, there was a spring that was getting tighter and tighter. At any second it could snap.

"Thank you, Victor," Ben said as he and Stella left him standing outside his door, with one hand on the knob and the other scratching his chin. He looked at Stella from beneath heavy lids but made no gesture, no muttering under his breath.

"What do you think of him?" Ben asked.

"A person of interest," Stella replied as they headed back to the office to return the key from room twelve to Ed Nepal.

Ben inquired about the tenant in room eleven.

"Vietnam Victor? He's harmless," Ed said.

"You sure about that?" Ben asked as Stella took more

notes. She looked around and spotted through the tinted glass window the young man who had been behind the counter when she and Ben first arrived. He was smoking a cigarette and pacing back and forth.

"Yeah. He's been a guest here for a while. Claims to have been in Vietnam but I don't think it's true," Ed replied. "If you get the guy talking, he'll tell you he killed over ten thousand Vietcong. He also says he's a blackbelt in jiujitsu. Maybe I'm being too judgmental of the man, but he looks like he can barely lift that mangy cat he keeps with him, let alone open a can of jiujitsu on someone."

"So why do you let him stay here?" Ben asked.

"Hey, a bird in the hand. He pays on time and he's not really a bother. He just needs to be told off once in a while. Like with those damn cats. The guy just doesn't listen," Ed shrugged and went back to shuffling some papers that looked like electric and water bills.

Ben handed Ed back the key to room twelve along with a business card. "If you come across anything, even if it doesn't seem important, would you give us a call?"

"Sure," Ed said and nodded a good-bye. When Ben turned around Stella wasn't there. She was outside talking to the lip-chewing nervous assistant, Latham Gree. When he stepped outside, he saw Stella giving him a business card too.

"What was that all about?" Ben asked.

"Nothing. The kid said that he didn't want his boss to know that he sometimes sneaks his girlfriend into the vacant rooms. They have a tryst a couple of times a week. He was afraid that if he said anything, he'd get fired but if he didn't tell us he might go to jail." Stella shook her head. "When I asked if he'd been in room twelve recently, he said no."

They walked around the back of the building to give it a

second look but there was nothing there. No footprints, no cigarette butts, no crowbar caked with blood, let alone the bloody knife used in the murder. The only thing they did see was Vietnam Victor staring at them from his bathroom window. Other than that, there was nothing to report to either the sheriff or to the brass in Chicago.

Chapter 7

Once back at the Open Plaines Motel, Stella went to her room. She unpacked her laptop, portable scanner, back-up .357 Magnum, and clothes, and then decided she needed a shower. The water was hot and made her feel better but there was, as Christine Lustyk had said, a burr in her side. Something wasn't right. Of course, the murder itself was a mess, and the fact that in a motel with at least a couple guests staying in the rooms, one being right next door, no one heard or saw anything was...

"Typical," she said as she stood under the running water. There wasn't anything happening in this case that hadn't happened a million times before. No clues. No witnesses who will come forward. Nothing to go on. But it was just the beginning. Why was she expecting this one to wrap up sooner?

"Because you thought it was going to be a cut-and-dry case of love gone wrong. Silly rabbit. Trix are for kids," she said as she spit out a mouthful of water. As soon as she stepped out of the shower and wrapped herself up in a towel her cellphone rang.

"Carrigan," she grumbled as she flopped down on her bed.

"You won't believe this. My room has a broken pipe under the sink. There is water everywhere," Ben said before a flurry of curse words.

"If you think I'm sharing my executive suite, you're crazy," Stella replied.

"I'm going to that B&B the sheriff mentioned in the middle of town," Ben huffed. "At least they'll feed me there. Do you know this motel can only get *one* delivery place to come to it?"
"So. You know the staff at the Washington Motel. That might not be a bad idea to stay there. Keep an eye on comings-and-goings. Just one delivery place? We're out in the sticks. I'm surprised it's

that many," Stella replied. "What do they deliver?"

"Pizza," Ben huffed.

"Sounds good to me."

"Fine, I'll save you one of the oatmeal raisin cookies they always have at B&B's."

"I'll take it. Hey, why do you think that Vietnam Victor shut his door like he did?" Stella asked as she looked at the Regina Phelps file on her bed.

"He had a cat in there. Why?" Ben asked.

"I'm thinking maybe we should take peek inside," Stella said. "Come on. The guy was right next door and says he didn't hear anything?"

"We'd have to get a warrant," Ben said.

"Not if Sally was going in to do her cleaning. Then we just happened to catch her while she was working and had a little looky-loo. Totally innocent," Stella said. "She starts her shift at ten in the a.m."

"I don't know about this, Stella. What if we come across something? How do we explain why we were in his room? You don't need me to tell you the lines we aren't supposed to cross," Ben said.

"Okay. How about we don't make a decision until we've both had something to eat and some rest. It's been a long day and I've got to make a couple phone calls including to the one and only pizza place that delivers here," Stella said.

"You come from the city known for pizza and you are going to trust your taste buds to Vandalia's one and only pizza delivery place?" Ben teased.

"Yes. Have fun at your bed and breakfast where you'll be

sharing a bathroom with three couples on their honeymoon," Stella teased back. She looked at the simple desk in the corner and saw the flyer for King's Pizza. There was a goofy cartoon character with a crown on exclaiming the pizza as the best in the land. No image of Italy like most pizza places have. No red, white, and green colors. She picked up her cell and dialed. It would be an hour and a half before her cheese and sausage would arrive. She was ordering at almost five o'clock. Rush hour.

Stella took out her notebook while looking at the file Deputy Winger was so reluctant to hand over. How did the assailant get Regina in the room without being seen? Did he just grab her off the street? He had to know that the Washington Motel was a little lax in its security. Even more than the motel she was staying in. And, if the assistant to the owner admitted to sneaking his girl in at random times and the cleaning lady admitted to finding squatters there on occasion, this guy could have been hiding in plain sight.

After slipping into a pair of sweats and a baggy t-shirt, Stella stretched out on the bed with the television going and the crime scene photos in front of her. It felt like she'd looked at them a million times already. She looked up at the television and studied it more than the show she had on. It had a built-in DVD/CD player. That was king of cool for a gizmo that was bolted to the ceiling.

"Regina Phelps. What were you doing all the way out here in Vandalia?" Stella asked the picture. For someone who didn't live here and from the initial report had no kin out this way there was no good reason for Regina to be here.

In addition to that, she had no priors or any kind of police record. There was a speeding ticket on file that she'd paid. From Stella's point-of-view Regina was an upstanding individual.

"And a foster parent in Chicago," she muttered aloud. That little bit of information struck Stella. After her own experiences in foster care, this made Stella frown. It was a weird detail. She couldn't say why exactly. Maybe she didn't want to. Thinking too much about that would mean looking into her own past and she'd actively pushed a lot of that into a dark corner of her mind to stay there until she was worm food.

This detail made Stella worry there might be children waiting for their foster mother to come home. She flipped through the file and found nothing to indicate she currently had any children. She let out a deep breath she hadn't realized she'd been holding.

"This is a weird case," she said. "Not that there is anything typical about any homicide."

Just then there was a knock on the door. Stella instinctively put her hand to her weapon.

"Who is it?"

"King's Pizza," came a squeaky voice from behind the door. Stella grabbed her money and yanked the door open making the young delivery man jump.

"Keep the change," Stella said as she quickly made a mental note of the delivery guy's appearance, grabbed her pizza, and shut the door. It smelled like a good pizza, not that Stella was choosey when it came to food.

She continued to study the file as she ate her pizza and was frustrated when nothing specific jumped out at her. Stella felt like she was looking at one of those puzzles with the hidden pictures in it. Each photo was a different angle of the body, the room, the items on the floor, the window in the bathroom. But none of it was saying anything other than Regina was murdered. Before she realized, she'd eaten almost the entire pizza.

Just as she was about to get herself a glass of water from the tap in the bathroom her phone went off.

"Carrigan."

"Stella?"

"Yes?" She pinched her eyebrows together with annoyance.

"It's Cole. I hope I'm not interrupting." He sounded so sweet Stella's face instantly softened. She had completely forgotten about him and their date the previous night. It made her feel a little guilty.

"Oh, hi. No, I'm just finishing some delivery pizza and studying this file," she replied thinking she couldn't possibly sound more boring. "How are you?"

"I'm fine. Hey, I won't keep you long. I just wanted to tell you I had a nice time yesterday and I hope we can finish our date when you get back in town," Cole sounded hopeful.

"Uhm, well, it looks like this case is going to take longer than I thought," Stella said. She wasn't really sure if this was true or not. She felt the need to hedge her bets with Cole even though he was smart, funny, and unbelievably handsome, a total gentleman. Still, something convinced her that he was probably too good to be true and that if he was worth his salt, he'd tolerate her game of not just hard-to-get but near-impossible-to-get.

"That's kind of out of your control, isn't it? It's not like you can send out a call for the guilty party to turn themselves in," Cole chuckled. "I understand."

"I'm serious. This could take a couple of weeks. Then there is all the stuff that comes after I solve the case. Assuming I do solve the case," Stella waiting for Cole to say good-bye and hang up. But he didn't. He was so damn optimistic Stella didn't know what to do.

"Hey, there are people relying on you to help them. I understand. Look, I couldn't help myself. I just wanted to tell you that I had a nice time and as soon as you are back, no matter how long that takes, I'm probably going to be ringing your bell again," Cole's voice was smiling and it made Stella smile, too.

"All right. I'll let you know when I'm back in town. Just don't expect it to be any time soon," she replied.

"Hey, you know there's this thing called a phone. You're on it right now. When you feel like talking you can just press a few digits and call me. You don't have to see me in person or anything," Cole teased.

"I get it," Stella smirked.

"Good," Cole chuckled. "Good-night, Stella."

"Night, Cole," she said before pressing the red button and dropping the phone on the bed. She looked at the time, yawned, and folded up Regina Phelps' file. Although she appreciated Cole's call, and he did offer a very sweet distraction for a few minutes, the last thing she really wanted was to be distracted from this case. There was a gnawing in the back of her mind.

"The gnawing worm," she said shaking her head. Something was there but she couldn't figure it out. Not yet. It would come in due time. It always did. But no matter how confident she was in her thoughts, there was something under the surface saying this time might be different.

Chapter 8

Before the sun rose the following day, Stella went for a run. With her hair tucked up in a baseball cap and a baggy windbreaker that almost reached her knees she didn't look like a police detective. Instead, she looked like a mom running to lose some of the fat she gained after having a baby. It was a good disguise because she looked harmless and almost helpless. No one would guess she was armed with her hip-hugger holster that made her weapon almost invisible across her tummy and a flashlight. After she started her journey, she soon became aware that Vandalia could be circled within an hour and a half if she were walking at a stroll. As she ran, she realized that she wasn't that far from the Washington Motel. The Washington Motel was plunked with two fields on either side of the row of rooms. The circular driveway was faded, buckled with weeds forced through the cracks. Every room had its curtains drawn tightly. There were a couple of rooms with empty bottles set neatly outside their doors.

Driving in a car it's easy to get turned this way and that. But out on foot, Stella was able to get her bearings easily and discovered just about everything was a quick jog away.

Without waiting for Ben or even letting him know her intentions, she slowed her pace as if she were fighting a cramp in order to inch her way past the motel and take that looky-loo she'd mentioned before. And as if it had been planned by Divine Intervention, Stella saw Vietnam Victor leave his room. He looked like he hadn't changed his clothes from the day before. He climbed into a car that was as old and worn out as he was. The muffler rattled, announcing its intention of falling off at any minute. He pulled away just as Stella slipped off the street into the weeds. Once the noise of the car disappeared Stella looked around and wasn't surprised to find no one else in sight. She jogged past the place then doubled back behind the tall weeds in the field on the northern side of the motel.

There was no telling where Vietnam Victor went or how long he'd be gone. Stella didn't waste time and made her way quickly to the back side of the motel. It looked as sad and depressing as it had the day before. The second window from the end that Victor had been staring at Stella and Ben from was just a black square. Holding her breath, Stella listened for the sound of Victor's car but only the sound of early morning crickets that hadn't turned in for the night could be heard. With a snap, the flashlight cut a beam through the dusk and then through the darkness of Victor's bathroom. As she pressed her face close to the glass, she saw clothes hanging from the shower curtain. On the floor by the toilet was a box of cat litter several days beyond its capacity.

Stella shined her light around the frame of the window and could see it had been moved before. After illuminating the area around the ground beneath the window Stella found dozens of cigarette butts, broken glass, flattened bottlecaps, broken bits of pens, plastic knives, a dirty blue t-shirt, and a nail clipper. She grabbed the clipper, pulled it open, and extended the useless file in order to jimmy it beneath the windowsill. Once it slipped beneath the window frame Stella was able to pry it up just enough to get her fingers underneath. When she stopped and listened for the choking muffler, she still heard nothing. There was some shouting from one of the units but even that stopped quickly.

Stella knew she didn't have much time. With all her strength she pulled up the window, stuck her head in, and looked around. It smelled like clove cigarettes, cat litter, and the same old carpet smell that was in the main office. There was one living thing in there, the cat. It came into the bathroom slinking lazily around the edge of the tub and looking up at Stella suspiciously.

Without wasting another minute Stella hopped up, leaning inside the bathroom, folding in the middle as she let her weight pull her inside as she kicked her legs up. One hand landed on the radiator, the other managed to brace herself against the edge of the tub. Sliding her legs inside was an easy final step. After wiping her hands off on her pants she carefully inched her way into the other room. Stella listened again for the muffler but heard nothing. She crossed the room and snapped on the lamp. Quickly, she surveyed the room. It was messy with stacks and stacks of paperback books everywhere. She picked one up, then another and another.

Her Scandalous Secret. Forbidden Lover. The Maiden's Lust. "Good grief." Stella flipped through one and saw part of it was highlighted. It was a description of a party. Another part that was underlined described a man's chest. There didn't seem to be any particular pattern to what Victor was noting. She put them back where she'd found them.

Stella looked over the contents of the desk. Empty fast food bags and cups, an overflowing ashtray of clove cigarettes, a few empty pill bottles for Xanax. There was a toothbrush and spent toothpaste tube. A couple of pieces of cheap men's jewelry. There were stacks of mail, uncashed checks from Social Security, and a dozen notebooks with scribbled notes in tiny handwriting. Grabbing one of them she tucked it under her arm and went to the closet. There was nothing that looked like a weapon, crowbar, or a knife. She looked at the bottom of the shoes in the closet and picked at a few items of clothing rolled into balls but there was no sign of blood splatter on any of them.

She was about to move on to the dressers when she heard the sound of the muffler and it was a lot closer than down the street. It was right outside the door.

Stella ran to the bathroom and tripped over the cat litter box sending it scattering all over the floor. She flung the notebook out of the window. Just as the engine stopped and the driver's side door slammed shut Stella slung one leg over the sill. She held her breath and folded her head down to tuck it under the window only after cracking the side of her head on the wooden frame. Unlike when she entered the unit with stealth and grace, Stella toppled out of the window, falling to the ground, her breath rushing out in a very unladylike grunt, into a semi-wet circle of gravel and grit. Just then the front door opened.

Stella had no time to close the window. The cat meowed like a fire alarm making her take off running hoping the creature didn't decide to follow. All she could think of was how curious Mr. Zarowny's cat, Cleopatra was. Vietnam Victor's pet might be the same way. With the notebook in hand, she made it to the bushes just as she heard a voice shouting out the open window.

"I see you!"

Stella ducked down, held her breath again, and waited. She didn't dare peek over the top of the weeds. Instead, she got as low to the ground as she could, peeled off her heavy windbreaker to reveal a runner's halter top beneath and removed her hat letting her black hair fall to her shoulders. It was a quick and easy transformation. As she crawled through the tall grass, she made her way toward the road past the entrance to the motel. Once her feet hit the cement, she doubled back at a leisurely pace as if she'd just been jogging along her merry way. As she passed the motel in an attempt to look inconspicuous, Vietnam Victor threw open his door in a rage with his cat in his arms.

He stopped when he looked at Stella, but she didn't think it was because he knew it had been her in his room. She was just a jogger. Hell, she could have been Detective Carrigan jogging. There was no law that she couldn't jog past his residence. As long as he didn't stop her, or see she had one of his notebooks in her possession, she was golden. But she could feel his eyes on her as she ran. She didn't dare look or pick up her pace. She just continued until she was around the corner, took a few detours down some residential streets, and after being sure he didn't tail her, she went back to her hotel drenched in sweat but feeling good.

She'd tell Ben about her visit later. Now she needed a

shower and breakfast over a little light reading of Vietnam Victor's private journal.

Chapter 9

Vandalia came to life in the morning. At least a couple places did. The police station was abuzz like every cop was getting suited up to attend the Macy's Day Parade. When Stella walked in with two cups of coffee she nodded to the receptionist, the same older redhead with the bossy attitude from the day before. She seemed a lot less bossy today and had purple eyeshadow to match her purple ensemble.

"Good morning, Detective," she said as if Stella had been coming to the station with coffee every day for years.

"Morning," Stella replied.

"Your partner, Ben, and Sheriff Darlow are in the conference room," the redhead said as she got the door for her.

"Thanks," Stella said as she walked in. Every uniformed cop in their bullpen looked up to see the big city detective who was helping with the murder at the Washington Motel. She spotted Deputy Clarence Winger standing near a corner cubicle staring her way with his arms across his chest. Another cop looked down but stole looks at Stella in between shuffling papers.

The whole scene reminded her of her first day at the 18th Precinct. Little did these guys know that she'd dealt with bigger and badder cops than them.

Without saying a word, she went to the conference room and was happy to see Ben sitting there alone.

"I went to Victor's," she whispered.

"You what?" Ben gasped.

"I searched the place. There wasn't anything," she

shrugged.

"Are you nuts?" Ben scolded quietly before looking at the door to make sure no one from Vandalia was coming in as he pointed out the problems that come with illegal search and seizure.

"He doesn't know it was me. I was careful." Stella waved Ben's concern away. "There was no sign of bloody clothes or shoes. Nothing that I'd call trophies or even any trace that a woman was in there within the last three years. I stole one of his notebooks thinking that maybe he'd have confessed to something in there. Turns out he writes romance manuscripts."

Ben sat there with his mouth hanging open for several seconds before he spoke. "You are determined to get us thrown off this case, aren't you? That way you don't have to admit you are stumped."

"No," Stella grimaced and shook her head. "I just didn't want to wait for a warrant. You know how long it takes when we are just down the street from the courthouse. Can you imagine if we are requesting it from Vandalia? Besides, no harm no foul. Like I said, Vietnam Victor didn't even know I was there."

"I'm at a loss," Ben muttered.

"No, you aren't. Have some coffee. I'll get you a danish. You'll feel better." Stella patted his hand like she was an old, concerned granny.

"If I make it to retirement with you, it will be a miracle," Ben said.

"How is the B&B?" Stella asked while handing him his coffee.

"It's very frilly and lacy and there is no television in the room," Ben yawned as he took the coffee.

"No television? What the hell did you do all night? Did you tell them you are a cop and there are certain amenities that this profession requires when we are off work, like sports on TV?" Stella chuckled.

"Are you crazy? It was lovely," Ben smiled.

"Okay, I'll get you another room at the motel as soon as I get back. Just get your things and..." Stella shook her head as she took a seat and a sip of her own large coffee.

"No. I mean it," Ben said. "I listened to some classical music. Then, I had forgotten I had a couple of books on CD that Rochelle had packed for me. I popped up *The Adventures of Huckleberry Finn* and had a wonderfully relaxing night. What did you do?" Ben batted his eyes at Stella making her chuckle as she shook her head and handed him the Regina Phelps file that he already knew she'd spent the night studying.

"I did some light reading myself. What are we waiting for?" she asked.

"Sheriff Darlow," Ben replied as he looked at the pictures.

"What for?"

"I don't know," Ben shrugged.

If there was one thing Stella hated it was the hurry-up-and-wait-game. She was about to get up and go rattle some cages when the sheriff walked in.

"Good morning," he said looking just as comfortable and country as he did the previous day in blue jeans and his badge.

"Sheriff? Are we waiting on something?" Stella asked.

"I was hoping to get a heads-up on what you guys discovered yesterday. Any news? Anything that might help me sleep better tonight than I did last night?" Sheriff Darlow asked.

Stella wasn't sure if she should feel bad for or aggravated with the man. Sure, this was his first homicide and it was a gruesome one at that. But this wasn't television. These things don't get solved in a day.

"Sorry, Sheriff," Ben stepped in as if he knew letting Stella answer might get them kicked out of not just the office but the town altogether. Tact and patience were not Stella's strong points.

"It's just too early," Stella scoffed, shaking her head like she couldn't believe the question was even asked.

"I understand," Sheriff Darlow replied. "But it doesn't hurt to ask. We've got some items in evidence that were taken from the scene. You guys can take a look at those. I'm going to back off. But if there is anything that you need, don't hesitate. My men and I are here to help."

Stella thought of the smug expression on Deputy Winger's face and thought, *yeah right*. But she didn't say anything and just nodded. Ben spoke up with a gracious thank you before they followed the Sheriff to the evidence room. It was more like the evidence closet.

"Here you go," said an old portly cop in plain clothes with his badge on his pocket.

"Counting the days until retirement?" Stella asked the man with a grin.

"You know it," he mumbled. "This is all they collected from the scene. Unless you plan on searching every house in Vandalia, I'm afraid you'll have an easier time finding a needle in a haystack. Sorry."

"Hey, we'll take what we can get. How come you aren't at the reception desk? I know... They keep all the good-looking guys hidden. I get it," Stella flirted. Ben stood back and shook his head as the old cop chuckled.

"You're a detective? You don't see very well, do you?" the salty cop replied with a chuckle. "Just sign here."

Stella signed for the item and was pleased when it was handed to her in a plastic baggie with vital information scribbled in black permanent marker. She said good-bye to her new friend and walked out with Ben.

"Now, how is it that you can make an old geezer like that smile but you're afraid to turn on that same charm with Mr. Mexican restaurant?" Ben needled.

"Are you kidding? That guy back there is harmless. He's got one foot in the grave and the other on a banana peel. It's easy to be flirty with someone like him because we both know it doesn't mean anything," Stella grumbled as she looked at the key through the plastic.

"Oh, and heaven forbid it means anything with someone your own age," Ben replied.

"What are you, my mother? Look, this key looks brand new. Very shiny and hardly any scratches. And the rubber grip has a name on it," Stella held it up to her face and squinted. "Morely's Hardware."

Within minutes Stella and Ben were driving through Vandalia to the only hardware store in town. At eight in the morning, the place was already hopping. A dozen pick-up trucks were in the parking lot, guys wearing blue jeans and steel-toed work boots were milling around hauling planks of wood, or bags of cement, or handfuls of nut and bolts, and boxes of nails. Construction work started early in the morning.

"Hi, can I help you find something specific?" a thin woman in blue jeans and a flannel shirt asked as soon as they walked in. Stella and Ben showed their badges at the same time as Stella introduced them.

"Can you tell me who cuts your keys?" she asked. The

woman looked worried but was happy to lead them away from the door, the cash registers, and the customers waiting in line.

"Trevor does all the key cutting," the woman said and pointed to the small cube housing a key cutting machine flanked by rows of blank keys hanging from pegs on each side. Like a ticket-taker at a carnival, a long-haired older man with calloused knuckles and perpetually dirty fingernails was leaning on the small counter talking with a fellow equally rough around the edges. When Stella and Ben approached the counter the conversation between the two men came to a halt.

"Can I help you?" Trevor asked and made no attempt to hide his judgment of the two people coming in wearing business attire.

"Trevor?" Stella introduced herself and Ben, flashing her badge and holding up the plastic baggie while asking for his last name, home address, and phone, and if he carved that key. Trevor's demeanor shifted quickly. He took the baggy and studied its contents.

"Yeah, I made this key. I didn't know the woman who bought it. I know pretty much everyone in town. Vandalia ain't that big," Trevor rubbed the back of his neck. "And there isn't a whole lot of house keys being made. People aren't coming and going like they do in the city."

"She was a stranger?" Ben asked.

"I'd never seen her before in my life, but she was getting a divorce," Trevor smirked. "She was more than happy to tell everyone within earshot about her no good, two-timing husband."

"Really?" Stella looked at Ben then back at Trevor as he shuffled through a file of receipts.

"Yeah. She gave him eighteen years of her life and all he did was make her feel bad about herself, talk down to her; he sounded like a real charmer. Of course, I was only getting her side of the story. Here we are. Barbara Casio. That's her," Trevor handed Stella the receipt. She gave it to Ben who copied down the information including address and cell phone number.

"This is really helpful," Stella said as Ben handed back the receipt.

"If I can ask...what has she done?" Trevor looked at Ben as if he might spill the beans to another fellow when Stella wouldn't.

"Thank you, Trevor. We'll be in touch," Ben said as Stella walked toward the entrance. She could feel all eyes on her but didn't mind. She and Ben did look out of place but there was a satisfaction she felt that came with a lead. Even a small one was better than nothing at all. As soon as she and Ben were in the car away from eavesdroppers, she said the obvious.

"A divorce? Two-timing husband?" Stella shook her head. "I told you it was going to be a love triangle. A dead body in a cheap no-tell-motel. We'll have this wrapped up by dinner."

"I hope you're right," Ben said as he slid behind the wheel. Stella lifted her chin and was sure that her gut instinct was correct, and she'd have another notch in her belt by day's end. But as with all best-laid plans, there was no way to stop a fly from getting in the ointment.

Barbara Casio was living in a ranch style home with pretty flowers blooming all around it. If there was a divorce and she wanted to keep her no good, two-timing husband out changing the locks was a good start. Judging by the neighbor's homes this was a nice neighborhood and the property value was probably high for this part of the state.

"You do the talking," Stella said. "She'll probably be happy to have a handsome guy like you to confide in."

"Yeah, you called that old cop at the station handsome. I don't know what the definition of that word is in *your* vocabulary," Ben teased.

They knocked on the door and rang the doorbell. The only answer they got was a frantic dog yipping from inside. Stella tried to peek in one of the front windows, but the curtains were drawn tight. While Ben stayed in the front of the house Stella walked around to the back on the off chance that Barbara was in the yard. The gate was a simple latch that opened with the flip of a lever. Stella went in and looked around. The backyard was also filled with pretty flowers and a small shed. There was a pretty back porch that led to a set of sliding doors. A long curtain was also pulled shut inhibiting her from seeing anything inside. After giving it a tug only to find the sliding door locked as well, Stella went back around front.

"I'm going to try her cell number," Ben said dialing and putting the phone to his ear. They both looked at each other when they heard the ringing. It was coming from inside the house. Without hesitating, Stella took the key from the plastic bag and inserted it into the lock. With a smooth click-click the door unlocked, and Stella pushed it open.

"Hello?" the only reply they got was from the dog. Frantic nails scraped on the linoleum floor and headed in their direction. The little creature making all the fuss was a Yorkshire terrier who quickly barked a salutation to Stella and Ben before turning back in the direction he came.

Chapter 10

"Her purse is still here," Stella said as she pointed to a table in the dining room that had a big purse on it as well as a cell phone next to it. Stella withdrew her gun as did Ben. Quietly, they split up and searched the house. There was nothing out of place in the two bedrooms or the bathroom upstairs. Neither did it look like any kind of struggle has occurred in the living room, dining room, or kitchen. But when Ben rejoined Stella in the kitchen and the dog was frantically scratching at a door, they knew there was one more place they had to look.

"Basement?" Ben asked.

"I assume so," she replied and carefully picked up the little dog in her arms. The little beast had a collar on with a tag that read "Lonnie." She stroked the dog and felt bad that it was trembling in her arms. She looked around and saw water in a bowl but no food in the one next to it. "Don't worry, buddy. We'll get you something to eat. You just hold on."

As she continued to survey the landscape Stella saw some sliced vegetables on the counter that had gone bad as well as a bowl full of oranges that were turning green with mold.

She set the dog back on the floor and as if he understood why Stella and Ben were there, he went over to his food bowl and sat. They both had their weapons in their hands as Ben reached for the doorknob and gave it a slow twist. It clicked softly. As soon as the door opened Stella and Ben were hit with the smell.

"Oh God," Ben wrinkled his face. They'd both encountered this smell more times than they cared to admit. Decay. Human decay. Stella stepped forward and, after spotting the light switch, flipped it on and headed slowly downstairs with her gun leading the way.

At the bottom of the stairs, she saw the body. The person was dead. But different from the first victim. There were no stabbing injuries. Were they dealing with two different people? Stella didn't dare think of that possibility this early in the game. She switched to autopilot and did her job first.

"Call the sheriff. Get the coroner here," Stella said as Ben reached the bottom of the stairs. The smell only got worse the further down in the basement they got. Stella scanned the room. It was an ordinary basement with a gray concrete floor and exposed wood and insulation along the walls. There were a washer and dryer in one corner and boxes marked Christmas decorations in another. A metal shelf had packages of toilet paper and paper towels stacked on it. A dry-vac was underneath it. The small windows were made of glass blocks, so no one was getting through them. They offered a creepy glow even though it was broad daylight. It looked like perpetual dusk through the thick pieces of glass.

As if the body in the middle of everything wasn't bad enough, Stella could hear the only living things beside Lonnie, upstairs, that were in the house. Flies. They were a disgraceful and disgusting companion to any victim. Stella wrapped her arm over her nose as she approached the body. She saw the flies swirling and swooping like tiny black tornadoes. It was enough to make even a seasoned cop like herself feel their stomach fold. But something else distracted Stella from the gruesome act of nature's composters.

"She's been posed," Stella said as Ben quickly gave the address and a description of the scene to dispatch.

Once he was off the phone Ben, careful to walk in a line behind Stella and stand close to her to minimize any cross-contamination, looked over her shoulder. It was easy to do since she was so much shorter than him. Then he pointed.

"Looks like marks on her neck. And the blindfold. What do you think? Some kinky sex game gone wrong?" Ben asked.

Stella hadn't seen the blindfold. But of course, she had. She saw the whole body as soon as she got to the bottom of the stairs. Then why did her heart race when Ben mentioned the blindfold? She looked at the victim who was covered by a scratchy looking old blanket that Stella was sure had smelled like mold and mothballs before the scent of death overtook it. She swallowed hard and instantly regretted it as the taste of death went down her gullet too.

"I don't know," she mumbled. It certainly would fit her scenario of a love triangle gone wrong. A lover killed in a motel room and the soon-to-be ex-wife offed in the house. The husband/lover probably killed both of them—unless he's got an airtight alibi such as he was with a third woman while these murders were being committed.

But as simple as that sounded Stella wasn't buying her own idea. If this was Barbara, her face was almost entirely covered by the blindfold. Her hair was wild and knotted with something Stella had originally thought were tangles. But as she leaned closer, she saw something was in her hair. Round things pale in color, and not normally found in hair.

"What are those things in her hair?" Ben asked as if he'd been reading Stella's mind.

"I can't tell," she said as she leaned in closer. For a second Stella was afraid she was going to fall head-first into the corpse. What was the matter with her? She'd seen dead bodies before in worse shape than this. Hell, she'd seen children and never felt the urge to pass out. She leaned back and shook her head.

"Are you all right, Stella?" Ben asked.

"Yeah, I think it's the temperature in here or something. I didn't eat any breakfast either," she swallowed hard. "I'm okay now. I think those are flower buds. What do you think?" she asked, happy to step back from the body and let Ben get a closer look.

"You're right. Rosebuds. Kind of a strange thing to have in your hair," he replied as he holstered his weapon and pulled a pen from his breast pocket. Delicately, he probed the buds in the woman's hair. They were tangled in there good. They'd have to wait for the autopsy to be finished before they knew exactly what they were.

"We've got a big problem here, Ben," Stella said as she walked closer to the stairs.

"You think?"

"She was killed first. The body in the motel was hours old according to Christine. But you can tell by the flies this one has been here a while. Technically, this is the first body," Stella cleared her throat. "I hear the sirens. I'll go meet the boys upstairs."

Ben let out a deep breath but said nothing more. Stella held onto the railing tightly for fear she might lose her footing. Even though she wasn't supposed to, when she emerged in the kitchen she went to the sink, grabbed a cup from one of the cabinets, and filled it with water from the tap. In three gulps it was down, and she got herself another one. With a few more shakes of her head, she was feeling a little better.

"You're coming down with the flu or something. That's all," she said but wasn't really convincing herself of that. What was it about the blindfold and the blanket over the body that was so bothersome? Stella didn't know. It had to be some kind of fatigue. Maybe she needed more time off than she realized.

"When this is solved, I'll take a month off. I've got the time coming to me. I'll do it. A month off. Just let me get through this case and bring it to an end," she said to the little white cup she was holding. She put it back on the shelf and went to the front door just as a coroner and two shiny clean squad cars showed up with the Sheriff emerging from one and Deputy Winger from the other.

"Did I hear dispatch right?" Sheriff Darlow asked as he

shook his head.

"I'm afraid so," Stella replied. She led them in and then looked at Winger. "There's a small dog. Probably hasn't eaten in a few days. Can you arrange for animal control to get it to a shelter until we can contact the ex-husband?"

"I'm sure you can handle that." Deputy Winger snapped back.

"Clarence," Sheriff Darlow muttered.

"What, Sheriff?" Deputy Clarence Winger was not happy.

"Just do what the detective says. We've got bigger issues than your pride," Sheriff Darlow whispered.

"But Don, I..."

"You're my deputy and you do as I tell you. I don't know what the bug up your ass is about with this detective but I'm not having it. Now get the damn dog to the shelter. Jesus, we've got two dead women. Are you kidding me?"

Stella had kept walking ahead, but she held her breath and listened to what the Sheriff was saying. When she held the door open for the men to come into the house, Winger glared at her before stepping inside.

The Yorkie sat in the corner of the kitchen. Stella pointed him out and Winger stomped up to the poor thing making it cringe. But just as she was sure he was going to manhandle the little beast, he dropped to one knee, reached out his hand, and let the dog get a good sniff before he scooped it up in his huge hands. It looked even smaller as he held it.

Stella caught his eye. "Thank you, deputy."

He grumbled something back and Stella couldn't be sure it wasn't an insult. But she didn't pursue it. Instead, she led Sheriff

Darlow into the basement.

"What's that smell?" he asked.

"The victim," Stella replied.

As he reached the bottom of the stairs behind Stella, Sheriff Darlow gagged. He put his hand to his mouth as he observed the woman still folded up in the fetal position, under a nasty, nappy blanket with flies buzzing around.

"Oh...m...my God," he stuttered.

The coroner's office had sent two men, but they waited upstairs in the kitchen with the stretcher until the sheriff gave them the go-ahead. Stella watched the sheriff as he inspected his boots more than the body.

"Who are you calling?" Stella asked as he took out his phone.

He held up one finger. "Hello, Tiffany? Yeah, it's Don. Look. Grab your camera and meet me at this address. Did you eat anything? Good. Don't." The sheriff hung up and looked at Stella.

"Sheriff, Trevor at the hardware store where this key was made said Mrs. Casio was getting a divorce. Do you know anything about it? This is a small town, and everybody knows everybody, at least that is what Trevor said." Stella asked hoping he'd say yes, the police had been called to the address on domestic disturbances at least once a month.

He shook his head no. "I've never seen this woman before," he muttered, his lips pulled down at the edges in disgust and distress.

"Do you know Mr. Casio?" Stella asked as she watched the sheriff put his fist to his lips.

"I've seen him around town. He always showed up at the

Glass Tap Tavern every couple of weeks. Not a daily drinker but certainly a monthly one. They all knew him there. That's where I saw him." Sheriff Darlow said quickly.

"Did he ever mention getting divorced?" Stella asked.

"Hell, I didn't know the guy was married. He didn't act like it," he replied. Stella was feeling better. The weird blanket and blindfold were just odd details added by an odd man who probably wanted to make it look like his wife was into all kinds of *strange* in order to throw the scent off himself. Although that was the direction Stella was sure the case was steering toward there was something about all of it that was sticking in her craw. Why did he put her in the basement? Why did he cover her with that old, stiff blanket? And if Regina Phelps was his mistress why did he leave the key to this house with her? It isn't like she committed suicide.

"Are you all right, sheriff?" Stella asked as she watched Sheriff Darlow turn green and dry heave into his fist.

"I need some air," was all he could mutter before he dashed upstairs.

Stella turned and looked at Ben.

"I don't know who I feel worse for, him or us," Ben mumbled.

"Why do you say that?" Stella asked.

"He's affected by this because he's never seen it before. We aren't because we've seen it so many times. Have we become that detached?" Ben shrugged before going back to his notes.

"He's a country sheriff. We're homicide detectives. There is a world of difference," Stella said unable to hide the defensive tone in her voice. She would never apologize for being able to keep her cool on a job like this. Someone had to. And she'd already had some heebie-jeebies just a few minutes ago so Ben had no idea what he was talking about. She was still affected by these crimes.

She just hid it well.

Chapter 11

Tiffany, the crime scene photographer was not at all what Stella had expected. Ruben, the crime scene photographer she saw on a regular basis in Chicago was a clean-cut fellow who wore khaki pants, button-down shirts, and sensible walking shoes to every crime scene. If she didn't know better, she'd think he would be on his way to sit at a desk and sell insurance after taking pictures of the latest victim of some gang shooting.

Tiffany, the crime scene photographer in Vandalia was a full-figured mother of three who, in between baking cookies for St. Mary of the Angels school fundraisers and her part-time job at the library, assisted the police taking crime scene photos.

"Oh, dear. Well, this is gross. Flies? Ugh," were the first words out of her mouth when she came down the stairs and saw Mrs. Casio. "This is going to take a while. Are you the folks assigned to this case?"

Ben said yes and made introductions.

"Well, detectives, I've got to call my kids and let them know that I'm going to be late bringing them KFC for dinner," she said, flipping her blonde bob haircut over her shoulder as she pulled out her bedazzled cell phone. It was pink with pink plastic sparkles all over it.

"No problem," Ben said as Tiffany stepped aside with her phone to her ear. He watched her study the body on the floor. Tiffany squinted and looked down her nose and tip-toed to the right of the body as she held her phone to her ear.

"What's going on over there? Who's yelling? Tell her it's Mom. I'm going to be late. This is going to take me longer than I thought. No, you have to do your homework first. No, I'm not promising anything. No, you can't. No. No. All right. I love your face. No. No. Good-bye, Good-bye Ryan," she said before tapping her pretty pink polished nail on the red button on her phone and slipping it into her back pocket.

"This is as bad as the other one at the Washington Motel. Do you think they are connected?" Tiffany asked.

"We won't know for sure until we have an autopsy," Ben replied.

"I can't imagine they aren't. We don't get this kind of action in the sticks. But when you are into the kinky stuff something is bound to go wrong. Looks like both victims were into the kinky stuff, too. With the whole blindfold thing," she pointed with her pink nail at Mrs. Casio's head. She raised her camera and snapped some pictures. With slow deliberation she inched her way around the body and, like a vulture circling before it dared get close, she captured the victim from every angle.

"This doesn't seem to bother you all that much. How come?" Stella asked Tiffany who smirked and shrugged.

"Detective Carrigan, I have four children. Three girls and a boy. Imagine your oldest girl gets her first period the same day your second child comes down with the flu, the third has diarrhea, and we find out the baby is allergic to peanuts the hard way," Tiffany chuckled. "I'm looking at the body of a stranger. I count my blessings and move on."

"Not many people would be able to do that," Ben replied.

"People do what they have to when they have to. I have to take these pictures. No use freaking out about it. I've taken pictures of deceased people before. Their suffering in this world is over. Now, if you'll excuse me. I'd like to get this done so I can feed my kids before they turn cannibal."

Stella and Ben chuckled.

Sheriff Darlow hadn't come back to the basement. He was

hanging around the front door, staying close to the fresh air. Ben was watching Tiffany and making sure she caught the same things he had noticed, and thought might be important. The knot on the back of the blindfold. The flowers in Mrs. Casio's hair. A few scuffs on the floor near the body. The print that was on the blanket covering her.

Stella didn't know what it was, but she was not feeling right. Like she was wearing shoes that were pinching her toes or a pair of pants that were just a tiny bit too tight. She couldn't get comfortable. She couldn't relax. She couldn't get into the normal groove she usually found when working a case.

"You still think this is a love triangle?" Ben asked as they let Tiffany finish her work.

"Don't you?" Stella replied.

"It's the only thing that makes any sense," Ben said. "I'll put out a call for the ex-husband to be brought in for questioning. Maybe we can get this wrapped up even quicker than we planned, and you can get back to your date with Cole."

Stella shook her head as she watched Tiffany pack up her things.

"I'll have the photos for you within forty-eight hours," Tiffany said. "I also do weddings, first communions, graduations, retirement parties. You name it. Just give me a call," she said as she handed Ben and Stella each a business card before going upstairs.

It took a matter of seconds before the crime scene investigators came down to measure, mark, and bag everything. Stella was anxious for them to finish. She wanted the body out of the basement and on a slab in the coroner's office free of the blindfold and that blanket.

There was something about the whole scene that was making her uncomfortable. Maybe she was getting claustrophobic.

Once again, she blamed it on not eating, not taking a break between cases, not getting enough sleep.

"Detective, can you help me get this blanket in the bag?" the CSI with a paunch and white gym shoes with black pants asked.

"Sure," Stella said as she grabbed a large plastic back from their duffle bag of supplies. There were also manila envelopes, tubes with red stoppers, rubber gloves, a ruler, and a dozen other instruments of the trade. She held the bag open but when the edges of the blanket scraped over her fingers before slipping into the bag Stella almost screamed.

"God, no!" she shouted drawing the attention of both CSI and Ben. Without even realizing it she yanked her hands away from the blanket and dropped the bag.

"What is it?" Ben asked. "Jeez, Stella, are you all right?"

She didn't want to admit that she was seeing spots and her body felt like a thousand pounds had been piled on her shoulders. Sweat dampened her armpits and forehead as a chill make her body shake all over.

The last thing Stella wanted was to faint in front of these country yokels. The news would not only spread to the sheriff and his deputy as quick as lightning, but it would get back to the 18th Precinct. The threat of being yanked off the case would be very real.

"I'm...okay," she said as her body started to shake.

"Come on. We've been down in this air for too long," Ben said. Although Stella wanted to put up a fight, she wanted to get out of the basement and away from that blanket even more. What was it about that thing? The fact that it was on a decomposing body? What the hell? Stella had touched stuff like that a million times before. And worse. She'd touched naked bodies of dead people that had been in partial water in the middle of July.

Nothing gave her a reaction like this.

Chapter 12

"I'm just worked up," she lied. "I feel like we've been doing a lot of hurry up and wait and you know how much I hate that."

"Yeah. Right," Ben replied, looking at her suspiciously. "Are you sure?"

"I don't know, Ben. I had sort of a flashback. Not a visual flashback, if that makes any sense. But the feel of that blanket," she whispered and pursed her lips before continuing. "It felt like a thousand spiders crawling over my skin. And that blindfold. I don't think that's any S&M toy. It looked old, used, like it was just torn from a bigger piece of black cloth that might have been in a dumpster or in a pile of rags."

"And you felt this before?" Ben asked.

"Yeah. A long time ago," she looked at Ben and waited for the answer to click in his head and show in his eyes. He was a good partner. Stella knew he had her back and right now she was hoping he'd understand what she was trying to say without having to come right out and say it.

"Are you talking about when you were a kid?" Ben asked carefully. When she nodded her head, he said the word that scared her. The only word that scared her. "The abduction."

"It was a million years ago, Ben. Why would anything here remind me of that?" When she finally spoke those words, she felt stupid, like a kid saying there were monsters under her bed even though she was too old to believe in monsters.

"You spent too much time in Mrs. Casio's basement. That's all. The air was tainted, to say the least. It's cramped and chilly. It's no wonder you felt uneasy. If I hadn't been taking notes on everything I was seeing I'd have gotten claustrophobic, too."

"Is that all you think it was? Claustrophobia?" Stella wrinkled her nose.

"What would you call it?"

The memory of being eight years old and pulled out of a dark place by a strong man in a police uniform popped to the front of her mind like the flash of the sun in a rearview mirror. She blinked it back, but it left its imprint already.

He wrapped his arms around her tightly. "You're safe now," the officer kept repeating. "You're safe." He smelled like new leather and clean soap. Stella never felt as warm and protected as she did in the minutes that man carried her out from wherever she had been. The memory was fuzzy around the edges like she was trying to focus on her reflection in water that was rippling. But she heard the gunshot as clear as day. It made her eyes widen. Ben didn't flinch. He didn't hear it. But Stella did. It echoed through her mind as her eight-year-old self was being carried to safety. The man who had grabbed her was shot dead.

"He's dead," she whispered as she tried to think.

"Who's dead? What are you talking about?" Ben asked quietly.

"I know how this is going to sound but the blindfold, the blanket. That stiff, smelly blanket, it's all too familiar. They remind me of when I was a kid," she looked up at Ben.

"Stella, that's just a coincidence. A blanket like that is probably in every cellar and basement in America. And you've seen enough deaths with blindfolds, that is nothing new to you. I'm not saying what you're feeling isn't legitimate. I'm saying that after seeing so much of it your mind might be overlapping things. That's all. Why don't you go out and grab some air? Get a few deep breaths in," Ben said.

Stella nodded but she didn't think it was going to help. Ben knew she didn't believe in coincidences. How could a cop believe in something like that? There was never a clue that didn't belong with its crime.

With her legs feeling rubbery she slowly walked to the door. As the fresh air hit her, she started to feel like herself again. Sheriff Darlow was standing with a uniformed officer chatting. Stella didn't want to talk to them or tell them anything yet. Instead, she took a look around the side of the house. There was nothing out of the ordinary there. Of course, there wasn't. The killer had the key.

"It would look odd to neighbors if the ex-husband was climbing in through a window or breaking down a door," she said but the words felt clumsy and awkward coming out of her mouth. Something was telling her this wasn't the husband, but it was the only logical conclusion. It was the only thing that made sense. She took another deep breath and finished walking around the house. She shook her head, gave herself a pinch on the arm to get her back to the present moment to try and focus. There was nothing out of place around the house anyway. When she got back to the porch the sheriff was waiting and asked.

"How's it going in there?"

"We'll need to have an autopsy done before we have any real news. I'm sorry," she said.

"No, I'm the one who should be sorry. I didn't mean to bail out on you down there. It's just that..." Sheriff Darlow started.

"You don't have to apologize. I needed some air myself." Stella was surprised she admitted this to Sheriff Darlow. On one hand, she didn't want him to see her as weak. But on the other, she didn't want him to feel like he was either. This was a bad situation and they both were going to be held responsible if a resolution wasn't found quickly.

"So, what are your thoughts so far?" he asked as he crossed his arms.

"All signs are pointing to a love triangle. I'm cautiously optimistic that if we bring in the ex-husband, we'll get a confession for both deaths," Stella said. "But there is always the chance that we are wrong."

"You mean this could be a serial killer?" Sheriff Darlow said those words as if they weighed a hundred pounds in his mouth and required all his strength to quietly say them.

"What I'm really saying is that I don't know. There are too many questions still out there. An autopsy and the ex-husband will definitely shed some light for us," Stella said.

Just then Ben appeared. He was leading the way as the CSI guys finished with everything. They carried out over a dozen bags of evidence. Stella caught sight of the blanket in its plastic bag and shivered. Only Ben noticed and asked to have a couple of minutes alone with her.

"Sure thing, Detective," Sheriff Darlow said politely. "The coroner will take over. We'll let you know when Christine is done."

"Thanks," Ben said as he slipped his hand around Stella's arm and gently pulled her to the side. "I think you should sit this one out."

"What?" Stella's mouth fell open.

"I think there is something going on with this case that isn't sitting well. You took one look at that bag with the blanket in it and all the color left your face. I'm going to call Captain Briggs."

"Are you insane? And tell him what? Carrigan hadn't eaten anything this morning and the sight of a crusty, dirty blanket over a dead body that had been in a basement for a couple of days made her sick to her stomach?" Stella snapped. "So help me if you call him I'll report you to internal affairs. I'll make some shit up. I don't care."

Ben looked around and then at his watch. "Fine, Stella. But

if I see you looking green like that again I'm going to make a phone call to the 18th."

They stood back as two men with the word 'Coroner' stamped in yellow on the back of their navy-blue jackets came out of the house with a stretcher between them. The body was covered in a white sheet and they were quick and as discreet as possible with the ever-growing group of gawkers collecting on the lawns around the house.

"We need to canvas the neighborhood," she said firmly, regaining her composure because she had to. Deep down it was obvious Ben was only doing this because he was her friend. But it annoyed her, and she shook off the feeling of unease and disgust as if she was pulling off an itchy sweater.

Chapter 13

Some of the neighbors had already been out looking at all the excitement and trying to get a glimpse of something tragic or gory they could call their friends about. The nearest neighbor was a man in his late sixties. He had dark skin and curious eyes buried under bushy eyebrows that were arched in concern. His name was Bill Medea and he had lived in his house for over forty years. It was obvious he was nosy but sometimes those are the best kinds of neighbors to have.

"What's going on over there?" Bill asked the detectives.

"We aren't exactly sure," Stella replied. "Can you tell us anything about the woman who lived there?"

"They were a couple of nuts," Bill rolled his eyes. "They were always arguing. I don't think a weekend went by where they weren't having some kind of shouting match."

"Do you know about what?" Ben asked as he took notes.

"Anything," Bill said. "Just a few weeks ago I was putting the garbage cans out and they were having a knock-down-drag-out screaming match over how he had parked his car in the driveway. It was a lot of stuff like that."

"Did Mr. Casio live there?" Stella asked.

Bill shrugged. "He wasn't there all the time, but I thought maybe he was a truck driver or had a job that kept him traveling. I thought he lived there at least up until their divorce."

"How did you know they were getting a divorce?" Stella asked. She had been studying Mr. Medea and decided he was credible. He was very honest and didn't hold back his opinion. His hands were rough from a lifetime of work. His sweatshirt was old and worn. But his yard was neat and simply kept. By the front door was a statue of a pug dog in a bandana. Bird feeders hung from every tree and windchimes hung from the corner of the roof and jingled happily.

"She told me. She told everyone who would listen. He had a girlfriend, I guess. We're only getting one side of the story, but that's what she said," Bill stated.

The story he told was the same from the other neighbors who were on the other side and across the street from the Casio home. But no one saw anything strange or unusual over the past couple of weeks. The only person who was seen coming and going other than the victim was the ex-husband.

Stella, who listened to the witnesses before writing anything down, was starting to feel like her old self by the time they finished questioning anyone who might have seen anything. The cool fresh air felt good and her stomach was starting to growl from hunger.

"Are you up for some food?" Ben asked as if reading her mind.

"Yeah," Stella nodded. They got in the car and she began to scribble her notes in her worn-out pocket notebook. "It isn't looking good for the ex-husband."

"No. But like that Mr. Medea said, we are only getting one side of things," Ben replied.

"That's a typical male response," Stella smirked. "You really think Mrs. Casio did anything that warranted getting killed for?"

"No. I don't think any victims do. But, if you leave a door unlocked, you are asking to get robbed," Ben replied.

Stella pointed to the sign for Blueberry's diner. They pulled in and continued their conversation as they walked in the restaurant and took a seat at a corner booth. As usual, all eyes were on them as they weren't just a black man and a white woman coming in together, but they are strangers in Vandalia.

"You know there are some people out there who will needle a person until they snap. We've seen it a thousand times. No, I don't think they should be murdered or beaten but sometimes a person doesn't realize continuing to poke the bear will wake that shit up," Ben said as he looked over the menu.

"I get it," Stella said as she looked at the menu quickly then slid it back between the sugar and napkin holder.

"If the victim was going around telling anyone who would listen that her husband was a lowdown dirty dog, well hell, she's the one who married him," Ben said in a low voice.

"I understand your point," Stella replied. "But we are saying this like it's an open and shut case. We still have to talk to the man."

The waitress showed up with a steaming pot of coffee and a pleasant smile. Ben ordered a ham and cheese omelet. Stella ordered a cheeseburger. Both had coffee and continued their conversation in hushed tones until their order came up.

"There's no hurry but here is your check," the waitress said. Her nametag read Bonnie. It was obvious by her casual manner and the way she floated around the diner that she'd worked there for some time.

"Can I ask you a question?" Stella said quietly as she held up her badge and gave a brief reason why she and Ben were in Vandalia. "Do you know the Casio's? Had they ever been in the diner?"

"Mr. Casio had been in a couple of times. There wasn't anything out of the ordinary about him. He was a lousy tipper and mostly kept to himself. I had seen Mrs. Casio around town. She'd never come in here. Not one for mixing with the riff-raff." The waitress said. "I remember Mr. Casio getting into an argument with a man once. It was over politics or religion. One of those things they say you aren't supposed to talk about in public."

"What happened?" Ben asked.

"Mr. Casio raised his voice and started shouting. He was calling the other guy stupid and ignorant," Bonnie shook her head.

"What did the other man do?" Stella asked.

"He kept telling Mr. Casio to relax and calm down. Finally, the cook came out and told them both if they couldn't behave, they had to leave. Mr. Casio calmed down but when he left, he called the other customer a couple of names as he walked out the door. I haven't seen him since." Bonnie shrugged.

"When was this?" Stella asked.

"It had to be about a month ago. Maybe three weeks. Not long ago. But that was the last time I saw him and like I said, he was in a few times, but I wouldn't call him a regular," Bonnie said.

When she walked away Stella looked at Ben with a smirk as she took a huge bite out of her burger. In her mind, she was wrapping up this case. Like she'd predicted, everything was falling into place with a bitter ex-husband who had enough of his wife's antics and did her in.

"But what about Regina Phelps?" Ben whispered so none of the locals would hear about the other victim. So far, they'd been able to avoid a lot of pressure and prying from the local press. The last thing they wanted was for it to leak out there were two bodies connected in a way the police weren't sure of yet.

"What about her?" Stella asked.

"How does she fit in?" Ben asked. "She was stabbed. There was no strangulation."

"If Casio had a temper, maybe she voted for the wrong candidate or goes to the wrong church. Who knows? But I'll bet we'll find out soon enough," Stella said. Before they left the diner, Ben got a call from Sheriff Darlow.

"You're going to love this," Ben said after hanging up. "Mr. Casio, the ex-husband, moved to Chicago about three months ago."

Stella rolled her eyes. So much of their job was spent driving around. It was those times that aggravated Stella because she'd think her cases to death. It wasn't just this one that she had to worry about. There were over a dozen more on her desk that needed follow-up and signatures and sign-offs by the top brass. There were emails to answer and phone calls to make and statements to collect and she didn't even want to think about the bureaucracy of the department and the hoops they were going to make her jump through for warrants and evidence and everything else she needed to eventually get a conviction. It was a mess.

However, this case was the one front and center in her mind, and she didn't like it. Not one bit. But she couldn't say another word about it. Not with Ben threatening to report her for a stress test or time off. She had to pretend it was all business as usual. As much as the feel of that blanket and the look of Mrs. Casio's black blindfold looked and felt familiar to her it was exactly what Ben had said. A coincidence. A freak similarity that was bound to happen in her line of work since so many murders involved the assailant covering or blindfolding the victim. It was nothing unusual. This case *was* typical and the only things different were the victim's names. But the motive was as old as the hills. Sex. *That* Stella was sure of. Or at least as sure as she could be while she was trying to calm her nerves. They kept their rooms at the motel and B&B and drove back to the city. By the time they pulled up in front of the bungalow on Trumbell Street, it was early evening. Supper time.

Chapter 14

It took Ben twenty minutes to find a parking spot. On the south side of Chicago, it was tradition for the people who lived in the neighborhood to put out a couple of chairs with a broom or an ironing board between them to mark their parking spot on the street. Anyone who moved those items to take that parking spot would come back to find their tires slashed at the very least. It was how things were done on the south side. And even if it was a cop car, or maybe especially if it was a cop car, that moved those territorial markers they would not be spared any vandalism.

"We practically parked at Midway," Ben grumbled as they walked to the Casio house.

"Why are you complaining? I thought you and Rochelle were all into this getting healthier thing," Stella teased. "We should have parked even further away. You ate a whole omelet this morning. The calories." She put her hand to her cheek and gasped.

"Very funny. But after driving all damn day I feel like I just need to get home and put on the television," he huffed.

In this area of Chicago, the sound of planes coming in for a landing and taking off could be heard at regular intervals. The jets flew over the houses low enough for you to see the passenger's windows. The "L" Train's orange line also rumbled a couple of blocks over and it was inevitable in this part of town to get stuck for a couple of blocks behind an exhaust belching CTA bus. People sat on their stoops when the weather was nice and waved or just shouted to neighbors as they passed by. The plots of property were small but in this particular area, they were neatly kept with flowers and bushes. It was highly probable that in the back yards were vegetable gardens thick with tomatoes, banana peppers, and zucchini.

When they found the house, they were looking for they saw all the lights were on inside and the front door was cracked open.

"So help me if there is a body in this one, too..." Stella said as they both pulled out their badges and held their weapons at the ready before pressing the little orange light that was the doorbell. An angry sound like a small school bell went off.

"Just a minute!" came a male voice from inside. After a few seconds, a man in black chinos holding a plunger came to the door. He was a handsome guy with short black hair cut close on the sides and longer on top letting a natural wave go through it. It was peppered with gray as were his thick eyebrows.

When he saw the badges, he rolled his eyes. "Let me guess. Barbara sent you." He pulled the door open while setting the plunger down. As Stella told him who they were he led them to a quaint kitchen that didn't have a lot of room but was cozy.

"Sort of," Ben replied. "Mr. Casio, I think you'd better have a seat."

"Call me Ned," he said as he shook his head. "If this has to do with Barbara, I'll stay standing. What has she told you? I'm harassing her? I won't stop calling? I'm driving by her house at three in the morning? Barb can't function if there isn't drama all over the place."

"Not quite," Ben tried to be diplomatic, but Stella grabbed herself a chair and took a seat before speaking.

"Your wife is dead, Mr. Casio," she said and watched his expression.

"What? No," he said and smirked as if he'd just heard a stupid, poorly timed joke. He grabbed a chair from under the kitchen table and slowly eased himself into it.

"Can you tell us where you were over the past week to ten days?" Stella asked.

"Week to ten days? Uh…" Ned stammered and looked from Stella to Ben and back again. "I work every day. I'm a plumber. I'm putting in a new toilet here and there's a problem with the water pressure I can't figure…are you sure you're talking about Barbara Casio?"

"Yes, sir. We're sure," Ben said.

"I've been working at a couple places, uhm…ten days?" he stuttered again.

"She was just discovered today," Stella said flatly. "She'd been in the basement for some time." The image of the blanket and the blindfold rushed her memory making her shift in her seat and clear her throat as she pushed them deep down and out of view.

"Did you say the basement?" Ned's eyes widened.

"Ned, did you know anyone who might want to do harm to your wife?" Ben asked.

"She was a hard pill to swallow sometimes but kill her? No. No," Ned replied.

"You didn't have fights with her that the neighbors could hear? No arguments in the driveway about parking the car?" Stella needled.

"Oh, I get it. You automatically think that I did it," Ned stiffened and sat up straight in his seat. Stella watched as Ned began to sweat and knead his hands together.

"This is all routine questioning," Stella replied. "Mr. Casio, did you know a woman by the name of Regina Phelps?"

Ned stared at Stella for a second then shook his head.

"No. I don't know that name," he swallowed hard then cleared his throat. Suddenly, he began to cry.

"Ned?" Ben pulled out the chair next to Ned. Stella got up and walked around the small kitchen before finding her way to the hallway back toward the front door. She passed through the dining room. The table was covered with the day's mail. The newspaper from the previous weekend was open with a partially finished crossword puzzle showing.

There were pictures in the front room across the mantel of the electric fireplace that had been installed when the house was built. There was a picture of Ned and Barbara, smiling with Hawaiian leis around their necks and glasses as big as fishbowls full of some blue cocktail in each hand. They looked happy.

Stella took a deep breath and walked back to the kitchen. Ned had his head in his hands. Ben looked at Stella without any expression which meant he had no idea what to think about this.

"Mr. Casio, when was the last time you saw your wife?" Stella interrupted forcefully.

"It had to be about two weeks ago," he sniffled and went on to say that he had been working in the city for the past two weeks. He had receipts and invoices to prove where he was. He told them that it was a remodeling job that kept him busy for several days in a row. Then there were a couple of broken pipes, clogged toilets, broken faucets that tied him up the rest of the week. It would have been impossible for him to go to any of his customers, slip away to Vandalia to kill his ex-wife, and come back in time to go to his next appointment.

"Was your wife seeing anyone?" Stella asked.

"No. She never..." Ned looked down at his hands.

"Stepped out on you?" Stella finished his sentence. "Did you?"

Ned swallowed again and looked up at Stella with narrow eyes. "Yeah. I had an affair. It was a mistake. I should have just left Barbara. We just couldn't get into a groove. One week would be heaven, the next would be like being in a gulag. But I'd never kill her. Hell, after the divorce I paid for her boob job and her alimony kept her in a nice house. She didn't have to work at all."

"Barbara had quite a bit to tell the neighbors and the guy at the hardware store about you," Stella continued. "Was there more to it than just cheating?"

"I'll bet she did. I cheated more than once. I promised to stop but I've got a problem. You know, a sexual addiction," Ned said looking for sympathy from such an honest confession.

Stella smirked. "Did any of these women feel Barbara was in their way? Maybe you made promises to someone who wanted to do harm to..."

"Uh, no. I paid for...the women."
"Hookers?" Ben confirmed as he scribbled in his notebook.

"Call girls," Ned corrected with a look of disgust on his face. "I didn't just pick them up off the street."

Stella shook her head. Inside she wanted to punch Ned Casio in the face. They drove all this way for what she thought was a sure thing to nail this case shut. But her gut was telling her this guy wasn't their man. At least she didn't think he was the trigger man.

You mean the blindfold and blanket man, her conscience mocked. She shivered again at the thought of Barbara Casio underneath that blanket with her eyes covered.

He was a jerk, for sure. But that wasn't a crime. Of course, she would verify his alibis and check his phone records for any unusual calls coming in or out.
Ben wrapped up the interview and left a business card with Ned with the instructions that if he thought of anything that might be helpful, even if it seemed silly or unimportant, to give them a call. Stella stomped out of the house and marched toward the car. Her body ached and the idea of getting back in the car was enough to

make her want to scream.

"That didn't turn out the way we'd hoped," Ben said when they got to his car.

"I think I'm going to take the "L" home," Stella said.

"Are you all right?" Ben asked.

"Yeah. I don't think we should discount Ned Casio until we check his alibis. If he's dipping his pen in the escort ink, there might be someone doing some of his dirty work for him."

"If you take the "L" you might not get home until after eight. Are you sure you don't want me to drive you?" Ben asked.

"Right, because the traffic in the city is totally light at this hour on a Friday night. Are you off your rocker? Go home. Surprise Rochelle and the baby," Stella urged.

"Okay, will you text me when you get home?" Ben asked.

Stella smiled. "I promise. But I might stop and get something to eat on the way so don't put out an APB if I don't contact you until the middle of the night." Ben nodded as he jingled his keys from his pocket. "And Darlow and the crime scene photographer said they'd have everything for us in forty-eight hours. Want to go back Monday morning?"

"Can't wait."

After a few more words Stella watched him drive off before she headed toward the Metro Orange Line that would take her to downtown Chicago. Once there she'd transfer to the Red Line and get dropped off about two blocks from her home. All for less than a gourmet coffee. She found a seat and stared out the window as the landscape of the southside whipped by. Stella made sure her badge was showing to ensure no one would try to talk to her. The gentle rock of the train as it stopped and started, as it swayed on the tracks that rode over traffic relaxed Stella. It was something she was used to and enjoyed. There were no surprises on the train. It wasn't suddenly going to veer off course and take her to a scary place she hoped to never see again.

Chapter 15

When Stella finally got home it was dark. The sounds of the city bounced off the buildings and down the alleys in a comforting symphony that only Chicago could produce. The air was cool and once inside her apartment Stella went to the window and opened it up. Within seconds Cleopatra was slinking across the fire escape to scold her for not being home.

"Hi, Cleo."

"What are you doing with my cat?" Mr. Zarowny yelled from his open window.

"Getting ready to dice her up and put her in a stew!" Stella yelled back and smirked as she heard the old man laughing.

Cleopatra stayed for a few minutes and quickly made her way back to her own home. Stella climbed out on the fire escape and watched the light change at the end of the street. Red. Yellow. Green. Red again. The air smelled like rain was coming. It was cool and would probably get downright cold at around one in the morning. She had to remember to bring some warmer clothes back to Vandalia. And a raincoat just in case it rained down there.

"You're small-talking with yourself about the weather. This is not a good direction to be heading in," she muttered. She took out her notepad and began to write. She let her thoughts run wild and the horrible truth that came into crystal clear focus was that as much as she wanted Ned Casio to be responsible for his ex-wife's death it still wouldn't explain what happened to Regina Phelps. If it wasn't him then there was a good chance a serial killer was on the loose. But there was Barbara's key in Regina's room. Regina was savagely killed. Barbara was strangled.

"Two women laid out like Regina and Barbara were can't be the end. It's just the beginning." She looked at her notes and tried to find a common thread but there wasn't one. Everything led her around and around in circles.

"Regina Phelps was a foster mother. Maybe there is something going on at the Department of Child and Family Services that will tie these women together." Stella scratched her head. As she sat on the milk crate she mused over her own experience in foster care. It was a part of her life. Once she decided to be a cop, she pushed all those memories aside. It wasn't that they were all bad. There were some wonderful families that she had been fortunate enough to spend some time with. But then there was the Haley family.

Stella sat and tried to remember what they looked like. A real image didn't come to her. It was more of a feeling. That feeling of being at a party where she didn't know a soul. She was alone, standing awkwardly in a corner while everyone else seemed to slip easily and comfortably in and out of conversations with each other. No, she didn't remember what they looked like, but she remembered feeling like a complete outsider. If she let the memory linger, she'd realize that she hated the Haley's. It was bad enough she was nothing more than a shadow to them, warranting nothing more than a casual glance out of the side of their eyes when she passed. But they let him take her.

Stella shook her head and focused on the changing stoplight. It was no use hating people who she hadn't seen in over a decade. They were the shadows now, and Stella was thankful for that. It was better she didn't remember their faces or voices or anything about them or else she might find herself looking for them in a crowd. Hell, she had the entire Chicago Police Department database at her fingertips. She could track them down tomorrow if she wanted to and find out where they were living, if they were still alive, or if they were still in the foster business. DCFS had a way of not vetting a good number of families looking to take in foster children. Better the kids get into *a* home. It couldn't always be a *good* home.

"This is too much. I've got clear my head," Stella muttered before standing up with a groan and climbing back inside her apartment. She looked around with her hands on her hips and decided that she needed more than just a hot shower and a glass of wine. That wouldn't calm her mind. If anything, it might make her feel more boxed in and jittery. She looked at her watch and decided a visit to the gym was the only thing that would help get the nervous energy out and hopefully bring some tranquility in. If nothing else, she could work out to the point of exhaustion and fall asleep as soon as she got home. It was as good a plan as any.

Chapter 16

Twelve to Twelve Gym was a twenty-four-hour place within walking distance of her apartment. Stella was a member because the gym at the police station was small and often too crowded for any serious workout.

As soon as she walked in, she was greeted by the owner, Mike. The t-shirt he was wearing was stretched to maximum capacity over muscles that bulged even when he wasn't flexing. He looked up when Stella walked in and smiled.

"Hi, Detective. I haven't seen you in a while," he reached out his hand to shake.

"I know. I'm sorry, Mike. Did you know there was crime in Chicago? I can't believe it either. I've been so busy I can hardly stand it," Stella smirked as she shook his hand.

"Well, I'm glad to see you. What are you in the mood for? Do you need a spotter?" he offered. No one would think such a big guy would be so considerate. He was the typical "big teddy bear."

"No. I'm not even sure what I want. If I need you, I'll give you a shout," Stella said as she walked toward the ladies' locker room.

"Hey, even if you don't need me," Mike replied with a wink making Stella smile and shake her head.

Once she'd changed into her workout clothes and stepped up to the first weight machine to work out her legs she felt better. There were mirrors on every wall and Stella was able to see herself from every angle. She'd stayed in shape not just for her job but just in case there was ever a national emergency. Doomsday prepping was her favorite hobby, if you could call it that. Part of her wished for the zombie apocalypse. First, there would be no more reason to pay bills. Second, she could use her gun at any time without worrying about being sued or investigated by the department's Internal Affairs. That was enough to push her into a daydream while she pushed fifty pounds of weight with her legs working her thighs, calves, and glutes. The burn felt good. The music was loud enough to motivate her to keep going. She moved on to a contraption that would give her arms a full workout. She felt her muscles tingle every time they stretched and contracted. Getting blood and oxygen to her brain was next. She hopped on the elliptical, cranked the tension up, and listened to the music piped through the place as she kept her movements in time with the beat.

The pain in her muscles, the burning of her lungs as she took deep breaths, and the sweat dripping down the center of her back were enough to overshadow any other thoughts in her head. She'd set the timer for ten minutes at a good incline that worked her entire body. When the little timer beeped Stella stopped pedaling and let the machine automatically return to its original starting position. When she finally stepped off the machine and turned to go get a drink of water from the fountain, she ran right into one of the other late-night exercisers.

"I'm so sor..." Stella looked up to see an all-too-familiar face.

"I thought that was you," Cole said with a smile. "I didn't know you came to this gym."

"Only when I can't get in at the station," Stella said nervously. She didn't know why but the sight of him in a tank top, shorts, sort of sweaty with a smile on his face made her heart race as if she were back on the elliptical. "What are you doing here?"

"I like to come later at night when it's less crowded." He just kept smiling. "Can I buy you a bottle of water or a Gatorade or something?"
Why was he being so charming? She'd told him she'd be out of town for a while and here she was *in* town. Where was the

suspicion? Where were the twenty questions?

"No. No, I was just going to get a drink from the fountain and go get changed and..."

"You don't want to drink from the fountain. Come on. My treat," Cole insisted and started to stroll toward the vending machine that dropped nothing but bottles of water.

"You don't have to," Stella said.

"I know. I want to. It's really nice to see you," he said as he pulled his wallet from a secret compartment on his workout shorts and stuffed a couple dollars in the machine. With a buzzing sound then a clump-clump-crack a bottle of water fell to the trough at the bottom.

"I am just in town for the day. We head back to Vandalia tomorrow afternoon," Stella said and waited for Cole to start his interrogation.

"How's the case coming?" he asked.

"Okay, I guess," Stella replied and folded her arms across her chest.

"Do you want to talk about it?" he continued. Stella was really starting to get mad at him for looking so good and being so interested in her. What was wrong with him?

"No. Do you think I wasn't really in Vandalia?" she snapped.

"Why wouldn't you be? That's where you said you were going?" he replied innocently.

Stella huffed. "Yeah, but I'm here now, and you...*caught* me in town when I said I was going to be out of touch for a while. Aren't you the least bit interested in why I'm here?"

"Yeah, but you said you didn't want to talk about the case,

so I didn't talk about the case," he folded his arms across his chest and rocked on his heels. "Stella, haven't you ever had a guy interested in you?"

Stella pouted like he's just asked her to name the capitals of all fifty states. "I think so?" she asked more than answered.

"This is what a guy does when he's interested in you. He asks questions about your job, the things you like and don't like. Your favorite movie or favorite color. He'll ask about your family and when things get serious, he'll ask more about your beliefs and values. We haven't gotten to that part yet so don't get nervous." Cole smirked making Stella smile despite her best attempt not to.

"You're a peculiar bird," Stella muttered.

"*I* am?" Cole stared at Stella as he pointed his index finger toward himself.

"Thanks for the water," Stella said as she raised the icy cold bottle he'd bought for her.

"Are you leaving?"

"Yeah, I have to get showered and changed because we are heading back downstate tomorrow." She didn't want to tell him about stopping at the DCFS office. That would mean she would have to tell him about the case and that she was stumped and if she didn't want to admit it to her partner of a couple years, she certainly didn't want to tell a prospective boyfriend she was having trouble. Did she really just refer to him as her boyfriend? That was a little premature. She'd barely kissed him. Actually, she *really* kissed him and had almost forgotten about it. And here he was standing in front of her looking better than the tall drink of water she had in her hand.

"Are you sure you don't have time to sit, finish that bottle of water?" he asked.

"No, I have to go," she replied, her cheeks flushing red. It was obvious that even though she was turning Cole down she was going against what her heart really wanted. He seemed to pick up on it as well.

"At least let me walk you to your car," he said as if reading her mind about the kiss they'd shared the last time he walked her to her car.

"I don't live far from here. I walked," she replied, instantly sorry she disclosed so much information about where she lived.

"Oh, well, let me walk you home," his eyes twinkled. "It can be dangerous out there and a little scary. It's not safe to walk alone."

"I'm a cop, Cole. I think I know how to handle myself," Stella replied with a smirk.

"I was talking about me," he replied making Stella laugh. "That's a nice sound."

"What's that?"

"Your laugh," Cole said.

"I appreciate your offer to walk me home. I'm going to hit the shower and then head on out. But..." She hesitated for a second then let the words tumble out of her mouth. "Next time you can walk me home."

"It's a date," Cole said.

As Stella stood under the running water of the shower, she wondered why she had said that to Cole. She didn't know if she really wanted him to walk her home. Heck, she wasn't even sure if they were going to finish their first date. It might have been better just to blow him off and never call again. Besides, what was with him? He wasn't asking any deep questions or even wishing her luck on the case. What kind of person was he?

Of course, she knew she was being unfair. The poor guy was damned if he did and damned if he didn't. Here he was being a hundred different ways of nice and sweet and even funny and that wasn't good enough.

"It's the case, that's all. The case has you tied up in knots," she said to herself, her words bouncing off the taupe colored tiles. When she finished and got dressed, she hoped she wouldn't run into Cole as she was leaving. It would be another round of awkward good-byes and uncomfortable small talk.

Her hair was still wet as she packed up her bag and hurried out of the locker room. She kept her eyes forward and when Mike asked her if she'd be coming back again soon, she shrugged and said she hoped so as she walked out the door. After scanning the parking lot, she was glad she didn't see any movement. No one was around. The sidewalks were relatively quiet and the traffic, although steady, not bad for a Sunday night in Chicago.

She hurried to her apartment and once inside let out a deep breath as if Cole had given chase down the sidewalk, calling her name while waving madly.

"You should have gone for a drink with him. It isn't Cole that has something wrong with him. It's you," she said as she slipped all the locks in place. There was nothing on television that held her interest. She put on the radio but there was nothing but commercials and crappy songs she either never heard of or heard too much of. She had heard the Rolling Stones song *Satisfaction* so many times in her life she was ready to puke.

So, she grabbed the file of material Deputy Winger was so reluctant to give up and hoped something new would jump out at her. It didn't. They were the same old details that led nowhere. The key that opened Barbara Casio's house was the only thing tying the women together. How did Regina get it and why did she have it?

Her mind felt even more tattered and worn out than it did

before she went to the gym. She paced around her apartment trying to think of something else to do. She couldn't look at the file anymore. She didn't want to read even though she had a couple of novels she'd picked up at a thrift store that were begging for her attention. She'd just had a shower so soaking in a tub or another shower sounded like terrible ideas. Even a glass of wine held no interest. Her mind just refused to settle. And to make things worse, the fact her workout was good meant she had even more energy.

At that precise moment, she remembered the CD Ben had given her. It was to help her relax. As much as she thought the New Age movement was hooey and these kinds of gimmicks were for people easily led, she relented. After pressing a few buttons, the disc was in her CD player and the sound of a trickling waterfall filled the room. Stella instantly liked the sound.

"If this works, I'll never tell him. I'll take it to my grave before I tell Ben this helped," she said to her apartment furniture. She stretched out on the couch, closed her eyes, and listened.

Chapter 17

The male voice that spoke over the waterfall was a deep, soothing voice that reminded Stella of Darth Vader had he done New Age voiceovers. At first, when he instructed her to get comfortable and pay attention to her breathing, she couldn't help but talk back.

"I tried this already. Don't you think I would have tried laying down, getting comfortable and breathing deeply already?" she stretched out on her couch as she argued with the CD. "It was the first thing I tried, pal. It didn't work then. I doubt it will work now."

After letting out a deep breath she continued to listen. As the narrator told her some mumbo-jumbo about the way her mind was working and what lies just beneath the surface of everyone's conscious thoughts all Stella saw were the faces of her victims. They swirled around, dangling over a black hole with nothing to connect them. There was no common thread and that was consuming Stella's thoughts. How was she going to solve this case? And worse yet, what if she couldn't? How would she go back to the 18th Precinct without a win in her pocket? She'd blow her image. The talk about her being gifted or special would disappear and she'd be just another average detective. That thought stuck in her mind like a popcorn kernel between two molars. It was tiny, thin, almost transparent but it brought such pain and discomfort she couldn't take it.

Could that really be what had been bothering her for so long? Her reputation? How the other cops might look at her? Suddenly, a wave of shame fell over her. Never in a million years did she think she was so superficial but here it was staring her in the face. Or at least ringing in her ears.

"So what if you don't get this case solved in record time like the others," she muttered. The real reason I want to get this wrapped up is because the victims deserve it. I've always thought that. That's what makes me solve them."

The narrator continued speaking every couple of minutes. His instructions were to feel every bit of her body sinking into relaxation one appendage at a time starting with her toes.

This kind of stuff she'd seen before on Lifetime movies where some pervy shrink would put a woman under hypnosis and when she woke up, she was pregnant. The thought made her chuckle. But she continued to listen, fairly sure she'd gotten as much out of the CD as she was going to. But still, she was feeling pretty relaxed and thought the worst that could happen was that she'd fall asleep. And that was what she had been hoping for all along. She continued to listen. Her body became more relaxed. Her mind cleared as she concentrated on her breathing. Soon, she was feeling light and warm and maybe even a little peaceful. With her eyes closed, she listened as the narrator instructed her to go to a place that makes her happy. Even if she'd never been there in real life, she could dream about it. So, Stella dove right in. She'd always thought that she'd retire to the mountains, live in a log cabin maybe not completely off the grid but pretty close to it. She'd hunt and fish and have a pick-up truck and wood-burning fireplace with a year's worth of firewood stacked next to the house. Big pine trees would guard her property and deer would stroll across the front yard and cardinals would frequent the bird feeders she'd have posted all over. It was her happy place. Her dream house.

Stella stayed there for as long as the narrator allowed her, with the water still trickling in the background and her body feeling comfortable and still. Finally, her mind had slowed down enough for her to rest. When the first chapter came to an end, Stella sat up feeling refreshed and ready to go lie down for a real night's sleep. As she climbed between the sheets, the cool material rustling against her legs and feet she took a deep breath and let out a long sigh.

"I'll never tell Ben it actually worked," she chuckled. "He'll never let me forget it."

Chapter 18

"You look well-rested," Ben said as they met at the 18th Precinct the next morning.

"Yeah, I went to the gym and hit the sack early," she replied. "So, I want to go to DCFS to ask around about our first victim."

"Do you mean the first victim found or technically the first victim murdered?" Ben asked. "I'm telling you that the whole thing had me in knots half the night. I finally broke down and had to tell Rochelle about it. It seems to help when I've got someone else to talk to. No offense."

"None taken," Stella couldn't help but remember Cole's offer to talk and she shot him down. Had she shared anything with him she might have found the same peace she did listening to Ben's CD. "How does Rochelle feel after you tell her about a case like this? I mean, two women are dead. It pretty grizzly and scary."

"First, Rochelle isn't a shrinking violet. She's pretty tough. But aside from that, she knows that my work is ugly. Can you think of any case we've dealt with that wasn't a heartbreaking mess?" Ben asked to which Stella shook her head no. Homicide detectives investigated murders. There was never any deviation from that. There was always a dead body and there was always someone responsible for it.

"So, when I talk to her we usually get some wine and make sure the baby is asleep, then we sit together and I talk and she listens," Ben shrugged.

"Does she ever offer advice? You know, tell you to look at one thing or another?"

"Usually she listens. Sometimes she'll tell me to put it all out of my head for a while. Sometimes she'll tell me to pray. But usually, she just listens," Ben said.

"You're a lucky man. You should send her some flowers," Stella suggested.

"You know what? That's a good idea. I'll do that," Ben snapped his fingers as he replied.

After Stella told him a little more about Regina Phelps, the foster mother, Ben agreed a trip to the Department of Child and Family Services was in order.

When they got there, Stella felt a wave of familiarity with the place as they walked in. Like most government facilities, there was one person manning a small podium who would tell you in which line you were supposed to go. That was the great thing about having a badge.

Stella walked up to the woman who gave her a look with heavy eyelids, already tired of working even though it was only nine in the morning.

"I'm Detective Stella Carrigan, this is Detective Ben Carey. We'd like to talk to someone about Regina Phelps," she said, holding up her badge.

"Just a moment," the woman said before picking up her phone and calling for backup by dialing with her extra-long acrylic nails. It was written on her face that she was not willing to take any responsibility for letting the police into this office. Someone else had to make the call and then anything that happened after that was that person's fault.

She turned to the right, thinking Stella and Ben couldn't hear what she was saying.

"Yeah, Joyce, this is Tammy at the front desk. There are two police officers here who want to talk to someone about Regina," Tammy said. "No, I didn't tell them anything. No, they didn't ask. Okay." Stella watched as Tammy hung up the phone, swiveled in her seat, and looked up at her.

"You can have a seat," Tammy said before she began to shuffle papers around and look busy. The DCFS office did look busy but Stella had a bias against the place. They were in charge of placing children in foster care. It may have been a different year with different people behind the desks, but it was the same red tape and C.Y.A. way of thinking as Tammy just proved.

Within just a few minutes Joyce appeared. She was a huge woman who was wider than she was tall. "Hello, I'm Joyce Keyes. Can I help you?" Joyce said with wide eyes but no smile.

"Hello," Stella said making introductions again. "We're here to talk to someone about Regina Phelps. Are you her supervisor?"

"I am the Operations Analyst and Public Service Administrator. I was already contacted by police on the phone and told them everything I know," Joyce said to Ben, sidestepping Stella. "She hadn't shown up for work for several days. I thought she quit."

"Did you work closely with her?" Ben asked as Stella began to take notes, not missing that Joyce was more interested in speaking to a male officer than a female.

"I'm the Operations Analyst and Public Service Administrator," Joyce said. Her response had Stella looking her up and down, taking note of her stoic expression and unwillingness to give any information that might stray from the company bullet points.

"Would you say you had conversations with her every day?" Ben asked.

"We discussed her work, responsibilities, expectations," Joyce said looking around nervously worried she might say the wrong thing resulting in a set of metal handcuffs being slapped on her wrists.

"You didn't chit-chat? Talk about plans for the weekends or what was going on in day-to-day life?" Ben asked.

"We weren't friends," Joyce continued. "She was an employee. I didn't know her well enough to say what she did on her weekends or when she left here."

"Can we see her desk?" Stella asked.

"What?" Joyce snapped, looking at Stella as if she were a pesky child interrupting the grown-up's conversation.

"Her desk. Where she sat and worked. Can we see it?" Stella said as if Joyce was nothing more than hard of hearing. Stella watched her swallow hard and pinch her lips together. Without uttering another word, Joyce led Stella and Ben to a two-person cubicle where a young man was sitting at a computer with a stack of files that looked a lot like the files Stella and Ben had waiting on their desks.

"Wes, make room for these people. They need to look at Regina's desk," Joyce ordered.

"Oh, okay," Wes said as he fumbled with the file he was working on, quickly shuffled it together, hit a couple keys on the keyboard, and clumsily stood up.

"It's all right. You can stay where you are," Stella said as she stepped closer to the desk that had been Regina's. It had already been cleaned off. There were no personal effects left behind. No pictures or inspirational quotes or calendar with kittens on it.

"The police already talked to us. We weren't told *not* to move anything." Joyce balked. "Those cases needed to be addressed. They were already behind by a couple of days. We have quotas to keep up and if we'd let them sit any longer there would have been..."

"Calm down, Ms. Keyes," Stella snapped. "You said you didn't talk with her about anything but work?"

"That's right," Joyce replied as if the words had a slightly bitter flavor to them.

"Then I think we are done with you for the time being," Stella snapped and looked at Wes who, by the subtle twinkle in his eyes, was enjoying the smack-down his supervisor was getting. "Did you work with Regina Phelps?"

"I did. For almost three years," Wes replied, looking nervously from Stella to Joyce and back again. Stella and Ben got the hint.

"Ms. Keyes, will you give us a moment?" Stella looked at Joyce who was pursing her lips. There was something going on at DCFS that Joyce was determined to protect. Stella had assumed it wasn't anything more than a company man protecting the company. It wasn't like anyone in Chicago could ever get fired from a government job once they had one. That was a rule everyone from the Windy City knew. But still, Stella was more than a little suspicious of Joyce's behavior.

"Ms. Keyes, I have a few questions for you myself," Ben said. "Do you have an office where we can talk?"

Stella watched as Joyce led Ben to a conference room and not her office. She was a tough old bird. Stella wondered if that was her own idea or protocol if the fuzz showed up to investigate anything.

"Is your supervisor always like that?" Stella asked Wes who had let out a deep breath once Joyce was out of the way.

"Yeah. She's always like that," he said and smiled sadly. Stella grabbed the empty chair that had been Regina's and took a seat facing Wes. She thought he was a pleasant-looking fellow. Not like Cole, but he had a boyish face that was easy to look at, and his body, although not toned like Cole's, appeared in good shape.

"What is your full name?" Stella asked in her 'just-the-facts' tone of voice.

"Wes Tyler," he replied as he watched Stella write it down in her little book.

"You said you worked with Regina a couple of years. What can you tell me about her?" Stella said, skipping right to the chase.

"She was great. I don't know what you know about the foster care business, but it has its trials. Sometimes, you can really get weighted down by the bullshi...by the garbage. Not every story has a happy ending, no matter how hard we try," Wes said.

"Yes," was all Stella said as she started to write in her notes. Wes had no way of knowing how much experience Stella had with foster care. But she understood his feelings on the matter and knew all too well that not every case had a happy ending.

Wes went on to tell her about Regina and what a great coworker she was. "I'm not saying she was Superwoman or anything. I'm just saying that she was a good person to talk to. She knew how to laugh when things got hard, and she was happy for you when things worked out. Not just *office happy* like Joyce would be. If something turned out well Joyce would say good job but you didn't get X-Y-Z so you need to focus on that. You could never be successful. You were always missing the mark. But Regina was genuinely happy if you got a good break or a successful adoption or a new family that really had everything going for them. Like I said, this is a hard job. Encouragement is necessary. Now that Regina is gone, all we have is Joyce," Wes, wiped his eye and smiled at Stella. "Don't be surprised if the next time you come here half the office has quit and been replaced." He chuckled but there was a hint of real sadness in his voice.

"Wes, did Regina say anything to you about going to Vandalia, Illinois? Did she have any family or friends there?" Stella asked.

"She didn't say anything to me. When I heard the news, I wondered myself what the heck she was doing out in the sticks. That's not even our jurisdiction so it isn't like she had a case there or was doing some kind of wellness check. It's really strange," Wes said and shrugged his shoulders.

"Did she mention anything about her home life? Did she have a boyfriend?"

"No. Her husband died young in some kind of car accident. If I remember right it was a rainy night and it wasn't anyone's fault. Just an act of God," Wes shrugged again. "But she didn't date all that often. And I never understood that because she was really pretty and just had such a big heart."

"Would she have told you about a boyfriend if she had one?" Stella prodded.

"I think so. I've told her about mine," he smiled. "You know how it is when you work this close to someone every day."

Stella nodded and thought that Wes and Regina were probably similar to her and Ben, minus the gun and life or death scenarios.

"So, she didn't say anything about having a date, or taking a trip to Southern Illinois?" Stella asked.

"Not to me. Nope."

"Did she have any hobbies that might have brought her to a small town? Antiquing or maybe she mentioned purchasing something online that she'd have to go pick up?" Stella was desperate for an answer that could lead her somewhere, anywhere where there might be some kind of link with Barbara Casio.

"Nothing like that. She liked to shop but not for anything she couldn't get in the city. She watched a lot of movies, too. But I can't see her taking a trip so far south for a movie," Wes replied. "I'm sorry I'm not more helpful. But I only know what I know."

"It's all right," Stella said softening her gaze but not smiling. Just then she noticed in the empty cubicle across from Wes and Regina was a vase of flowers with blooming rosebuds. She remembered the dried up dead flowers in Barbara's hair and had to ask. "Where did those flowers come from?"

"A family just officially adopted their foster kids last week. They sent that to one of the other case coordinators because they helped facilitate the foster care. They were thankful for the help. We get flowers or chocolates or little gifts sometimes from grateful parents. It isn't always but sometimes," Wes said. "One time I got a box of cigars. I don't smoke. But it was the thought that counts."

"Was Regina involved with this family?" Stella asked seeing just a slim line of connection that was more like a spiderweb between two trees. In the right light, you might be able to see it, but it was mostly invisible, undetectable, and easily broken.

Wes turned to his computer and banged away on a couple of keys before he shook his head. "According to this, she didn't touch that case. It was Maggie Dillon. She's on maternity leave now. That's why the flowers are over here instead of at her desk. Joyce said she'd send it to her but has yet to do so."

That canceled out the possibility the rosebuds were the same as the dried ones in Barbara's hair. Stella swallowed and looked over her notes.

"Tell me, is Wes short for something?" Stella asked. She didn't know why and wasn't even sure where that question came from. But it came out before she could give it much thought.

"No. Just plain Wes," he shrugged again. "Detective, do you think you'll find who did this to Regina? I'm not trying to be a smartass or anything. It's just that it always seems to happen to the good guys, you know?" Wes said, his eyes getting slightly red around the edges.

"Yes. I know," Stella said and stood up from her seat. "I can assure you that we are doing our best. If you think of anything else that you might have forgotten, even if you think it's unimportant, please, give me a call," she pulled a business card from her back pocket and handed it to Wes.

"I'll do that," Wes said. He didn't seem all that impressed with her standard reply. But it was true. She and Ben were doing their best. And they wanted to solve the case. But it seemed everywhere they turned they were coming up empty-handed. Still, Wes didn't need to know that. Maybe Ben was having better luck with Joyce in the conference room.

Stella shook his hand and was surprised such a soft-spoken guy had such a firm grip. He smiled at her and she gave him a nod and a smirk, the best she could do under the circumstances. Had he given her a lead she might have cracked a smile. As she walked to the conference room, she did notice a couple of desks had bouquets on them. That was a nice gesture. It was more than she ever got for solving a case.

Once at the conference room door she knocked, then turned the knob, opened the door, and walked in. Joyce looked up angrily. She wasn't used to anyone else calling the shots in the office and wasn't happy about any of this.

"So, are we done here?" Joyce said, forcing a grin that made her look more seasick than anything else.

Ben stood and handed her a business card and told her if she thought of anything else to please call the precinct. As they walked out Joyce immediately picked up the conference room phone and called Wes, demanding he come to the conference room. Stella and Ben saw themselves out.

"There was a vase of flowers with rosebuds on it in the cubicle across from where Regina sat. Some woman on maternity leave got them from a grateful family, Wes told me," Stella said. "They looked like the same kind that were tangled in Barbara's hair but..."

"But that isn't enough to charge anyone with anything," Ben said.

"So what did you learn from Joyce?" Stella asked.

"Aside from the fact that she wasn't going to say shit without written approval for each sentence from the head of the department?" Ben replied.

"What? Did you tell her she could be charged with obstruction if she didn't cooperate?" Stella huffed. "Do we need to go back in there? Because I'm ready to crack some skulls. Something funny is going on in that place and Joyce knows it. I say we take her downtown and have a little chat in *our* conference room."

"All Joyce knows is how to say yes to the higher-ups. She's an empty suit," Ben said. "After I asked her how long she worked for DCFS she started to let out a little more information. She's been here for eight years. She started where Regina and Wes were in a cubicle handling individual cases. Then she got a promotion. But get this, she didn't know how adoptions were done because she never had any family adopt. She didn't know how many cases Regina had when she disappeared, other than a lot. And she had a cousin in City Hall who is married to someone in the Parks Department."

"That sounds about right. The City of Chicago's hiring procedure, it isn't what you know but who you know," Stella griped. There were more than enough examples of nepotism in the police department. Seeing it in other places where everyone knew no real work was being done made Stella mad.

"But truthfully, I don't think Joyce knew anything other than what she's been told. She's not an independent thinker. She wants her job and the salary and to quietly go about her business. Regina being murdered isn't nearly as upsetting to Joyce as the fact that now she has to divvy up the caseload until she hires a replacement. And she's in no hurry to do that because she'll be saving the department money if she can work the other employees to death," Ben said. "We've both seen it before."

"I don't know, Ben. I get a weird feeling about this place. Like something was quickly covered up with a blanket in the hope we might not peek underneath," Stella said.

"I think that is your past causing you a little anxiety. And rightfully so," Ben replied.

"Maybe. But one thing is for sure, that place is not operating like the well-oiled machine it's supposed to be and all I can think about are the kids on the receiving end of it," Stella sighed as they got to the car.

Chapter 19

When Stella and Ben walked into the precinct Stella felt like everyone was looking at her. She hadn't solved the case yet. Normally she'd have some kind of update or report saying they were closing in, but she had nothing to offer at all in this case. She felt like she was being judged and that made her mad. She stomped to her office with the intention of checking her phone messages and email but instead found the toxicology report and forensics findings on Regina and Barbara had been completed and sent to her.

Quickly, she shut her door. It wasn't that she didn't want Ben in on it, but she wanted to see everything first, chew on it, digest it, all the while praying there would be some kind of connection that not only linked the women together but pointed to a common person they had missed or maybe didn't even know about.

"Okay, Regina. What have you got to tell me? You were strangled. Yes. The bruising pattern on your skin says by a rope or bungee cord. So, the perp probably took it with him since it wasn't at the scene," Stella said to her empty office. "No trophies appeared to be taken like jewelry. The lock of hair was yours. Weird. The scratches on your neck were self-inflicted. Obviously, you were trying to pry up the rope around your neck."

Stella took a seat and a deep breath before letting it out. Her ritual was to read over every word slowly to make sure she could see as clear a visual in her mind as possible. If she had the movie running in her head, she was less likely to forget the details of the report.

"No fingerprints at the scene. Of course, there weren't," she muttered. "But, Regina, you were killed somewhere else and brought to the room at the motel. How in the world did that happen? The real question was how did it happen that no one saw a damn thing?"

Stella continued to read the file like she was reading a best-selling book and was talking out the details to help her understand what had happened.

"Regina was killed sometime between midnight and three on Friday morning. She wasn't in the room when Sally Greene checked the place at six-thirty a.m. but she was there when Sally returned around six-thirty in the evening. How did he get her in the room?" Stella shook her head. Reluctantly she moved on to Barbara's reports and braced herself for more questions and no answers.

Barbara was killed two days before Regina. Strangled in the same manner and with the same or similar rope or bungee cord. Similar scratches. Now Stella felt her heart starting to pound harder. As she read over the file it became more and more apparent that there was no real connection between the two women. They were strangers to each other. That could only mean one of two things.

The killer had somehow seen both of them and tied them together in his mind. They both had blonde hair. Maybe that was enough for him. Serial killers had stranger ways of picking their victims than that. Hell, maybe the voices in the guy's head were all there was standing between him and the choice of his next victim. At this very moment, he could be staring at two ladies in a drug store and the voice says *take the one in the pink blouse, not the one wearing running shoes*. And there the choice would be made.

"A serial killer," Stella muttered. She'd gone after people who left a trail. Usually a paper trail or computer trail. This was different. As creepy as it sounded this killer was more organic, prowling around like any predator looking for the perfect opportunity more than the perfect victim. She'd never dealt with a serial killer, but she knew enough to know that at any moment they could just stop. The urge will recede like sea anemones when the ripple of the water indicates danger is coming. He'll blend into the scenery and vanish until one day, after the cases of Regina Phelps and Barbara Casio are coated in a layer of dust in the cold case archives, his urge will burst forth with more fury and force than a volcano erupting. And by that time Stella might be retired or dead or stuck behind a desk pushing a pencil. Who knew?

Suddenly, the feeling time was running out washed over her. As she looked around her office everything came into sharp focus. Did she really want to continue to pursue this? Something was wrong with the whole case and maybe she wasn't the person cut out to solve it. It would require swallowing a huge slice of humble pie to pass it off. Not to mention that Ben might be pissed if she did. But there was a nagging feeling that just wouldn't let up and no matter what angle Stella tried to look at the case from she came up with nothing. How could there be no angle to lead anywhere? Not even a long shot, one-in-a-million chance? Every way she looked was a dead end. Was this just fate's way of telling her she'd met her match? Maybe a more seasoned detective should take the reins? She called Ben in and went through the file with him, sharing her fear and taking a little comfort in the fact he felt it too.

But as if that wasn't bad enough, Stella got a call from Captain Briggs. At first, she thought Ben had made good on his threat to report her odd behavior to him. But it had nothing to do with Ben. Mr. Victor Gaines had called the Vandalia Police Department to say a woman had broken into his home and stole his property and she looked an awful lot like Detective Stella Carrigan.

"The window was left open," Stella lied to the Captain. "I was just jogging around the crime scene. You know how the culprit sometimes returns to the scene of the crime."
"And what was Ben's part in this?" Captain Briggs mumbled as he looked at some random documents in front of him.

"Uh, Ben wasn't there. I was up before the rooster. I just

took a jog. Vandalia's not that big of a town. Before I knew it, I was around the building and saw the bathroom window open. The occupant of the room next to the murder scene has a reputation of being a bit strange, claims he murdered over thousand Vietcong, says he didn't hear anything but was happy to tell us initially that he can hear "them" all sneaking around. Why would I not take a peek?" Stella shrugged.

"According to the report by Deputy Winger of Vandalia he's got a very upset resident who feels he's being harassed. You're only saving grace is that the man did not file a report with the deputy. Otherwise, I would have yanked you off that case so fast you'd have whiplash," Captain Briggs hissed.

"Yes, sir," Stella replied. "I thought a double murder was enough for probable cause. I'll know better next time."

"You're on thin ice, Carrington," Captain Brigg's finally looked up at Stella, his eyes were as hard as glaciers and his jaw muscles pulsed. "I told Deputy Winger if there were any more problems, he was to call me immediately."

Great, Stella thought but said nothing and just nodded. "I really thought I had something with that guy, Cap. You won't have any more problems."

Captain Briggs let out a deep breath. "Stella, this kind of thing is done when a detective is starting to buckle to the pressure. You've got no leads and the clock is ticking. You've had a good run but maybe this case should be handed over to someone with more experience. It's not to say you haven't done a good job. You have. Everyone knows it. It's impossible to ignore that you've cracked your share of cases. Yes, Stella, you are a good Chicago cop. But there comes a time when all good cops get the feeling they need to slow down and take a break. And if you don't see it then I've got to make that call. Do I need to make that call now?"

"No sir," Stella said immediately. "No. This won't happen again. I promise."

Briggs nodded and looked back down at his papers without saying another word until Stella stood up and went to the door.

"I've instructed Deputy Winger to contact me," he said.

Stella stood with her back to the Captain and her hand inches away from the doorknob. She froze. Then, in defeat, she dropped her hand to her side and turned around to face him.

"You know he doesn't like me. He didn't like the idea of a Chicago Detective being sent to work on the case. And I asked him to take a dog to the shelter," Stella sighed.

"What?"
"A dog. One of the victims had a dog and it needed to be taken to the shelter and I asked him to do it. Sheriff Darlow made him do it because I was working the scene. He didn't like that. Not one bit," Stella admitted.

"Making friends wherever you go, I see," Briggs huffed. "Get out of my office. And don't let me get another phone call like this last one or you'll find yourself suspended without pay. Do you understand me?"

Stella nodded her head, felt for the doorknob behind her, and opened the door. Briggs didn't stop her so she quickly slipped out and headed back to her office where Ben was waiting.

Chapter 20

"At least we haven't gone backward," Ben said as he rubbed the back of his neck. Since Briggs didn't ask for her to send Ben in, she decided to spare him the gory details and said that her discussion with him was just a rehash of a whole lot of nothing happening.

Stella started to laugh as she sat back in her chair. "What if this case is what it appears to be? A serial killer with no rhyme or reason for the victims he chooses except that they are female and blonde at this point."

"We don't know if that's what we've got yet. Maybe if we go back to reinterview the ex-husband, or go back to Vandalia and talk with the people at the motel... Vietnam Victor might be worth a second glance," Ben said.

"Right. That will get us kicked off the case and suspended for sure," Stella replied.

"I don't know. He sure did know who to call when he was angry. Like he wanted to have everything turned around on us to distract from what he was actually up to," Ben said.

"That still wouldn't explain how he knew Regina or Barbara," Stella said but caught herself. "But maybe that doesn't matter. He was a regular at the motel so maybe people in town knew him. If anyone at the hardware store encountered him, we might have a connection to Barbara. And he was staying right next door to where Regina's body was found. It's a stretch but you might be right. A second look wouldn't hurt."

Ben pulled out his cell phone. "I'm going to let Rochelle know we're going back to Vandalia."

Stella nodded but before Ben called his wife she

interrupted with a grave look on her face. "I think we should run this through the criminal database and see if there aren't any cold cases in Illinois, maybe go as far as Indiana, Wisconsin and see if there are any matches to the M.O."

"Stella, I don't know if we have enough to go on. Strangulation is a pretty common method of murder," Ben said. "And Regina was beaten and stabbed in addition to attempted strangulation. I'm afraid we can't rule out two separate murderers."

"Yeah, but in both cases, it was some kind of rope that was used. They were both blonde and positioned. I think it's worth a look. Maybe someone has come out of hiding. Our time might be running out." Stella hated the words she just spoke. They left a bad taste in her mouth and a queasiness in her stomach. Still, it was all she could come up with to narrow things down. That was funny to her: she was going to open the floodgates in order to find a needle in a haystack. Brilliant.

"You might be right," Ben said sadly. "I'll let Rochelle know and then I'll meet you in the lab to submit the information to..." just then the telephone rang, making them both jump.

"Jeez," Stella muttered angrily. "Carrigan," she barked in her phone.

"I'm sorry to bother you, Detective," it was Sheriff Darlow.

"That's okay, Sheriff," Stella waved Ben back to shut the door and sit down. "Detective Casey and I were just discussing your situation in Vandalia."
"I'm afraid I've got bad news," the sheriff said, his voice wavering.

"What bad news?" Stella said while she looked right at Ben.

"We found another body," Sheriff Darlow replied.

Within half an hour Stella and Ben were on the expressway driving back to Vandalia. The cold case lab would have to wait. It was the middle of the afternoon on a Monday and traffic was a nightmare. Of course, an accident caused a back-up on the Dan Ryan and then construction on I-80 pulled everything to a near halt.

"This kills me. I don't think there has ever been a time in all my years in Illinois that I-80 wasn't under construction," Ben said as he eased the car to a stop after moving only about three feet.

"Take the next off-ramp and we'll go through suburbia. Once we get past a certain point it's all cornfields anyway," Stella said as she relaxed in the passenger's seat. "I don't know how you could complain about driving a car like this. It's like floating," she teased.

"You hungry?" Ben asked.

"Not really. I can wait until we get to Vandalia. I think stopping at the diner again to ask around about Vietnam Victor might be a good idea after we view the latest victim," Stella said as she closed her eyes. Crazy as it seemed, she was mentally doing the relaxation technique she'd listen to the previous night and was enjoying her thoughts about her cabin off in the mountains. She dosed off the for the majority of the trip. But once they crossed the line into Vandalia her eyes automatically popped open. This time they weren't heading to a house or motel. This body was found in a park.

Chapter 21

The sun had started to sink behind the tree line making the branches and dry leaves still clinging to them look like pulsing black veins against the orange horizon. Someone was burning leaves and the air smelled good reminding Stella of fall and school. Halloween was less than a week away and the cool night temperature made Stella glad she'd brought some of her thick, bulky sweaters along.

She called Sheriff Darlow to tell they'd made it back to town and he gave them directions to the park with the promise to meet them there.

"Sheriff Darlow doesn't sound good," Stella said.

"What do you mean?" Ben asked.

"He's got that distant sound in his voice like he's had enough. This is getting to him, too," Stella said.

It would have been hard to miss the location of the body since there were over a dozen cars parked a distance from the scene roped off with yellow tape.

"Jeez, this is every cop in town lined up here," Ben mused. "If we have any integrity of the scene left, I'll be amazed."

They parked, got out of the car, and marched up to the group, their badges showing for everyone to see.

"Hey, make room!" It was Sheriff Darlow shouting at his men who were primarily just milling around. Tiffany was back snapping pictures and the crime scene investigators were also carefully tiptoeing around the perimeter with flashlights and baggies in their latex-covered hands.

"Sheriff," Stella didn't believe in niceties at times like this. "Where is the body?"

"Detective, I don't mean any disrespect," he said and stopped her from proceeding by standing in her way. "But this has turned into a real shit-show. I've got the press and the mayor breathing down my neck that this is going to either end badly or worse yet, not end at all. Now, after you look at this and my men have cleaned everything up, I need you two to tell me what your plan is. Are we supposed to just sit here with our heads up our asses until this maniac waltzes right up to the station to turn himself in?"

"I understand your frustration, Sheriff, but..."

"Do you?" Sheriff Darlow barked.

Stella squared her shoulders and stared at the sheriff for several seconds before speaking. "Sheriff Darlow. I'm here to do a job and you people are the ones who called us. Believe me when I say I'd rather be in Chicago than down here in shit-kicker central. Now, do you want to show me where this latest victim is, or should my partner and I just turn around and drive back to the big city and let you and Barney Fife handle this?"

Sheriff Darlow stared back at Stella then looked at Ben. It became instantly clear to the sheriff that Ben was in agreement with his partner. He shook his head, looked down at his boots, and said nothing more except a grunt to follow him where the body was.

Stella didn't know where this tiny town came up with five huge floodlights to illuminate the area, but they were extremely helpful as they approached the body. All the men parted and formed little cliques away from Stella and Ben so they could whisper about the outsiders in their town doing nothing to solve this case.

"This one has dark hair. There goes one theory out the

window," Stella muttered to Ben. The body was positioned, like the others. No stab wounds. There was bruising around her neck but until Christine Lustyk could confirm it, they couldn't be sure it was strangulation or if it was done with the same kind of rope as the other victims. That was when she saw the beans.

"Stella, you okay?" Ben asked. He'd been talking and Stella didn't reply. "Stella, don't make me put you in the back of that ambulance here in front of everybody."

The sight of the kidney beans made Stella's stomach curdle. She took a couple of deep breaths and looked away for a second.

"I'm all right. But this is just too strange," she said putting her hand to her mouth as if she just might puke.

"What is?" Ben asked. "Do you know this woman? Because you look like you've seen a ghost."

"I hate beans. Hate them," Stella replied just above a whisper.

Ben looked around. "That doesn't make any sense. What do you mean you hate beans? So what?"

But she didn't say anything for several seconds. Ben looked like he was about to risk their reputation and have the EMTs check her out, so she snapped out of it.

"What are her hands tied with?" Stella asked as she looked up at the sky taking a few deep breaths.

"It looks like some kind of twine. Not rope but twine," Ben said as he looked back at Stella who was back to staring at the woman. Really, she was trying to see the victim when in reality all she could see were the beans. She tried to study her face, her position, the disruption of the area surrounding her body. But the beans were there, staring right at Stella and making her remember that smell, the fuzzy taste they had in her mouth. How many years had it been since she thought about eating those things? She avoided them at all costs. There was no stopping the intrusion of the memory about these things from bursting into the forefront of her mind like that red guy in the Kool-Aid commercials burst through walls.

She'd been forced to eat those for days. But no one knew that. No one had any idea why she'd freak out over the sight of beans scattered on and around a dead body. Stella shivered from the thought but played it off like she was just cold. She walked around the body and began to search the area for any footprints or distinguishing marks that might be important later.

"I'm almost done with the pictures, Detective," Tiffany said, snapping Stella out of her trance.

"Are you sure you're okay?" Ben whispered.

"I've got a strange feeling about this," Stella replied. "But I don't want to talk about it yet. Not with all these people around. What did you say her hands were tied with?" She looked at the men who were the police force of Vandalia. Aside from her and Tiffany, there were no other women. Except, of course, the victim. She couldn't be sure, but Stella got the distinct feeling they were talking about her. Which one of them knew Stella would freak out at the sight of beans? Which one of them had peeked into her background, searched her files, and found out that tiny detail in order to throw her not just off this case but maybe out of her mind?

"It looks like twine. The kind of stuff you can find at a craft store. It's not very strong. I can't imagine that it was a useful restraint. Maybe the assailant tied her hands after the fact. Like he was presenting a gift."

"A gift," Stella muttered. "For me."

"What's that?" Ben asked.

"Nothing," Stella cleared her throat and pretended to be

herself again but inside she was screaming. Inside, her blood froze in her veins and she felt helpless, vulnerable, and surrounded by scary things. But she couldn't let anyone know it. She bit down on the inside of her cheek until she was sure her mouth was going to start bleeding. The pain cleared her head and allowed her to focus on everything but those disgusting beans scattered everywhere.

"So, Detective?" Sheriff Darlow carefully walked up to Stella.

"So what, Sheriff?" Stella snapped back. "Have I solved the case? No. Not since you had your little tantrum."

"I'm sorry about that." Sheriff Darlow said. "I'm just really feeling the squeeze, that's all."

"Right. And that's what is most important here. Did you ever stop to think what these women felt right before they died? We've got three women who were alone with a monster just before they were strangled. What did they think of? Did they think of their family or their friends, or dreams they'd had, plans they made just before their candle was snuffed out? No. They thought 'How can we make this more difficult for Sheriff Darlow,'" Stella snapped. "You know, sheriff, you can tell you never had to get your hands dirty the entire time you've been sheriff of this town. Where I come from, we call that kind of man a pussy."

Sheriff Darlow clenched his jaw. If Stella had been a man Ben would have been picking him up off the ground along with several of his teeth. He walked up, inserted himself between the sheriff and Stella, and stared down the local authority who scratched his jaw and walked back to his squad car that didn't have a speck of dirt on it.

The other officers who heard the entire exchange were ready to hogtie the two city slickers and dump them off at the edge of the city limits.

"Are we almost done here?" Ben shouted to Tiffany who

nodded her head. The CSI crew went to work quickly but aside from the beans and the twine around her wrists, there was nothing worth collecting. Ben saw them pick up a couple of cigarette butts but those could have been on the ground for months. This was a public park after all. As if he'd just had words with a sassy teenager, Ben slipped his arm around Stella's shoulders and squeezed hard.

"I'm okay," she muttered.

"No, you aren't. Something is wrong and I'm not qualified to diagnose you, Stella. I don't know if you are well enough to keep going on this case," Ben said in a low voice so no one else would hear him. "But you are scaring me."

"Why, just because I told off a yokel cop who wouldn't know his ass from a hole in the ground? You've seen me tell people off before," Stella replied.

"Yeah, but you never called another member of our fraternal order a pussy," Ben hissed.

"Was that too harsh?" Stella asked. She didn't think it was but perhaps Ben had a different opinion.

"It was uncalled for and disrespectful. You need to go make it right. If we are going to solve this case, we are going to need the help of local cops and they aren't going to help some female detective on a power trip," Ben said. "Go fix this and fix it quick."

Stella swallowed hard and looked around. The remaining cops looked at her with contempt meaning Ben was right. They weren't going to help. She took a deep breath and loudly called out to the sheriff so his men would see her.

Instead of studying the scene where the body was dumped, Stella was being forced to play nice in the other kid's backyard. Part of her knew it was the right thing to do. The sheriff was out of his league and never felt like that before. But part of Stella still thought the guy needed a swift kick in the ass. But she held that part of her observation back and instead, begged for mercy.

"Sheriff Darlow, I'm sorry about that," she said loudly. "I didn't mean it. This case is bigger than I thought, and I'm frustrated and running out of ideas. I apologize for that outburst. You didn't deserve it."

The sheriff adjusted his jeans, shifted from one foot to the other, and then cleared his throat. Stella looked him square in the eye and waited for whatever reprimand he wanted to give her. She'd already made things harder for her and Ben. Maybe it wouldn't be as bad if she accepted a public tongue lashing.

"I'll have the coroner and photographer hurry up their reports and have them available at the station tomorrow morning," he said and looked over her head like she was barely there.

"I do appreciate that," Stella replied.

"Detective Carrigan," the sheriff said before Stella could turn and walk away.

She looked at him and braced herself for the one-two punch she was sure she was going to get. Instead, he shook his head.

"If you think I don't care about what happened to these women you are mistaken. Unlike you guys from the city I'm just not used to this kind of thing happening," he said. "I don't know how a person is supposed to act when there is one unexplained death, let alone three."

Stella nodded her head. "I'm sorry to tell you that we are not any closer after examining the first two victims than we were when we first got the information on the case. There are some things that stick out to me but nothing solid enough for me to give you any encouragement that this will soon be over. I'm sorry."

"I am, too." Sheriff Darlow stuck out his hand and Stella

shook it. it was soft and she thought that she probably wasn't far off with her comment about him not ever getting his hands dirty. But she turned and went back to her car where she opened the door, took a seat, and pretended to make notes. The truth was she didn't want to go back to the body with the beans still there. She let Ben take the lead and when he returned to the car and the body was transported to the coroner's office, they had a few minutes to talk before he dropped her back at the motel.

"That was a good deed you did. Especially since you could have gotten us in even more hot water," Ben said.

"What, calling the guy out? Was I really wrong?"

"No. But you don't call out the sheriff of a tiny town like this in front of his men and then expect help when we need it. That deputy has it out for us all ready," Ben said.

"He's not going to do anything," Stella smirked.

"You don't know that. Stella, this case has infected you with something. I'm afraid for you. I said I was going to call Briggs if you had another episode and—"

"Ben, this case is especially *for* me."

"Stella, that doesn't make any sense. What are you talking about? What does that mean? Especially for you?" Ben started the car and began driving in the direction of the Old Plaines Motel.

"I know it sounds crazy but the blanket, the blindfold, and now those...beans," she dry-heaved as she said the word. "Someone knows about me. Or at least someone knows about that incident and they are at it again."

"Stella, that man who kidnapped you was shot dead that night. He isn't around. It's impossible. This is just another weird coincidence. Maybe victim number three had gone to the store specifically for those beans. Maybe the bag broke in the scuffle. We just don't know what happened to her yet. But we do know what happened to you and the man responsible. He's dead. He's been dead for years and he isn't coming back. You are safe, Stella. You're safe." Ben said before pulling into the motel parking lot. "Do you want me to stay with you?"

Stella thought about it for a minute then shook her head. "No. I'm a big girl. Thanks, though. Sheriff Darlow said the report and photos would be done fast and ready in the morning."

"Okay. See you when the rooster crows," Ben said and waited until Stella was inside her motel room before pulling away and heading off to the bed & breakfast he was staying at. He didn't know it but as soon as Stella had the door closed and locked, she ran to the bathroom and threw up. Bile burned the back of her throat, sweat saturated her armpits and forehead and her eyes watered terribly making the white porcelain blur in front of her.

When nothing more would come up and her body ached from throwing everything in reverse, she flushed the toilet and leaned back against the bathroom door. As crazy as it seemed she felt better. The tile floor was cool through her pants, so she stayed there for a while thinking about the case and the beans, no longer feeling queasy but still confused and angry that they were at the scene. Was it just another coincidence? Could it be this was the one case that was rife with coincidences that didn't mean anything? She couldn't believe it but imagining someone from this tiny town was trying to mess with her head was just as unbelievable.

Stella took a hot shower then watched television until she couldn't keep her eyes open. Within minutes of shutting off the light, she was asleep and didn't wake up until the following morning when Ben was pounding on the door. She didn't dream and was glad.

"Time to go already?" she asked as she yanked open the door. Ben was there with coffee and donuts.

"You look like some of the tenants here, Carrington," Ben

said as he stepped inside, shut the door, and took a seat at the little desk and chair by the window.

"Yeah, I'll bet I do. I slept like a log last night. I could have used a couple more hours," she said as she took the coffee and grabbed some fresh clothes from her overnight bag before going into the bathroom. In ten minutes, she was out with her hair in a ponytail, wearing tight black jeans and a t-shirt with her badge on its chain around her neck, and her weapon already fastened at her hip.

"Wow. What are you trying to do? Get Sheriff Darlow's attention? Those jeans will work." Ben teased. "Do you think I should go back and change out of this suit? Maybe put on a pair of bib overalls and a straw hat."

"Yes, Ben, I think that's a fabulous idea. Get some pointy-toed cowboy boots too while you're at it." Stella said without cracking a smile. Ben chuckled as he sipped his coffee.

"The twine around our last victim's wrists. Where do you get stuff like that?" Stella asked before grabbing her donut from the bag on the desk and taking a huge bite. She pulled a pair of boots out of her bag, took a seat on the bed, and quickly slipped them on while chewing.

"It looks like the kind of stuff you'd get at a card shop or craft store," Ben said after he swallowed the last of his donut.

"Is there a craft store in town?" Stella asked.

"I don't know. Only one way to find out," Ben replied.

They drove into town and noticed there were new orange, yellow, and black banners advertising the Harvest Festival. People had stacked pumpkins, dried corn stalks, or bales of hay outside their businesses. Halloween decorations of old-fashioned jack-o-lanterns, ghosts, and skeletons hung in windows, and even the flowers in the cement planters had been replaced with rust and plum-colored mums with orange pips and green gourds arranged in them.

"This looks amazing," Stella said suddenly feeling rather festive.

"Yeah. Rochelle would love this. She likes all this artsy crap," Ben said.

"This is baby's first Halloween," Stella said. "You are going to have to cut a pumpkin and take him trick-or-treating. And get dressed up. Now, what would be a good costume for the three of you? Let me think," Stella tapped her chin.

"Don't even start, Carrigan," Ben shook his head.

"The Marx Brothers, and you would have to be Harpo," Stella chuckled.

"Enough," Ben shook his head.

"Three blind mice? That would be adorable," she continued. "No! I have the best idea. You could all go as bags of jellybeans. You get clear plastic bags and put them around your stomach then fill them with a bunch of blown-up colored balloons!" Stella laughed and slapped the dashboard. "I'd pay money to see you dressed like that! I'm going to call Rochelle and tell her you suggested it."

"Don't you dare," Ben grumbled.

"I'm going to and you can't stop me. You just got through saying she likes all this crafty stuff. That would be a perfect project for her and what a family photo!"

"What about you? You don't think you're getting out of my son's first Halloween, do you?" Ben snapped back.

"Of course, I'll stop by, but you know the weirdos come out on Halloween. I'll be home before the sun sets. If I want candy, I'll go buy myself a bag. My days of begging door-to-door are over,"

Stella chuckled as they pulled into the police station.

Stella thought it looked like there were a lot more squad cars in the parking lot than the last time they arrived.

"Looks a little crowded today," Ben said.

"Do you think that's my fault?" Stella asked.

"Oh, it's probably a good assumption," Ben shook his head. "How many times have I told you not to go racing into a place without your backup knowing what you are going to do? Do you see why I ask you to do that?" Ben huffed. "Detective, can you be on your best behavior? Don't call the sheriff of Vandalia a pussy today. Maybe don't ever say that again."

"If the shoe fits..." Stella started but when she saw her partner's serious expression she stopped and smiled. "I promise. That wasn't me last night. I was having a bad time but I'm doing better today. A lot better. Don't worry."

They got out of the car and entered the police station. Everything came to a stand-still the minute got to the front desk. The red-headed receptionist was back to her purple eye-shadow and gave Ben a pleasant smile that faded the instant she looked at Stella.

"The sheriff is waiting for you," she said politely to Ben.

Everyone gawked at the two detectives from Chicago who thought they could come and disrespect their chief. It didn't matter that Sheriff Darlow had approached Stella with the same hostility she gave back. This was a good ol' boys club. Certain things just weren't done and calling the sheriff a pussy was apparently one of them. Stella squared her shoulders and slowly strolled through the bullpen to the conference room.

"Morning!" Stella said to the entire bullpen of cops but and got no reply. "Where are we going?" she asked Ben.

"Darlow said to meet him in the conference room," Ben said as they wove their way through the office. Stella nodded. She was the lead detective on this case, but the sheriff had called Ben. *That's what you get when you act up and smart off to the sheriff, young lady*, she scolded herself.

As they walked past the entire Vandalia police department glaring daggers at her Stella hated to admit that the juvenile part of her was ready and willing to give them all the finger but because Ben was there and she'd promised, she said and did nothing. Like a gentleman, Ben opened the conference room door for her as if nothing was out of the ordinary. The sheriff was already there waiting with the new file and pictures in front of him. He looked like he didn't sleep a wink all night.

Chapter 22

"Morning," Sheriff Darlow said without any emotion. "Here are the pictures. Here is the file. Christine was up all night getting this done. I'm afraid it's the same as the other two. Death by strangulation. Some kind of rope or bungee cord. But this one had one thing different."

Stella took a seat next to Sheriff Darlow who was at the head of the plain long table. Ben sat across from her. The conference room was nothing special. It had no windows, two whiteboards on the walls with some random notes from meetings past still scribbled on them and a corkboard with some McGruff flyers tacked to it.

"What's different?" Stella asked, her mind switching into gear.

"This woman had those kidney beans in her throat," Sheriff Darlow said sadly. "Thankfully, Christine said it looked to be post-mortem. She didn't choke on them. She was already dead when they were put in her mouth."

Stella coughed and looked at Ben. A million thoughts went through her head. What was going on here in Vandalia that could have such a strong connection to her in Chicago? She'd never even been to Southern Illinois before this case. She had no family or friends who moved here. But yet how many strange things were happening that seemed designed specifically for her? Instead of letting nausea overcome her Stella bit her tongue, hard, and shook her head.

"Do we have an I.D. of the victim?" Stella asked taking the report and leaving the photos for Ben to review.

"Yes. It's all in there. Therese Foley. Thirty-seven years old. She just moved here," Sheriff Darlow said. Stella looked at him.

For a moment, their eyes locked, and a mutual feeling of respect and compassion was exchanged, like a quick note being passed in school while the teacher's back was turned.

"Have you notified the family already?" Stella asked.

"No family. She was all alone. Can you imagine that? Moving to this small, close-knit community where everyone knows everyone and still dying alone? And like this?" he replied.

"I'm sorry, Sheriff. I'm sorry about my behavior last night and I'm sorry this is going on," Stella cleared her throat and shifted in her seat before focusing again on the file. "What was used to bind Therese's hands?"

"It was a twine like they have at craft stores," Sheriff Darlow replied.

"Is there a craft store in town?" Stella asked.

After a few more preliminary questions Stella and Ben were on their way to the only craft store in town. Hollie's Hobbies was located in the downtown part of Vandalia. It was decorated to the hilt with glittered and bedazzled pumpkins and corn stalks outside the front door in unnatural colors of pink, red, and teal.

When they walked into the store every inch of the place was drenched in Halloween and fall decorations. The customers milling through the store all looked up to see who had set off the bells over the door. The arts and crafts community of Vandalia had to be fairly substantial based on the amount of material in the store and the number of customers in so early. But it was obvious by their stares they knew Stella and Ben didn't belong.

"Good morning. Can I help you find something?" Even the cashier at one of the three registers was eager to give them directions and send them on their way. She wore a pink apron over her blue jeans. She was in her late fifties and forced a grin that seemed almost painful.

"Hi," Stella smiled as she held up her badge and introduced herself and Ben. "Do you carry decorative twine?"

The few patrons who were in this early inched their way around the store to get a good look at the police officers and eavesdrop on what they were saying.

"Of course, we do," the woman chirped. "What color are you looking for?"

"It isn't for me," Stella replied. "Have you had anyone buy it recently?"

The woman in the apron looked at Stella and then to Ben as if they had suddenly both grown horns from the middle of their foreheads.

"Uhm, yes," she replied nervously.

"Do you know the people who did?" Stella asked as she took out her pad of paper to begin writing.

"Uh, well, just about everyone in town," the woman replied and pointed to the window. The entire town suddenly seemed draped in the stuff. Stella looked at Ben who rubbed the back of his neck and looked at his shoes.

"That's right," Stella muttered. "The Harvest Festival. What is that exactly?"

The woman went on to describe a fun country tradition of pumpkin carving contests, store decorating contests, multiple food vendors, and hayrides through the pumpkin patch and around the park.

"It's just a lovely time of year and people come from all over the state to see it," she chirped proudly.

Stella thanked her for her time but as soon as she was out the door a string of obscenities left her mouth making Ben just shake his head.

"What was I thinking? Of course, everyone in this town has the same kind of twine around. It's just staring me in the face, Ben. I'm losing my mind. I should have let you call Briggs and had me shipped back to the city. This case is too much. And did you hear what Darlow said? Therese had beans in her throat. Ugh! I could puke just thinking about it." Stella said as a few locals looked at her suspiciously. "Good morning. It's a beautiful fall day, isn't it? Enjoy the fall festival."

"It's the Harvest Festival," some smart-ass replied back making Stella pout her lips and shake her head. Ben chuckled.

"What's so funny, Detective? This is a mess," Stella snapped. "This twine is all over the place. Our perp could have gotten it from anywhere. Same goes for the beans," she frowned as she said the word.

"Have you had anything to eat? You're looking a little green in the gills again," Ben said.

"Just the doughnut you brought me. No, I haven't had anything real. But I'm not hungry," she said. The last thing she wanted to do was eat. The kidney beans first thing in the morning killed her appetite.

"Come on. Breakfast on me," Ben said.

"Would you mind dropping me off at the motel? I need a shower and to look over the new files. You get something to eat and I'll catch up with you later," Stella said.

"Okay, I'll take you back," Ben looked worried but knew better than to argue. Once Stella made up her mind there was no talking her out of it.

Back at the motel, Stella was happy to see her room had already been made up. She tossed the new file on the desk, pulled off her clothes, and stretched out in her underwear across the bed.

There was that familiar pit in her stomach again, like she used to get in high school just waiting for the test she didn't study for or the call to the principal's office for skipping school the day before. It was the waiting that was the worst part. And what made it unbearable was that Stella had no idea what she was waiting for. Another body? Got that. Something even more gross than the beans around it? Got that, too—the nasty morsels were put in her mouth. What for? What was the killer trying to say? And why did Stella keep feeling like he was talking directly to her?

In a fit, she hopped off the bed, took off the rest of her clothes, and jumped in the shower. The water wouldn't get as hot as she liked it. She wanted it to sting a little, turn her skin pink and burn through to her muscles. All she got was warm and it slowly but surely got colder by the second. As she dried off, she was feeling tenser than before. She slipped into stretch pants and a baggy t-shirt and tried some stretches but all she really wanted was to be back at the gym working out until her muscles screamed and her mind was flooded with endorphins. Maybe she'd see Cole again and maybe she'd let him walk her home this time. But she wasn't at home to go to the gym. She was in Vandalia, Illinois trying to solve a homicide that was definitely being perpetrated by some kind of serial killer who had an artistic talent for posing corpses and leaving gross trinkets around that only Stella could see for what they were. Signals? Messages?

"You're losing your mind," she muttered. As she slipped back in her career as a detective and even before that as a beat cop, she'd seen plenty of death. She'd seen junkie parents who killed their own children and never had such a reaction. She'd seen rape victims as young as twelve who couldn't speak after their assault. It broke her heart and enraged her at the same time, but Stella could still think straight. It wasn't that none of that phased her, it all did. Every criminal she hunted down and laid a trap for became an obsession until they were finally apprehended. But it was like she was playing a game of chess and knew exactly what the bad guy was going to do next. It wasn't that they were predictable, it was that Stella could think clearly without her emotions getting in the way.

This case had her emotions hanging out like a flag on a pole at the top of a lighthouse and the winds were picking up.

Stella looked down and saw she'd worried a hangnail, tugging at the skin until it pulled a wedge so deep it was bleeding. She cursed and went to her overnight bag to find a nail clipper.

Inside was Ben's relaxation CD.

"What the hell," she muttered. She grabbed it slipped it into the television dual DVD/CD player. She pressed play and heard the familiar voice of the narrator urging her to relax again on track two. She heard his voice. She tried paying attention to her breathing. But the file that was on the desk kept calling to her. There was the hair cut from the first victim and the way she was pointing to the key. There were the dried rosebuds in the second victim's hair along with the blindfold and the scratchy blanket that wasn't fit to line a garage floor, and then there were the beans. Again, the thought made Stella sick. But what was worse was that she was seeing something else as if looking through beveled glass. There was a form, an image but it was distorted and confusing. Why was it there? Who was sending her these messages and how could they be? The man who used all these things, the blindfold, the beans, the smelly, dirty blanket was dead. He was dead! She knew it! She saw it! There was nothing left of that man so how was it possible that all these things were pointing at...*him*?

Stella sat up, with trembling hands stopped the CD player and began to cry. No one else saw what she'd seen all those years ago so they wouldn't see them now. Coincidence, Ben said. No. Stella was being haunted by something and it was determined to tear her mind apart like he'd tried all those years ago. She sobbed even harder until she was sure there was nothing left inside to get out. She was tired. Getting all that emotion out made her feel better.

The file was still sitting on the desk, but Stella couldn't look at it. Not yet. Not now. She put the television on and watched some boring house-hunting show that numbed her mind until Ben called. He was going with Sheriff Darlow to Therese's house.

"I'll be at the motel in fifteen to pick you up," he said.

"No. You go ahead and take the lead on this one. I'm working on these files," she lied.

"Are you sure?"

"Yeah, Ben. I'm in the zone and could really use the hours to get a grip on the new information." She wasn't sure if he bought it. He said okay but Stella was sure he knew something was wrong. Ben was good that way. It was no wonder he and Rochelle were so happy together. He was a good man and had a steady head on his shoulders. Stella felt she owed it to him to get her head together on this case. But she wasn't going to look at the file now. She'd wait until this evening and order some pizza. She peeked out the window and decided her only venture outside would be to the liquor store across the street.

Chapter 23

The next day Stella woke up with her head cloudy and a bad taste in her mouth. The Boone's Farm peach wine sounded like a good idea at the time. Never again. But Stella felt the hangover was just what she needed. It may sound strange, but she'd been trying to crack this case with a clear mind and common sense. Maybe it required a cotton-head and distorted view to understand what was going on.

She only looked at the file last night briefly. When she studied the pictures and read the report it all came back to her. The rope or bungee cord used around her neck and the beans around the body and in her mouth. The body was posed.

Something was coming into focus. Not about the case but something in Stella's memory was swimming up from the murky black. Just as it was about to break the surface her phone rang making her jump like a cat.

"Carrigan," she snapped.

"You're up," Ben said.

"Yeah. Yeah, I'm up," Stella muttered, shaking her head in annoyance that her thought completely vanished.

"Saddle up, we've got some people to talk to," Ben said.

"What did I miss?" Stella asked as she pulled on her jeans and a flannel shirt. She looked in the mirror and thought she'd blend right in with the fine folks of Vandalia and the upcoming Harvest Festival.

"I'm out front. Got coffee for you," Ben said.

Stella peeked out her window and saw his luxury car

parked in front of her room. She waved, hung up, grabbed the files, her boots, and darted out the door.

"Therese Foley was a grade school teacher at Maple Park Primary School," Ben said with a smile.

"This pleases you?" Stella asked.

"She moved to town and made a big splash with anyone and everyone she could. Lots of contacts. Lots of associates. Just by the law of averages, we're bound to get a solid lead out of it," Ben said.

"I like your optimism," Stella said and rubbed her eyes as she squinted against the sun.

"Did you have a good time last night?" Ben teased.

"Yeah, I took a trip to Boone's Farm. It was nice on the way there but turned bad. They duped me, Ben. It was not a magical place. It's a place of sweet, peach-flavored lies," she rubbed her head again with a smirk on her face as Ben chuckled.

Maple Primary School was a traditional brick building in the shape of a rectangle with a playground in the back and two shiny buses. As soon as they walked in Stella flashed back to her school days. The smell of paper was prominent. The halls were decorated with goofy looking frogs made out of construction paper, essays written in clunky letters, the grade numbers of each class stuck to the doors. The teachers and children could be heard in their classrooms.

The principal's office was guarded by a long counter that required everyone to stop and get clearance from the secretary stationed there. When Stella and Ben stepped up, they were greeted by a pudgy woman in blue jeans and a white blouse.

"Remember the days when teachers and administrators dressed like they were going to work, not shopping at the mall," Ben whispered.

"I do," Stella said. She let Ben do all the talking since he was the one who had called ahead to say they'd be arriving.

"I'm Detective Ben Carey. I think we spoke on the phone," he said politely to the woman behind the desk.

"Yes, I'm Pam Turner. Mrs. Swanson is expecting you. If you can just give me a minute," Pam said as she picked up the phone. All it took was a quick whisper into the receiver and Principal Swanson emerged from her office that was tucked in the right corner.

Stella thought she looked like a principal. She was heavy set with purple-framed glasses and a face that could be either kind or stern depending on who was standing in front of her. She looked at Stella and Ben nervously as introductions were made.

"Please, come in my office," she said. Stella and Ben each took a seat in front of Mrs. Swanson's desk. "We are still so shocked about the news. Sheriff Darlow let us know last night. I got the call around two in the morning. It's just so devastating."

"Did Therese ever talk about having any problems with anyone in Vandalia?" Ben asked.

"Not, not to me. Therese was a God-send. She loved her job and it showed because the kids loved her. She was one of those kind souls that saw beauty in everything. And she was very creative.

"I'm sorry to ask you this, Mrs. Swanson, but did Therese ever mention feeling uneasy around any other teachers or parents?" Stella asked.

"If she had any of those feelings, she never told me. All I ever saw was her with a smile on her face. She really was a good person. I don't think the reality of the situation has even sunk in. She's gone, I understand. But I don't think I've even fully registered what that means. We haven't told the children and have sent an email to parents that there was an incident. But Sheriff

Darlow asked that we not disclose the graphic nature of the situation until they have a little more information.

"Sheriff Darlow is my cousin," Mrs. Swanson said with a tired smile. "You'll find that kind of thing a lot in small towns. He knows I won't say anything until he gives the go-ahead."

"We appreciate that, Mrs. Swanson," Ben said.

"What's even worse is that Therese was involved in so many school projects and volunteered to help organize the Harvest Festival. I don't know what Janet is going to do without the extra helping hand," Mrs. Swanson shook her head. "You just don't come across people who really want to help. Therese was like that. She'd help anyone who asked."

Stella looked at Ben. "Did she ever mention a boyfriend? She wasn't married and had no children. A woman without those kinds of responsibilities who is as friendly as you say might mention a relationship."

"Again, if she spoke to anyone about it, it wasn't me. But, since you mentioned it, aside from school, I do know that Therese was spending most of her time helping with the Harvest Festival. It was almost like a second job she'd said. That sounds about right since Janet Steeple-Gazak was organizing it and she likes to use the volunteers as if they were her own private employees," Mrs. Swanson said.

"You don't think Therese and Janet had any kind of altercation?" Ben asked.

"I just know that Janet has a way of taking advantage of people who are just trying to do the right thing," Mrs. Swanson leaned forward across her desk. "She's very wealthy and can be very generous. But only if she's allowed to do things her way. There have been several families who have complained about her behavior, but it never does any good. I don't know what people expect. A leopard doesn't change its spots. She's mean but she's been that way her whole life."

"How old is Mrs. Steeple-Gazak?" Ben asked.

"If I had to guess, she's maybe in her fifties," Mrs. Swanson said. "Oh, this is all a mess. I just don't know what else to say. Therese is going to be missed by everyone. And she had a bright future as a teacher."

"Do you know where we can find Mrs. Steeple-Gazak?" Ben asked.

Mrs. Swanson wrote down Janet Steeple-Gazak's address and gave it to the detectives. Then she gave them directions to what was considered the historic part of Vandalia.

"She lives in the biggest house on the block. What she needs all that space for, I don't know but she's quoted as saying she'll never move out and no one else will ever live in her house. She's leaving it to the park district as a historical monument or something," Mrs. Swanson shrugged. Stella and Ben thanked her for her time and left to visit the historic part of Vandalia.

As they followed the principal's directions winding through Vandalia they knew exactly when they had hit the historic area. Not because the houses were old fashioned but because there was a huge sign that said Historic District and a plaque hanging from the bottom that read donated by Janet Steeple-Gazak.

"Wow. I am not getting a good feeling about this woman," Stella said.

"Do you think she had something to do with it?" Ben asked. "You know how rare female serial killers are."

"Rare, yes. Non-existent? No. Actually, I don't know if she had anything to do with it or not. We didn't dig up any connection with any of the other victims with a wealthy widow who likes to do community service. I'm just thinking on a purely investigative level that I have the feeling this woman is going to be a handful."

Stella said.

"Okay, let's just remember how things turned out with the sheriff when you mouthed off. Let's not do it again with Vandalia's rich and famous," Ben teased.

When they pulled up to 801 Vine Street in the heart of Vandalia's historic district Stella thought the house looked like one that would belong to a rich old biddy. It was a three-story white Victorian with black shutters and a red front door. The lawn and bushes around the front yard were perfectly manicured.

"This is great. I'm underdressed for this interview," Stella grumbled. "You look nice. You're in a suit."

"Yeah, but a black man in a suit won't impress a small-town widow with money. Don't be surprised if this interview takes place on the porch through the three inches of space the door chain allows," Ben chuckled, adjusted his jacket as they walked together to the front door.

"I don't know if I like the way you said that, Detective," Stella replied just before ringing the doorbell.

The woman who answered the door was exactly what Stella had envisioned except shorter. Janet Steeple-Gazak wore large square glasses in a tortoiseshell design, had her hair so Aqua-netted in place it could withstand hurricane winds, and had a bosom so large Stella was sure the woman hadn't seen her feet since puberty.

"Yes?" she looked at Stella and Ben as if she were watching a tennis match.

"Mrs. Steeple-Gazak, I'm Detective Stella Carrigan, this is Detective Ben Carey. We're here investigating a series of homicides and understand that you worked closely with one of the victims. Therese Foley," Stella watched as Janet didn't even flinch.

"You really need to come back later. I'm extremely busy

and..."

"Mrs. Steeple-Gazak, we need to talk to you about a homicide," Stella said firmly. "If you like, we can take you to the station to talk. Perhaps you'll have more time for that. Most people like to discuss things in the comfort of their own home."

Janet looked at Stella with eyes wide enough to say *who do you think you are talking to, outsider?* But Stella remained calm and stared back.

"You wouldn't believe all the things that have to get done for the harvest festival in a couple of days. You said Therese was the victim of a homicide?" Janet asked, squinting her eyes as if she might have heard wrong.

"That's right. She was found last night?" Stella said.

"How did she die?" Janet asked, her eyes narrowing.

"We aren't at liberty to say," Stella said and rocked on her heels. "Can you tell us what you know about Therese?"

Janet looked Ben up and down then focused on Stella again. "Yes, I knew Therese. I knew all about her," Janet said without making any gesture to invite them into her house.

"Can you tell us a little bit about her?" Ben asked politely. Janet looked Ben up and down again. Stella waited to see if she made any kind of inappropriate comment that might set him off. But she didn't.

"Therese only just moved to Vandalia about eight months ago. She inserted herself into the community as if she'd been here her whole life. It was rather strange but, I knew what she was up to," Janet said then pinched her lips together.

"What do you think she was up to?" Stella asked.

"She was never married. She had no children or family. She

had been seen on occasion at the tavern that I'm sure you passed on your way into town. That's the kind of person she was," Janet said.

"But she was helping you with the Harvest Festival. Volunteering, I understand. You didn't want her help?" Stella asked.

"She was bossy."

Stella nearly choked when Janet said that but was able to pass it off as just a cough, a hitch in her throat.

"She came barging in on the scene trying to take over and run things as if she had been in Vandalia her whole life. My family can be traced back to the founding of Vandalia in 1805. There has been a Steeple on the books ever since. At this moment, my great uncle Ernest Steeple is on the city council. One of my cousins was the youngest person to run for alderman of this area."

"Did he win?" Ben asked.

"No. He lost by only one vote and I know who that was," Janet sneered.

Stella shifted from one foot to the other as she pulled out her notepad and began to take down Janet's information.

"Can you tell us about your experience with Therese?" Stella steered the conversation back to the homicide. She could tell by Janet's look that she was offended Stella didn't see the injustice of her cousin not becoming alderman.

"Like I said, she was new in town and seemed to think that entitled her to join any and all community programs that Vandalia had to offer. I know she was a schoolteacher and that is just fine and dandy. But there is a certain level of professionalism and traditionalism that comes with tending to things like the Harvest Festival. She'd already signed up for the Country Christmas and was trying to get the hardware store to put a float in the parade.

Can you imagine? The hardware store?" Janet shook her head and snickered.

"So, you didn't like her?" Ben asked and the question sobered Janet up quickly.

"It isn't that I didn't like her. She just wasn't...the same caliber as I am used to."

"Mrs. Gazak, you don't seem too broken up about Therese being murdered. She was strangled to death. Do you recall anyone who might have shared your opinion of her? That she was not the same..." Stella checked her notes. "*Caliber?*"

"That isn't what I meant," Janet stuttered. "But I'm not going to pretend she was some kind of saint just because she went and got herself killed. I'm not being cruel. I'm just being honest."

"Can you tell us if anyone else felt the same way you do? Anyone who may have had an issue with Therese? Anyone who may have validated your opinion of her after you'd shared it?" Ben asked. Janet looked at him as if she were a deer in the headlights. But it only took her a second to narrow her eyes and look back at him.

"No," was all she said.

Stella didn't want to, but she gave Janet her business card with the instructions if she remembered anything else to give a call. They weren't off the porch before they heard the front door slam shut.

"What a piece of work," Ben said.

"Yeah. But small towns like this always have a Janet Steeple-Gazak. Remember the Gomez case on the northside? Remember when we had to deal with that Louanne woman who was president of the Edgewater Community Council?"

"Oh yeah, we crashed their fundraiser and she was singing

a song about how she single-handedly got the hookers off the corner of Sheridan and Granville. The song was set to... what was the tune?" Ben asked as he laughed.

"Wasn't it '*My Kind of Town*'?" Stella laughed.

"I think it was. Yeah, neighborhoods in Chicago are no different than these small towns when you really think about it," Ben replied.

But as they pulled away and Stella saw Janet peeking out her curtains to make sure they were leaving she realized the worst part of the interview. That although Janet was a mean old broad, she left her and Ben with nothing more to go on. Again, they were back at square one. Three bodies with nowhere to turn to find who did it. The walls were starting to close in.

"It feels like we've been working on this case for months and we've only been down here for a week. Why is that?" Stella mused.

Chapter 24

"What are your plans for tonight?" Stella asked Ben after they finished discussing Janet Steeple-Gazak and the three victims over an early dinner at the Blueberry Diner. The waitress gave them a friendly hello welcoming them back.

"I'm going to go back to the B&B and listen to some classical music while I soak in the tub," he replied without skipping a beat.

"Does Rochelle know this is what you are doing? I'll bet she'd like to soak in a tub listening to classical music after tending that baby all day," Stella teased as she took a sip of Coke to wash down the last of her burger.

"Her mother is staying with her while I'm gone," Ben replied. "Which means my sister-in-law, brother-in-law, a couple of cousins, and an auntie or two are probably all at the house passing my child around while Rochelle gets her nails done, her feet rubbed, and all the chocolate ice cream she wants."

"Well, she had a baby," Stella laughed.

"We adopted," Ben replied before starting to laugh himself.

"That sounds nice. It's good to have family so close," Stella replied. She'd never had any family. Except for Ben. The foster families had not left enough of an impression on her that she ever felt the need to stay in touch. Stella always felt like more of a bother to those people than anything else. But she felt as welcomed as she'd allow herself to feel with Ben. She considered him and Rochelle family but even they were not allowed completely into her heart. There was the possibility of her being transferred, or Ben getting a promotion, or as with every cop on the street, death could sneak up at any time. She'd jump in front of a bullet for Ben but told herself it was more out of duty and not because she cared so much about him and his family.

"You want to hang out after this? Go have a drink or something?" Ben asked.

But she quickly told him no. "I'm going to go for a run. Vandalia's not a big town. I'm going to walk to the park and take a long run down the paths. Maybe stop in and see Christine Lustyk at the coroner's office and pick her brain." Stella lied about seeing Christine. She didn't want to talk to anyone. She wanted to clear her head and exert herself so she could sleep without dreaming or waking up to some irrational fear about being somehow involved with the case.

"Okay. If you learn anything new, let me know. Keep your cell on you. Just in case," Ben said as they paid their bill and left Blueberry's.

Once at Open Plaines Motel, Stella went to her room and changed her clothes. She tucked her phone into the secret pouch on the thigh of her running pants. There was a path that picked up just three blocks from the motel, a wooden sign reading Little River Meadow Bike and Running Trail with a crude map of the area showing red lines weaving through simple green triangles of trees outlining the path a bike rider or jogger could take. It was a ten-mile loop around the perimeter with offshoots of trail that cut the path into two-mile chunks. Stella felt like running ten miles. She'd be exhausted on the walk back to the motel, but it would be worth it. As she stretched her muscles her mind began to fill with all the images of the case. As soon as she hit the trail and started running rather than try and push the images out of her mind, she put them in order. Starting with Barbara Casio, Stella took inventory of all the clues they had so far and how that brought them to Regina Phelps, and then to Therese Foley's body, the only one left outside.

The scenery was very pretty with thick pine trees, majestic oaks, and a myriad of other trees that were blooming in brilliant fall colors. The reds, oranges, and golds looked even more intense on the backdrop of a gray sky. It was nearly silent except for Stella's gym shoes hitting the sidewalk and her breathing. Even as she reran everything in her head, she saw no connection. As she ran it was like she was chasing something that was constantly out of reach. She was the rabbit chasing the carrot on a stick. She pushed herself harder. Sweat coated her whole body and even with the release of endorphins, she couldn't see anything more clearly. She saw this case slipping away from her.

It's because it's too personal, the voice inside her head screamed over her heavy breathing. It was so loud she stopped and whirled around sure she was going to find some ghoul behind her, grinning demonically and ready to pounce. Tears filled her eyes as she stood there, looking over her shoulder and desperately trying to catch her breath in order to hear if anyone was creeping up on her. The sun was setting. Soon it would be dusk. Stella felt her heart starting to race.

"What's wrong with me?" she asked finally getting her breathing under control. She stood still and that was when it happened. She started to cry. While standing alone on the Little River Meadow Bike and Running Trail Stella cried for herself. She couldn't recall a time she'd felt so helpless and scared as she did that minute. Not because she was alone on the path but because this case was personal. Someone had her in mind even if no one believed it. There was an invisible monster that could see her. Not only could she not see it, she felt helpless to stop it. There was going to be another death and it was also going to have something familiar to Stella and only Stella.

Once her breathing slowed to almost normal, Stella listened and heard nothing out of the ordinary. She looked down the path in both directions and saw nothing out of the ordinary. Except, off in the distance, she saw several old cabins tucked in between the trees in the hillside. They reminded Stella of summer camp although from what she could see of them now they looked more like sets in some scary movie with sex-crazed teenagers trying to outrun a machete-wielding loon in a ski mask. They were sad and scary looking with their black windows staring in Stella's direction.

Suddenly, a memory jumped into the forefront of Stella's mind making her gasp. When she had been kidnapped as a child there wasn't just one person. Yes, she was grabbed by a man, and that man was shot dead when the police finally rescued her. But there was someone else.

He fed her the beans. The very thought made her shiver and she felt her stomach ripple with disgust. But it was real and true and now she remembered it.

"They are a superfood. Good for you. She'll stay alive and healthy for a long time. Make sure she eats them all." The voice was as clear as a bell echoing through Stella's head. She froze. Her mind was racing with images of someone lumbering up behind her to grab her and throw her back into that dark place. But she couldn't move the slightest muscle. Her eyes flooded with tears. The sweat that had coated her body seemed to freeze on her skin. She violently trembled as she pulled her legs from the invisible cement holding her in place. Finally, with every bit of energy she could gather, Stella broke into a run. She remembered. She remembered now what had been lurking just below the surface and she cried again as she ran but not because she was afraid or even scared. But because she could see it all now.

When she made it back to the motel, her shirt and leggings soaked through with sweat, she fumbled with the plastic key card. Finally, after sliding it into the slot three times she got the little green light, heard the click-click, and opened the door. She slipped inside, slammed the door shut behind her, and slipped the deadbolt and chain in place.

She slipped out of her clothes, turned on the shower, and finally felt like herself again. While she was blindfolded, under that scratchy, dirty blanket in that cold, dark place, someone else was always there. Someone who had fed her those fucking beans.

Chapter 25

The next day after freshening up Stella slipped into her jeans and a t-shirt, over her hip-hugger holster and completed the look with the flannel shirt. With her head feeling clearer than it had for days, Stella left the motel early and headed to the police department to talk with the sheriff. She had rehearsed what she was going to say since things were still a little tense between them. But like all best-laid plans, when she showed up the sheriff wasn't there. But Deputy Winger was.

"You're here early," Stella said after she went into the bullpen to help herself to a cup of coffee. It was early and in Vandalia, it wasn't necessary for too many cops to be on duty. But there were a few who looked at Stella knowing she was the big city detective with the hard-ass reputation who had called out their beloved sheriff just a few days ago.

"That's my job. Along with taking dogs to the animal shelter," Clarence said, smirking.

"I do appreciate your doing that," Stella said as pleasantly as she could pretend. She didn't like Clarence. He was a jerk. But she didn't want any more problems and was really trying to play nice on the playground. "I know it was a hassle. You really helped us."

"Yeah, I bet," Clarence said, trying to stare Stella down.

"Okay, enough of the pleasantries. Those cabins in the park not far from the running trail. What are those used for?" Stella asked firmly. And just to add a bit of spice she took out her pad of paper and pen and began to write as he spoke.

He squinted at her, but he had no reason not to answer. "Those were used a long time ago for all kinds of things," he cleared his throat. "Businesses had teamwork seminars there.

Vacation bible camps were there. Some people booked them for fishing trips on the lake or vacations. But the main one caught on fire. When that happened no one really took the time to maintain the other ones."

"I bet. Vacationing in Vandalia probably isn't on most tourists list of places to see before they die," Stella couldn't stop the words. They just tumbled out of her mouth without thinking.

Clarence narrowed his eyes and shook his head. "You city people are all alike," Clarence sneered.

Stella put her hand up and shook her head. "Spare me the wholesome country living routine. I'm investigating a triple homicide in *your* town. Chicago has three million people. Some are bound to not get along. This is a place where everyone knows everyone. Where did *you all* go wrong?"

Clarence stopped speaking and clenched his teeth.

"Tell the sheriff I'm looking for him," she continued before she turned around and walked out of the station. Just as she was stepped out the door Ben was walking in. He was carrying two large coffees from the diner but his relaxed face slipped into a mask of concern.

"Don't bother. The sheriff isn't in," Stella huffed.

"Is that what has you upset?" Ben asked handing Stella her coffee.

"Kind of. Ben, there is something about this case that is in direct relation to me," she said. "Hear me out, please."

"Stella, you've never been to Vandalia. You don't know any of these people. And the only person who would have any intimate knowledge about your abduction is dead. You're starting to scare me, partner. I'm not going to lie. You are," Ben said and looked past her into the police station.

This response from Ben made Stella want to cry. But she didn't. She showed no emotion, made no pleading remarks, begging for him to believe her. Instead, she shook her head and shrugged.

"The facts are what they are. I'm not making any of it up. Now listen and just tell me what you honestly think," Stella said calmly as she continued and revealed to Ben what she remembered the night before. "I'm not making any of it up. You know me, Ben. You know me better than anyone else. Would I ever make a case about me? Did I ever insert myself in it like I was some kind of victim? Ben, if it weren't for you how many people even talk to me at the 18th? Briggs, when I'm in trouble. A couple of uniforms who I've worked with. But no one talks to me."

"You don't really mingle, Stella. What do you think is going to happen? It's called the Fraternal Order for a reason. We have a bond as cops and when someone does things a little differently on purpose, well, you have to expect that you're going to be treated differently," Ben took a sip of his coffee. "And look, it works for you to be a lone wolf. I get that. But I'm just worried that by isolating yourself you are starting to see things that aren't there."

"This is *there*, Ben. The blindfold. The blanket. Those fucking beans. Someone was in that dark place feeding me those beans. Making sure I ate them. Ben, I'm telling you the truth," Stella was not sure how much longer she was going to be able to control her voice or the tears.

"Stella the man who kidnapped you, the man who kept you blindfolded in that place and fed you beans was *lunatic*. He lived in a shed, had no running water or electricity, shit and pissed in a bucket, ate beans out of cans, and I'm sorry to say it, made you do the same. But Stella, there is a big difference between you and him. You are still here, alive. He's dead. Shot to death by an earlier version of us. People who cared about you. People who wanted you safe and were only too happy to pull the trigger and put an end to that monster. Stella, not only is he never going to hurt you, but he's never going to hurt anyone ever again." Ben's words were true. Stella knew that. But something was going on and she was going to have to embrace the idea it was nothing more than a coincidence until she could prove otherwise.

She stood on the sidewalk for a couple of uncomfortable seconds keeping herself composed when all she really wanted to do was scream. Instead, she sipped her coffee and looked off in the distance.

"I think I'll go back to the motel and check on a few things," she muttered.

"I'll go with you," Ben said quickly.

"No. You can talk with the sheriff. Maybe the deputy will be a little more open with you. I've got a couple of things I want to check into," Stella said and began to walk.

"Let me at least give you a lift," Ben added.

"It's only a couple of blocks. This town isn't very big," Stella replied as she shook her head. Before Ben could say anything else, she was already out of sight. Stella knew he watched her walk away, trying to spot some sign of cracking-up like her talking to herself or maybe pulling out a couple handfuls of hair. Funny, now that she'd really let it all out, she felt better. Even though Ben, her partner and closest, if not only, friend didn't believe her. She could hardly blame him. It sounded crazy. But Stella knew that sounding crazy and actually being crazy were two different things. And it reminded her of a person she knew. Okay, so she had two friends. Ben and a fellow by the name of Sean Householder. She hadn't talked to Sean in a couple of months but one thing about him, the end of the world was always coming, so it was easy to pick up where you left off. He was always in the same place. Six feet under with room for one more.

Chapter 26

"Who is this?" came the familiar gravelly voice on the other end of the line. There was no hello, no friendly greeting of any kind.

"Don't you ever say hello?" Stella purred into the phone.

"Ha, ha! When I saw a private number from Illinois, I had a hunch it might be you. Stella Carrigan, love of my life," Sean growled back. He sounded rough around the edges, but Stella could see him clear as day with his camouflage pants and army issue boots traipsing through the wilderness with a bow and arrow like some kind of upgraded Robin Hood.

"How's the world treating you, Sean?"

"Like shit. How 'bout yourself?" he chuckled.

"I can't complain. No one will listen," Stella replied in kind.

"Now, you know that I've got room here for you. Anytime you want to get off the grid and come stay with me I've got you covered. I've made some improvements to the place. It's like paradise," Sean said.

"Oh, yeah? Sound like you've been keeping busy," Stella replied.

"The honeymoon suite, that's what I like to call it. It's got fresh running water fitted with my own purification system. I stole a few tricks from Dean Kamen but he's never going to know," Sean said, and Stella could hear the smile of pride in his voice.

"I'd love to see it," Stella chuckled.

"And the view. The bulletproof, reinforced glass allows the sun to come in every morning and the stars every night. It's very romantic," Sean was not just a doomsday prepper. He was a doomsday survivor. There wasn't any emergency he wasn't ready for and had Stella not liked being in the city so much where she could blend in and not be seen in plain view, she might have taken Sean up on one of his many invitations to join him in luxury to await the end of the world.

"You mean to tell me you haven't found a woman to hunker down with? Maybe you should try Match.com," Stella chuckled.

"Right!" He boomed with laughter.

"Seriously, Sean. I have a favor to ask you. Can you still tap into some of the state databases?" Stella asked carefully.

"Yeah, of course, I can. What do you need?" he cleared his throat.

"Can you pull up a file under my name in Ottawa from twenty-three years ago?" she said the words as if they had sharp corners and was afraid of slitting the sides of her mouth with them.

Sean immediately knew what she was looking for. "Why are you looking into that, Stella?" his voice although gravely and rough, at this moment was tender with concern.

He knew about Stella's past. When they had met it was completely by chance. Stella had gone home to Ottawa for a baby shower of all things. She had finally escaped the foster care system by the miracle of turning eighteen. When she was just about to turn twenty the biological daughter of her last foster family was having her first baby. It was the last thing Stella wanted to do and it made her a thousand shades of uncomfortable. But they had been the only family she knew for the last four years of her life, the longest Stella ever stayed with anyone, so she felt an obligation. She bought a pack of diapers, some powder, and baby wipes for the mother-to-be. As soon as possible without being rude, blaming her quick departure on junior college classes, homework, and tests that she had to study for, Stella left the house she spent her high school years in and went to the nearest tavern.

She was never a big drinker. But the idea of just having a beer seemed right. She sauntered in, took a seat at the bar, and was hard to miss among the regulars. One of which was Sean. Aside from being easy on the eyes, he was a real charmer. And, as if things couldn't get any better, he was a prepper. Stella had yet to make the jump to full-on prepping, living in a self-contained bunker with twenty-five years of food and water as well as ammo and firearms stockpiled. But she thought it would make a wonderful retirement hobby. She was still too addicted to the idea of catching the bad guys and making them pay for their crimes.

Sean's and Stella's bond was almost instant. They exchanged information and amazingly kept in touch over the past several years. As Stella inched up the food chain in the Chicago Police Department, Sean slipped more and more off the grid. But they found that they sort of needed each other to be reminded of what life had to offer.

"Sean, I've got a gut feeling about something. It won't let me go and the truth is it's chewing me up inside. I hate to ask you to poke your head above water, but I really need a solid," Stella said.

"Yeah, okay. You don't need to explain it to me. It will take me a while. Probably by this evening. Are you at the same email?" his voice was all business.

"The Chicago PD isn't much for change. Yes, same address," Stella smiled. "I need you to pull everything on my case. All of it. Even if it's just a blurb after the hoopla died down. Anything that has to do with it and...with him."

"Stella, you'd tell me if you were in some kind of trouble, right? You know I'd let you know how to find me, right?" Sean said.

"I know that. But you forget, Sean, I'm a detective. I'd know how to find you," Stella bragged making Sean laugh.

"I'll have it for you in a couple of hours. But my services aren't free," Sean said and clicked his tongue.

"Let me guess. Dinner in the city?" Stella teased and again Sean laughed.

"Nope. You have to come and see my place. I'll send you a map and a compass and when you get here, I can tell you, you aren't going to want to leave," Sean said. "All the modern conveniences. None of the government interference. I'm living the dream, Stella."

"It really sounds like it. Okay, I promise," Stella replied. She certainly would love to see Sean's bunker. But that would require time away from the force and the 18th Precinct and her job, the people relying on her, the victims. It would be difficult, but a weekend hidden from everyone, with an arsenal of firearms for target practice, and MREs with some wine sounded like a good time. But Stella knew as well as Sean that as soon as she had a break in her schedule there would be another case, another emergency, something that needed her undivided attention and she'd have to postpone indefinitely.

"Okay, I'll send you a text from a burner with the email address it's coming from. It will probably go to your spam so check there first. And that address won't be accessible once you open it. Sort of a kill switch gets thrown," Sean said proudly.

"Sounds good. You probably don't need to go through all this trouble. I think everything is on public record. I just don't want to wait by going through the regular channels," Stella replied.

After a few more pleasantries Stella reminded Sean he'd been on the phone long past his usual limit.

"Hey, there isn't a war going on. I'm just living off the land at the moment. A regular patriot who knows forewarned is forearmed. Is that against the law?" Sean teased.

"Not yet. You're a peach, Sean. I'm glad you've kept this number. I don't know what I'd do if I couldn't reach you," Stella chuckled.

"You won't have to worry about that, darlin'. We'll talk soon," Sean said before reminding her to give him a couple of hours to collect everything she needed. As soon as Stella got off the phone she felt better. Sean really was a peach and the best, most well-kept secret in her life. No one knew about him because if they did, they might do some digging and find that he hadn't paid his taxes in forever and probably owns some questionable firearms. Nothing Stella would consider bad, but the *law* had its own definition and it was written in several legal books with no room for interpretation.

She went back to her motel room, got her computer juiced up, and waited. True to his word Sean sent the email under a mysterious email address that ended up in her spam folder. When she clicked on the attachment and opened the file there was no friendly greeting, no well wishes. No one would know it was sent by Sean.

"Where did you get all this?" Ben asked later that evening when she called him to her room to help her look through it.

"I've got a few connections in the records department. Is that wrong?" she fibbed.

"No. But Stella I'm worried about you looking into this when we are supposed to be looking into this situation we have here in Vandalia. Your case is closed," Ben replied.

"Believe me when I tell you this is about this case. I just know it. But I need you to look over this with me. I started to read these files and I started getting a little nervous. Not cracking up, Ben. Before you jump to conclusions that I'm having a breakdown I'm just telling you I'm not. I'm asking for you to read these files over and let me know if you read anything that mentions another person." Stella looked at Ben, her eyes steady and clear.

"Okay, I'll take a look," Ben said before taking a seat at the desk. Ben started to read through everything. There was a description of the man who had kidnapped Stella. His real name was John Budrene. He was a quiet man. Aren't they always? Neighbors who knew him, coworkers who saw him every day, never gave the man a second thought. Only once in a while would he mention going off into the woods. It was just his "thing" to live simply out in the woods in a shack he built with his own hands and called his vacation home with a chuckle and innocent shrug of his shoulders. It was too late when people discovered it was also his "thing" to kidnap little girls. According to police, they found the remains of two other young girls around eight or nine who had never emerged from the basement. The same place Stella had been under a blanket, on a cold, cracked cement floor with a blindfold around her face that she was too terrified to remove.

As Ben scanned the information his heart broke. He knew what happened to Stella. Everyone knew a little bit about it. But there were some details here he didn't know about. The stash of urine and fecal matter the man kept in jars. The weird number of clocks he had upstairs all set to different times that meant something in his twisted mind but that no one else could figure out. Of course, there was pornography in neat stacks under the bathroom sink.

Ben looked at Stella who was reading over his shoulder like the words might jump out, take hold of her, and throw her back into that place. Her eyes skimmed the words, looking for one in particular and not lingering on the others for too long as they would piece together the nightmare she tried to put far behind her.

They were at the end of the file. Stella let out a deep breath as she started to read but Ben turned to her and wasn't going to look at the file any longer.

"Stella, I don't understand why you wanted to put yourself

through that again. Look, it's obvious to me that something has brought all this back into focus and you aren't doing well. You're focusing on this...this...imaginary person from this event and giving him power over you today."

Stella stared intently at the computer screen, barely listening.

"I know you don't want to hear this. I know that you are the best cop I've had the pleasure to work with. But there is no second shooter from the grassy knoll, Stella. I've got to tell Briggs that I think you need a break," Ben sighed. "I won't go into all this. I'll just say you're burnt out. I'm not wrong. Stella, there comes a time when all of us need a break or else *we'll* end up in a shack out in the woods surrounded by bottles of our own shit and piss treating them like trophies."

Stella smiled faintly at Ben's words as she looked up at him through tears. His image warbled like she was looking at his reflection in a funhouse mirror. She pointed to the computer screen. At the very bottom of the last file was an article about John Budrene being shot at the scene. His young son, Henry Budrene, was taken and put into foster care. There was no other family. There were no close friends. The boy was all that was left.

"There was someone else there," Stella whispered.

"Looks like you were right," Ben replied.

Chapter 27

The next day Stella showed up early at Ben's bed and breakfast. It was not a long walk, as nothing in Vandalia was far from anything else in Vandalia. It was a beautiful fall morning. She could see her breath as she walked along the sidewalk. The colorful decorations in the shops and in front of the houses popped against the overcast sky. It was inevitable in any town across America that there were those people who celebrated Halloween with carved pumpkins, a ghost, or maybe a skeleton. And then there were those who broke out the fog machine and strobe lights to accompany their zombie apocalypse scene complete with bloody, decomposing zombies chewing on bits and pieces of their victims. Stella saw enough gore in real life. Besides, she wondered what these people were thinking. And what little girls dressed like princesses or little boys dressed like firefighters thought when they saw this stuff. Stella had a theory that if she went into any of those gore-themed houses she'd find several laws being broken that could probably get the owners at least thirty days in the slammer. But that was beyond her authority.

As she walked up to the B&B it was also decorated with cute pumpkins, stalks of corn, glittery black bats hanging from the porch ceiling, and a plastic skeleton holding the sign that read Burr Oak Lane Bed and Breakfast. When she stepped inside, she was instantly hit with the smell of cinnamon and apples. It was nice and before she had a chance to ring the bell on the counter for someone to assist her, Ben came rushing downstairs.

"Hey, slow down," Stella said. "You don't have to rush, I'm right here. Good morning. Buy you a coffee?"

"We've got some news," Ben replied. "And yes, you can buy the coffee."

"What happened?" Stella asked.

"The sheriff called me about ten minutes ago. It turns out that Therese Foley was a teacher in Chicago who left abruptly," Ben said. Stella listened and pretended not to notice that the sheriff had called Ben and not her.

"At first I thought she had an affair with a student. That will get them chased out of a school quickly," Ben said.

"Yeah, to be hired just as quickly at another school," Stella smirked.

"That's what I thought, too. But no. She left because she was being harassed by a student. According to the statements she made to the school superintendent she was terrified that this kid was going to come and get her. He left her notes. He waited around her car. He posted images of her on social media. And when these gestures of affection didn't work...he didn't take it too well," Ben shook his head. "According to her statements she was in fear for her life. This young Romeo threatened her more than once, in front of classmates, until finally, she reported him to DCFS. She was sure there was something going on at home that a boy his age, sixteen, could be allowed to run around the city. He'd show up at her home around midnight or one in the morning to peek in the windows and he'd leave notes in her mailbox. He wasn't very subtle about anything nor did he try and pretend it wasn't him who was doing all this."

"Okay, we're sure there wasn't some kind of tryst that took place?" Stella asked skeptically as she and Ben left the B&B and walked toward his car.

"Whether it did or it didn't doesn't really matter. What matters is that the boy's father is Ned Casio's cousin," Ben said.

"You don't say," Stella gasped.

"It's a small world, isn't it?" Ben said. "And that's not all."

Stella shook her head and put her hands on her hips.

"Turns out that the troubled boy's father owns the house that Ned is staying in," Ben said. "And, I had to get this off my chest with Darlow, I told him if there were any more developments, he was to call you first. They might play games like this in the country but in the city, you are the lead detective on this case and he is to behave accordingly."

"How did he take that?" Stella asked.

"Like any young man caught acting a fool. Embarrassed. But he nodded and I think he got the point," Ben said. "So, should we get the food to go?"

"You get yourself something to eat. I'm going to stay behind," Stella said.

"What for?" Ben asked. "Are you sure that's a good idea?"

"I think you can handle it. Besides, the last time we both went to the city we came back to another body. I think it might be best if one of us remain behind. It'll be all right. I've got a few things I can do. Besides, a little time at the diner or maybe at one of the local watering holes might help us out. I'm not going to hold my breath but you never know where a good tip might pop up. Besides, if something happened it wouldn't look good for one of us not to be here. Not when we've got three bodies and not a single halfway decent lead other than this one." Stella said.

"I'll call you when I get downtown," Ben replied.

"Yes," Stella said and watched as Ben got in his car and drove off in the direction of the highway. She headed to the Blueberry diner and took a seat at the counter. Bonnie was serving coffee and gave Stella a wave. Within seconds she was behind the counter pouring Stella a cup of coffee.

"How are things coming along, detective?" She said pleasantly. A couple of the regulars looked in Stella's direction.

"Can't complain. No one will listen," Stella joked. "Don't

they ever give you a day off? Every day I come in it's always just you working."

"Yeah, no rest for the wicked they say. What can I get you?" Bonnie asked as she pulled a pen from behind her ear and put it to her order pad. Stella ordered some pancakes and once Bonnie disappeared into the kitchen, she looked at the fellows sitting along the bar who were sizing her up.

"Good morning," Stella said loudly nodding her head.

A couple of them mumbled a good morning to her. The man sitting one stool over looked at Stella skeptically. "Morning. You ain't from Vandalia."

"No sir," Stella replied. "Are you born and bred here?"

"Sure am," the man said.

"So, you know everyone and everything going on in town?" Stella thought she might have just bellied up to the right place.

"Not quite," he replied. His eye-glasses were round and amplified his eyes making him look like a wide-eyed owl. He didn't smile at Stella and appeared to be slightly offended that she was not only in town but sitting at his restaurant counter.

Just then Bonnie brought Stella her plate of pancakes. "Earl, leave this lady alone. She's trying to eat."

"It's all right, Bonnie. I enjoy talking to the locals." Stella said. "Earl is your name?"

"That's right," he snarled back.

"Earl, have you seen or heard anything strange around town over the past couple of days?" Stella barked loud enough to make everyone in the diner look up and take notice.

Earl looked around at everyone staring and shook his head.

"Earl, you had a lot to say before. Now you aren't talking. See, that's what my partner and I run into a lot. People complain the cops don't do enough but when we need help, you dummy up," Stella huffed.

"Now there's no need to pick on him. He was just asking questions," another man in a Cubs baseball hat said.

"Funny, I ask lots of questions. I ask everyone I know questions and they give me smart ass responses or tell me they don't want to be involved. It's not easy being a cop.

Earl threw his money on the counter and walked out to the shouts of his friends telling him not to leave.

"BYE!" Stella waved. Her temper had gotten the best of her and she should have never acted this way. But there was such a heavy cloud hanging over her she didn't know what was going to set her off. It just so happened to be a couple of old guys at Blueberry diner.

Chapter 28

After dealing with the locals, Stella was beginning to wish she'd gone with Ben back to the city. At least there she knew how to handle things. There was a strange incestuous element in little towns. Everyone knew everyone or maybe it was more accurate to say everyone knew the rumors about everyone. There were probably only a couple of people who knew the truth. Certainly, the guys at the diner weren't them and Stella learned long ago that any stories heard in a tavern were forty percent accurate, if that.

It was another cool, overcast day and Ben texted that he'd be staying in the city. Turns out Mr. Ned Casio's cousin didn't come home last night.

"I can't leave until I talk to him. If anything has happened to this guy, too, I'll..." Ben started but Stella quickly cut him off.

"Don't say it. Just keep me in the loop," she instructed. After hanging up Stella got on her computer and checked her work email for any fires that might need to be put out. She made a couple phone calls regarding a couple of other cases she'd wrapped up prior to starting this one. When she thought of the schedule that she'd been keeping she realized that Ben was probably right. She was burning the candle at both ends. It was dangerous. But now that she'd discovered proof that there was someone else with her when she was held in that dank, hopeless cellar she wondered where the connection was with these cases. Had those women suffered the same experience at one time? What would be the chances of that? It would have to be one in ten billion at least. That suspicion was too far-fetched.

"No. I'll bet it has something to do with the bad kid and his father. Some parents can't believe their kids could do anything wrong even when the whole world is pointing to their mugshot on the wall," Stella muttered to herself. She got dressed but was feeling listless and stir-crazy. She went for another run.

Just as she got back, her phone rang. It was Ben and he didn't sound happy.

"How was the interview?" Stella asked as she opened the door and walked outside.

"Boring," he replied.

"But that was just the drive, right? Tell me we've got a connection with the troubled kid and Therese Foley's murder," Stella said.

"I'm not sure. I got no answer at Ned's place to ask him about his cousin. I camped out for most of the night but there was no movement." Ben said.

"You don't think he flew the coop, do you?" Stella asked, her eyebrows pulled down tightly.

"No. Not at all. I saw not just one, but two women walk up to his door and ring the bell. They got no answer either. From the looks of them, I'd say they were hoping for some company. I don't know what kind of cologne the man wears but it has an effect on the ladies." Ben sounded disgusted.

Stella could tell he was frustrated. She was too. But there was nothing they could do. It was better that Ben stay in the city. He could be close to family while he was tracing down the leads and there was no harm in that. Little did she know it would be another day before he got anywhere on the case and drove back to tell her. Stella met him outside her room when he drove up. Ben started talking right away.

"I went back to the house on Trumbell and Ned Casio was there along with a female writer from some local rag doing an interview. When I walked in Ned said I could have a seat in his living room. You looked around a bit in there, didn't you?" Ben asked.

"Sure did. Why?" Stella replied.

"Well, he'd done some redecorating after we left. There were quite a few pictures of Barbara around. And I listened to the interview as it wrapped up. Our boy, Ned was really just one big fuzzy ball of heartbreak," Ben shook his head.

"Really? How did he react when you asked him about that little detail about a cousin with a troubled kid?" Stella rubbed her hands together wishing she could have been a fly on the wall to see Ned's response.

"First, I had to chase the reporter out of there. She was an annoying twerp. Ready to change the world with her own opinion oozing off every word," Ben replied. "But once she was gone and I had Ned alone I asked him if he knew about his cousin's kid stalking a teacher. Of course, Ned asked what that had to do with him."

"Of course, he did," Stella replied.

"I'm starving. Mind if we walk to Blueberry's?" Ben asked and started to step away from his car.

"Oh, I had a little talk with the regulars there a day ago. I'm not sure they will be very happy to see us, er...me. They probably won't be too happy to see me," Stella shrugged and shook her head, wincing like the words smarted a little as she said them.

"I was gone for less than twenty-four hours and you got us banned from the only breakfast place in town?" Ben rubbed his stomach then put his hands on his hips.

"Okay, we can go there. Maybe they'll be nicer if you're with me. They did mention that you seemed like a pleasant enough negro," Stella teased.

"Tell me they didn't say the word negro. This town isn't that hillbilly. Is it?" Ben asked.

"No, they said colored. And no, they aren't *that* hillbilly," Stella joked. "Look, they certainly don't mind you. They had a hard time accepting a female cop asking about their friends and family and one of them made reference to the sheriff being a relative or neighbor. I'm going to pay for that exchange with Sheriff Darlow until we leave this place, aren't I?" Stella let out a deep breath.

"You brought that on yourself. I was born this way. I can't help it God made me so pretty," Ben said while smoothing back his black hair that was short like he was in the military.

As soon as they walked into Blueberry's all eyes were on them.

"Morning, Detectives," Bonnie saved the day. "There's a spot for you right by the window."

"Thanks, Bonnie," Stella replied and looked to the group of regulars she'd had the exchange with the previous morning. She smiled at them and gave a sweet nod. "Gentlemen."

Almost in unison, they grumbled back at her. It was like Bonnie was keeping watch over the troublemakers in her classroom. She cleared her voice and pursed her lips at the men who shook their heads, shifted in their seats, and went back to drinking their coffee.

"Well, that wasn't so bad," Stella smiled broadly. "Now, tell me the rest of what happened in the city."

"Ned knew his cousin's kid was having some trouble but according to him, it was just puberty. The kid was sixteen, he was having all these emotions and problems, he wasn't doing great in his classes. Normal teenage stuff. But when I brought up what had happened with Therese Foley, Ned looked a little green around the gills," Ben said.

"Do you think he knew about it?" Stella asked.

"No. I think he suddenly saw his poor, lonely, widow act

slipping away. So, without grabbing me by the scruff of the neck and tossing me out he told me that if I had anything more to ask about his cousin's kid I'd have to talk to his cousin. Jimmy Molitor." Ben replied after ordering a short stack with bacon and coffee. Stella had the same hoping no one would spit in their food or worse because she'd upset the yokels.

"You spoke to him?" Stella asked.

"Ned practically handed him over to me. He gave me the construction site he was working on, his home address, his lake house address in Wisconsin, his home phone, cell, his kid's cell, and his ex-wife's cell and address just in case," Ben chuckled. "I wish all our people of interest were as accommodating as this. I mean, if I had said his mother was involved, he would have handed her over."

"Classy," Stella said before taking a sip of coffee. Ben took out his notebook. He'd called Jimmy Molitor and spoke to him on the phone. He seemed like a pleasant enough guy and he was on the job but welcomed Ben to come and talk with him.

"He was a regular guy. Anyone you might see on a construction site. Big. Dirty pants and boots. Hands like baseball mitts. Skin brown from the sun, tattooed from his younger days and calloused from working," Ben said.

"Any telltale ink on him?" Stella asked.

"No gang affiliation that I could see. But he confessed he's been in and out of jail. Just a guy who didn't have his head screwed on too tight," Ben said.

"What did he have to say about his kid? Did he know about it? That his son's behavior caused our latest victim to leave her job and town and start over in Nowhere's-ville, Illinois?" Stella asked.

"Yeah, he knew. Said there wasn't anything he could do. He talked to his kid and told him he'd have to wait to date a woman Therese's age," Ben read from his pad.

"He'd have to wait to date women Therese's age? Good thing he told him." Stella shrugged. "That's what passes as parenting, huh? I guess I don't know since I don't have any children. What did he do when you told him Therese was dead?"

"He shrugged and said he didn't know the woman but from what his son had said she was a little more than friendly with a lot of the students. But that his son, Joshua Molitor, wasn't as well off as the other kids she cozied up to. When I asked if this was in the files at the school, Jimmy just shrugged. It didn't matter, he said, because they'd believe the teacher over his kid every time," Ben replied.

"Body language? Did he appear to be hiding anything?" Stella saw her game piece being moved back to the beginning.

"He didn't seem to care about any of it. When I asked him if I could talk to his son, he told me the boy had gone back to live with his grandmother in Indianapolis two months ago. If I could get past her, she was the ex-wife's mother, I could talk to him," Ben replied. "Jimmy made it clear he was not happy the grandmother had custody. She was awarded the kid due to the fact the mother was in and out of rehab and according to Jimmy had nothing nice to say about him."

"Nice. Did you call the grandmother to verify the boy was there?"
"I did. Her name was Betsy Benson and she confirmed not only had the boy been with her but that he was spending some time in the juvenile detention center there for breaking into a house and trying to steal a television. She turned him in. He's been there for the past ten days," Ben said.

"Fine. Back to square one," Stella suddenly didn't feel hungry. When their breakfast was on the table, she pushed hers around on her plate while she thought. Finally, took a small bite. It went down okay so she continued to eat. Before she realized it, she was halfway through her breakfast.

"Did Jimmy have any opinion on Barbara Casio's death?" Stella asked with a full mouth.

Ben wiped his mouth with his paper napkin before continuing. "He said that Barbara had made Ned miserable. She strung him along and used him for his money and when he cheated on her it was only because she wasn't putting out."

"This guy is classy," Stella chuckled.

"Isn't he? He didn't seem to be all that upset about her death either. I don't know what it would take to rattle the guy. But he admitted he didn't like her. Never did. He thought she was a busy-body up in Ned's business and anyone else's who happened along. According to Jimmy, all they did was fight and fuck. Jimmy reported hearing Ned say the fucking wasn't all that great anymore. Jimmy said he didn't kill her but isn't surprised she's dead."

"Okay. So where was Jimmy when Barbara was killed? If he had such a strong opinion of her, he had to know we'd think he was a suspect," Stella said.

"He was in the city working. His timecards prove it. There would be no way for him to get off work, drive the five hours to Vandalia, hope to catch Barbara alone, kill her and then make the five-hour drive back to go right to work. Even if he could manage a construction job on zero sleep. It doesn't seem likely."

Stella surprised herself and finished her meal before Ben. "I just don't know where to go from here. I think that we should just forget everything and start over from scratch. Like we just walked in on the case today." She shrugged and shook her head. Whoever was responsible for this was making a fool out of her and she couldn't swing or kick or bite at a vapor that seemed to be the most likely culprit at the moment. Every time something was promising, like a love-sick teenager or an angry ex, a solid alibi ruled them out.

"Yeah, I agree. I haven't checked back in at the B&B. I'd like to go wash up and take some aspirin. I was driving into the sun almost the whole way here," Ben said. "I had tried to keep this migraine at bay but after eating I can feel it settling in."

"No problem. I'm going to roam this lovely little town of Vandalia. I'll see what I can stir up," she smiled and blinked her eyes.

"Try not to get us run out on a rail," Ben said as he took out his wallet and tossed the money on the table before standing up. "I'll leave the car at your place. But the keys are coming with me."

"You don't trust me after all this time? I'm hurt." Stella grumbled.

"You'll get over it," Ben said and walked out of the restaurant. Stella took a sip of her coffee and looked at the counter. None of the people were paying any attention to her. She was glad as she stood up, handed Bonnie the money, and headed toward the door.

"Good luck, today, Detective," Bonnie waved.

"Thanks, I think I'm going to need it," Stella said and nodded toward the line of regulars before leaving.

Chapter 29

Stella left the Blueberry Restaurant and decide she was going to do a little canvassing. The main street was beginning to come to life as the stores, shops, and boutiques began to open. Stella wondered if she could ever settle down and live in a place like this. It was quaint and, aside from this horrible triple murder, had been untouched by the dirt and grime that comes with a big city. She would probably be safe in a place like this where neighbors learn your routine not so they can burglarize your home but because they care enough to make sure you are able to bring your garbage cans in on time or keep your lawn cut.

Her first stop was a bakery. Even though she'd already eaten she stopped in. There were places to sit and enjoy coffee and a pastry. The little handmade signs read "Baked Fresh Daily" and "Try our flavored coffee daily special." The woman bustling behind the counter was a full-figured gal with blonde hair and red lipstick.

Stella hung back until the couple ahead of her had finished their small talk, got their coffee and scones, and took a seat. When the blonde woman looked up with a smile, Stella smiled back and held up her badge.

"I'm Detective Stella Carrigan. I'm investigating a string of homicides in the neighborhood. I'm asking around about the women who were killed and if anyone had seen or heard anything strange over the past couple of days. Any strangers in town?" Stella watched the woman's reaction.

"Oh, I did hear about that. My God, what is the world coming to?" the woman said. She introduced herself as Jacqueline Tovis. This was her shop and she'd been in business for over eight years. "Detective, I hope you'll understand when I say that I don't want any trouble. I don't have any information that could help you. I'm just a business owner. I know pastries. I don't know anything about the murders."

Stella thanked Jacqueline for her time and gave her a business card in case she remembered something or saw something. The couple watched her as she walked out like they were expecting her to suddenly burst into song and sashay her way out the door. Neither of them made any attempt to talk to Stella.

She continued down the street stopping in a paint shop where there were a couple of fellows hanging out in front of the register. Their matching red vests told Stella they worked there. They smiled as soon as she walked in, all too eager to help the new female in town who didn't have a wedding ring. But when she showed her badge as she looked around at the handful of other people inside, now all of them looking her way, she got the same response as the bakery. It went the same for the hair salon, a sandwich shop, and the eyeglasses store. Everyone gave her the same reply. No, they hadn't seen anything strange and the only strangers in town were her and the tall black guy she was always traveling with. Everyone seemed nice on the surface, but the fact that there wasn't even the slightest inclination to report on a neighbor was telling. These folks were scared of something. They had to have been reading the news. Even this small town had a paper and it was impossible to keep a lid on three dead females for long no matter how discreet Stella and Ben tried to be. This is what grapevines thrive on.

Just a couple of blocks off the main drag the scenery took a turn. The houses had security gates on the windows and front doors. Weeds crept up across the foundations and through cracks in the buckling driveways. Old beaters sat in the driveways. Vandalia had a poor side of town. Stella looked around. There wasn't anyone on the street but that didn't stop Stella from getting the distinct impression she was being watched. This area was far from Barbara Casio's house. The park where Therese was found was directly on the other side of this neighborhood and the Washington Motel was opposite that. It made a triangle. But Stella knew every case with three victims makes an ominous-looking triangle when pinned on a map. This wasn't helping her.

Without hanging around for too long Stella turned around and started to canvas the other side of the busy main street when all of a sudden, she saw one of those spotlessly clean squad cars rolling up on her with Deputy Winger behind the wheel. He pulled in the alley just feet in front of Stella and got out of the car.

"Hi, Deputy," Stella said cheerfully. "Have you been to Jackie's bakery over there? Yum. Although I can't personally vouch for the food or coffee, it smelled like heaven."

"I know Jackie. I know her and the regulars at the gym and the sandwich shop. It's safe to say I know everyone in town, Detective. And they are all telling me the same thing. You are making them nervous," Deputy Winger replied.

"Good. They should be nervous. There's a killer out there who isn't making it easy on us and if I didn't sleep with a gun on the nightstand I'd be scared, too," Stella said.

"So, I can assume you haven't made any progress," Deputy Winger looked at his watch and then at Stella.

"When the people of this town are more concerned about upsetting the applecart than offering the detectives on this case any help, it is a safe assumption that no progress has been made," Stella replied sweetly. "What's the hang-up with everyone, Winger? No one will talk all of a sudden. The guys at the hardware store were happy to tell me about Barbara Casio's business. Her neighbor was a nice enough man who had a good bit of information. Hell, the people at your favorite no-tell motel were like open books compared to the upper tier of people in this town. What gives, Deputy? You're the law in these parts. I've seen first-hand how dedicated your men are to you and the sheriff. Can't you shake some trees and see what falls loose?"

"My job is just to assist you in any way I can," Deputy Winger said.

"Great. Then let the people know we need their help if we are going to get this wrapped up," Stella said. In the city, it was expected that people were hesitant to help but when Stella had connections, she had paid squealers and she wasn't afraid to use them. Hell, in a pinch she reached out to Sean who was more than happy to put the drop on some bad guy. But she had nothing to go on here in Vandalia. Three bodies and no clues.

"Isn't that *your* job?" Winger said. Stella stared at him and saw behind his eyes a shift. His cocky attitude melted, and he realized he'd gone a step too far.

"I see where you are planting your flag, Deputy Winger," Stella said.

"I'll see what I can do. You don't…"

"No. I'd hate to drag you away from your warm office where nothing ever happens and the worst you have to deal with is teenagers humping in their cars on the outskirts of town. Don't worry, Winger. When I have news, you'll be the first person I notify." Stella walked around the squad car and continued up the street. Suddenly, the decorations didn't look so festive. Instead, they looked like too much make-up on an old woman trying to look attractive and young again. What a shame. Stella had been enjoying herself. But now she realized there was more going on here. Vandalia was doomed to suffer more tragedy before this case was solved. She could feel it in her bones.

She crossed the street, just to make sure Deputy Winger couldn't easily catch up to her.

After a few paces, a fellow who was in the paint shop when she stopped in came sauntering up to her.

"Excuse me, you were just in the paint shop a couple of minutes ago?" he spoke like Stella might not have remembered.

"Yes," she replied, looking at him suspiciously.

"The Harvest Days start in two days. Is something going to happen?" he asked nervously. Stella wondered if there wasn't something wrong with the young man.

"I don't know. What do you think?" she replied. He returned with a shrug, his eyebrows raising to the middle of his forehead. There wasn't anything particularly striking about the young man aside from his question. Stella had encountered people like him before. They were annoying. Tough guys who felt they got a raw deal in life because their high school sweetheart dumped them or their boss didn't take them seriously enough to pay them six figures with nothing more than a college education. A lot of them had fantasies of being cops solely for the purpose of being able to carry a gun and shoot at people. If Stella had a nickel for every time she pulled her weapon she'd be rich. But if she had had the same deal for every time she actually pulled the trigger, she'd starve to death.

Thankfully, guys like this one lacked the dedication needed to become a member of the thin blue line. Or they wouldn't make it past the psych eval. Stella was a little surprised when she made it considering all the baggage she had. But the head-shrinker told her that her unique experience as a child could come in handy on the force. He called it a "unique experience." Stella called it hell. But that was water under the bridge.

"Have you seen anything strange or different around town? Anyone who seemed like they didn't belong?" she asked. He shook his head and shrugged. "Well, if you do, let Sheriff Darlow know. He'll get in touch with me."

"I'll do that," the man said with a nod and smile.

Stella turned and continued walking down the sidewalk when her phone rang. It was Ben. She couldn't wait to tell him she came up with absolutely nothing while asking around the neighborhood.

"I've got good news for you," he said.

"I could use some. This town is keeping its mouth shut. Not a single person will talk to me. I just don't get it. They want the cops to help but they think we can just wave a nightstick and the clues will all fit themselves together. It's crazy," Stella vented. "What have you got for me?"

"It's not about the case, Stella. On a hunch I called the librarian from the town where you were…you know…held," Ben said carefully. Stella's stomach seized up. "She had the same name as a friend of Rochelle's from a couple years back. Anyway, as a favor, she pulled a couple of articles about the man who kidnapped you. These weren't in your case file. They wouldn't have been. You know that crossovers of departments didn't start until recently."

"Yeah," Stella muttered.

"Well, it's not a lot but it's a few things about his previous life. It isn't about you. This is prior to what he did. I thought it might help you get a grip on things. Those might be the wrong words to use but I think you catch my drift," Ben said.

Stella felt a lump in her throat. It was the last thing she expected but maybe the thing she needed most. Just a kind gesture to validate her feelings. Ben was the best partner. Even if she could have designed her own perfect version of a police detective she couldn't come close to one as good and decent as Ben. She'd never forget this.

After clearing her throat, Stella replied. "I appreciate that, Ben."

"My pleasure, Stella," Ben said. She could hear the smile in his voice, and it made Stella smile back. "Just keep your phone on. I'll meet up with you in a couple hours."

"Yeah. Okay," was all Stella said before hanging up. Although Stella believed in the Almighty, she wasn't what anyone would call a church-goer. But at that moment she whispered a tiny prayer of gratitude for Detective Ben Casey.

Chapter 30

As the fire crackled, Henry watched the tiny sparks as they swirled up into the air. The smell of the smoke mingling with the cold air of the season made him feel romantic. If only Stella were here with him, next to the fire, under a black sky with nothing but the stars to witness what they were doing, he would be able to die a happy man.

"It won't be long," he muttered as he imagined her snuggling up to him to stay warm as he poked the logs to keep them burning. There was nothing he wouldn't give her. He would stand in the middle of this campfire if she asked him to. He would set the world ablaze if she whispered it was her desire to watch it burn. Even though he knew she'd never ask him to do that, he'd love it if she did. But he knew Stella was more reserved than that. She was the kind of woman who would be thankful for a kind gesture. That he remembered. The kindest, simplest gesture made her whisper thank you. He remembered how her lips pouted and trembled. She wanted to see him. He knew it. She'd tilt her head back and peek when she thought he wasn't looking, and he never told. It was their secret. She would have seen him eventually had things not gone off the rails like they did. But that was okay because it gave him time to prepare. Had things gone on back then it all would have been clumsy and awkward, and it could have been ruined from the start. This was better.

The wind blew, rustling the dried leaves still in the trees and along the ground gently pushing them along like a crinkling brown and gold wave in the light of the fire. That light made everything look beautiful, golden, and soft. The gift Henry had for Stella was next to him. It had taken a lot of thought to find just the right spot for her to find it. Vandalia wasn't a big town, but it was big enough that he needed to carefully consider all kinds of possibilities. How many people could possibly see it before she was called? Would the weather cause it to be damaged? Would anyone else claim responsibility for it? No. Of course not. Besides, Stella would know who it was from and that it was for her. They were connected. His father had told him so just before he died. His father was a prophet. A shaman. He was all-wise and touched by God. There was never a dishonest word that came from his mouth. Even when Henry was being scolded, even beaten, he knew it was all leading up to this. It made him stronger because only a strong man would satisfy Stella. And he was determined to be that.

He thought of Stella's eyes once she saw his gift. They would glaze over with that heated look as the fire of lust burned inside her. She'd have to walk away from her partner, from the scene, lest they see how turned on she was. But he'd know. She'd look around the area, looking for him like a wolf prowls for its mate. But he wouldn't make himself known. Not yet. He'd make her wait. It wasn't cruelty, just part of the game. She was playing it just like he was but this time she wouldn't be able to hold back any longer. Once they were reunited, she'd give herself to him. He'd fuck her. That was for sure. But then, once the initial lust was satisfied, he'd tenderly take her again. While in their own world he'd whisper sweet words to her about how he gathered these gifts, how he placed them thoughtfully for her to find. Like a playful treasure hunt. She'd laugh and say his name over and over until they'd exhausted one another.

An owl hooted high up in the trees and another answered off in the distance snapping Henry out of his daydream. He poked the fire with the stick he'd been holding then poked the plastic garbage bag next to him. A smile of true happiness spread across his lips. He hadn't always been this happy. Those years of searching for her were hard. But they weren't as hard as the time after he finally found her. Watching Stella from a distance, following close enough behind her that he could reach out and touch her but not daring to do so. Those times were worse. But he knew she was aware of him. She knew it by the subtle signals when she flipped her hair or took off her jacket, or when she'd wear the exact color he'd expected her to on a day he was feeling particularly lonely. It was all part of the game. It would be crazy for him to expect her to run to him and jump in his arms, wrap her legs around him with a crowd of people around. As much as the idea thrilled him, he knew it was impossible. Waiting was all either of them could do.

"But it won't be much longer now. Not much longer at all," Henry said and smiled, feeling true happiness and a delicious longing wash over him like the warmth from the fire.

Chapter 31

Wednesday, another gray morning greeted Stella as she got up to hit the running path and clear the cobwebs from her head. She'd thought about Ben's phone call before she fell asleep. Although she had no idea what she was going to find out she was comforted by the fact that there was something more to learn, something to help fill in the blanks to this gruesome part of her past. She wanted to see it the way a doctor has to look at a festering wound in order to clean it out. She had thought that pushing everything aside was the right thing to do. The idea of taking out her frustrations on the perverts and abusers she routinely arrested seemed like a fine therapy. It had worked up to this point. But this case was different. There was a personal element to it and although she didn't know exactly how she fit in with things she knew she did.

As she stretched her muscles groaned like the wooden hull of a ship that had enjoyed calm waters until now and was being tested against a strong wind. Her breath came out in white plumes and she shivered against the cold. It prompted her to get moving and within a few minutes, she was traveling at a good pace, her body warming, and her head clearing.

The leaves had either suddenly turned overnight or it was the first Stella had noticed that they were in their brightest fall array. The red and orange colors of the trees were Stella's favorite as they seemed rarer than the golds and purples and browns. They immediately pulled her eyes toward them. But the quilt the fallen leaves made across the ground was even prettier. While she was out running Stella felt free enough to dream a little as her body became hot and her breath came in a rhythm. The impulse of running and jumping into a pile of leaves that someone had carefully and meticulously raked into a pile on their lawn was overwhelming. Of course, she'd never do it. How would that be for public relations? The town of Vandalia had already decided the big city cops weren't the quick fix they'd hoped. But maybe, before she left town, she'd do it. She chuckled a little as she rounded the first bend of the Little River Meadow Bike and Running Trail. And as her mind continued to roll like a movie still in progress her eyes saw something that didn't belong.

Stella looked down the path ahead of her and no one was there. She looked behind her and confirmed she was all alone. The sound of her gym shoes hitting the pavement was muffled. Even though her legs were still moving Stella felt like she was slowing down, trying to run through glue. She saw it there on the ground, but her mind didn't register it. Even as she jogged closer and closer she didn't think it was real. This was a dream. She hadn't really woken up yet. In just a second her eyes would pop open to the familiar view of the closed curtains of the motel room and the slit of daylight coming through the middle. The smell of lemon cleaner that never really left the place would fill her nostrils and the plain white bathroom would be off to her right. Her weapon, unholstered with the safety off on the nightstand. Any second now that was going to happen. Her eyes would pop open. She wouldn't be looking at another victim.

She certainly wouldn't be staring into the cloudy gray eyes of Janet Steeple-Gazak. Stella swallowed hard even though she had no spit in her mouth. The smell of burning leaves caught her attention and she saw a couple of yards into the nature preserve a small campsite was smoldering. Whoever did this was here long enough to set a fire. Carefully, Stella walked around the body but before she got to the ashes still emitting thin strands of curling smoke, she saw Janet had been posed with her hand stretched out. The thumb and pinky had been cut off.

"In three days, you'll be mine," she said the words but had no idea how she knew them. "I don't know them," she muttered. But she did and where they came from was a place that terrified her. If she focused on herself Stella was sure she'd lose her mind right then and there. She had to focus. This was a crime scene. It wasn't some kind of trick or flashback. This was happening now, and she needed to assess the situation and get the sheriff and Ben on the scene as quickly as possible before more runners or bicyclists or families hit the trail for an early morning walk.

Stella began to pace, her body quickly losing the heat it had generated just a few minutes ago. Was it minutes? Maybe it was just seconds ago. Or maybe she'd spent an hour there, staring at those three remaining fingers and muttering "In three days you'll be mine...in three days you'll be mine...in three days you'll be..."

"Get a hold of yourself." Stella pulled her cell phone from the side pocket of her running pants. Her hands were shaking as she dialed Ben's number.

"I knew you were going to wake me up," Ben grumbled.

"B-Ben, we've got another body," Stella stuttered. "It's Janet Gazak."

"Are you all right?" Ben asked.

"Yeah, as all right as I can be considering this is what I came across first thing this morning. Whoever left her here stayed with her for a while. There's a campfire just a few yards away, still hot," Stella swallowed hard again. Ben..."

Stella was about to tell Ben that she was certain this was a message for her. "In three days, you'll be mine" kept rolling over and over in her head like one of those perpetual motion gizmos they show at science fairs and at the Museum of Science and Industry in Chicago. It wasn't like having a song stuck in her head. This was different. There was a scariness to it. Stella looked at her phone, then over her shoulder, and was sure she was going to see some maniac running toward her with a machete or a chainsaw or, worse yet, just his bare hands. His eyes would be black like there was nothing behind them and he'd be grinning sadistically. But when she looked, the phone still up to her ear, she saw no one.

"Ben, there looks to be rope marks around her neck. She's

got two fingers missing from her right hand and she is posed so we'd take notice of it. Her hands are bound with the same kind of twine." Stella let out a deep sigh.

"Stella, you have to stay there until I get the sheriff. Are you still with me?" Ben asked nervously. It was obvious by the shakiness of his voice that he was trying to get dressed while talking on the phone.

"Yeah, but hurry, Ben," Stella muttered as she tried to watch all around her at once. She felt as vulnerable as if she'd ventured outdoors completely naked. After hanging up with Ben she withdrew her weapon from her hip-hugger pouch and waited.

It felt like hours that Stella was left alone with Janet Steeple-Gazak. It wasn't the fact she was there with a corpse that had Stella pacing nervously back and forth. It wasn't even the fact that any second now an innocent person could come jogging around the corner and see this. It was the words that popped into her head. Ever since she started Ben's relaxation tapes, she'd been remembering things. Bits and pieces of her life were snapping into focus so quickly they almost hurt.

"In three days, you'll be mine," she mumbled, and it caused her body to tremble as she remembered it. A boy. A boy in foster care told that to her. No, that wasn't right. He didn't just tell her a cute little ditty to make her smile or offer her comfort. It was like a threat. Every time he saw her, he said it and something else. There was more to it. What was the rest of the saying? Stella couldn't bring it up. It was still buried deep, deep down under a million other memories.

Finally, after what seemed like hours, Stella heard the sound of sirens in the distance. The Parks Department should block off the trail. She hoped the Sheriff had enough sense to post a couple of uniforms at the trail entrances. If she remembered right, there were about three of them.

Stella tried to concentrate on the situation at hand but the sickly feeling she was getting from the poem or song she remembered was taking over her thoughts. Where had she been when she heard it? What was the rest of it? And why did she even want to know? It was obvious from her reaction that she wasn't going to like it.

"Oh my God!" a woman screamed from the north side of the trail. Stella whirled around to find a jogger, standing in shock, staring at Janet's dead body. With eyes wide and terrified she looked at Stella, put her hands up, and started to back away.

"Wait, hold on," Stella ordered and fumbled for her badge that was also in a special slot on her hip-hugger case. "I'm Detective Carrington. Ma'am, I need you to calm down. I have to ask you some questions."

There was no way this woman would ever know it, but she saved Stella from completely freaking out and having some kind of episode right there on the path. The poor lady, who was fifty-four-year-old Melanie Hobbs, was on the verge of tears when Stella began to question her.

"Ms. Hobbs, did you see anyone else on the path?" Stella asked firmly. The sirens were getting closer and Stella was sure she could hear radios and voices not far off.

"No. No one. Oh my God. I just can't believe this. I don't know what to say. I mean, she's really dead? That woman? She isn't just sleeping or maybe having some kind of epileptic fit? I've heard people sometimes have these fits where they appear dead and then snap out of it at the funeral parlor," Melanie muttered.

"Do you jog here regularly, Ms. Hobbs?" Stella continued. She had to stay focused in order to keep her own composure. "Have you ever noticed anyone who looked out of sorts? Someone who didn't look like they were jogging or walking or maybe they behaved strangely?"

No, no, and no, the woman replied back. She was in shock

and unfortunately, she hadn't seen anyone leaving the area. Stella would have passed anyone who was coming from the other direction. Either the person responsible left before the trail officially opened or perhaps, they were still there, hiding in the trees, or lurking just out of view with a pair of binoculars, watching, listening, and laughing.

Just as Stella was about to let Melanie Hobbs go another pair of bicyclists were coming through. With her badge up she nearly got run over as she stepped into their path. At first, they were ready to argue until they saw her badge and what she was guarding.

"What is that? Is that really...?" the man in a black helmet and blue shorts choked on the rest of his sentence. The woman with him, in a pink helmet that matched her shorts, stared in shock. Before Stella had the chance to ask the two any questions a squad car rolled up the wide path. The coroner's car was behind it. Another unmarked vehicle behind that and she could only guess how long the parade went on.

Ben climbed out of the passenger's side of the squad car accompanied by Sheriff Darlow. Deputy Winger stepped out of the squad car behind him. Without hesitating, Ben hurried over to Stella to help with crowd control.

"Looks like you are handling things," Ben said with a grimace on his face.

"Yeah, good morning," Stella replied and explained she'd already taken a statement from Ms. Hobbs but the other two just showed up. Ben passed them off on one of the uniformed officers who had come along.

"There's the body and a campfire that only recently went out," Stella said and jerked her head in the general direction without looking right at it. It made her feel nervous like it had been just a cozy place for the killer and his victim. Now with Ben there, Stella let out a sigh of relief. Hell, she would have been thankful even if only Sheriff Darlow or Clarence Winger had shown up. There was an oppressive air over the place and gave Stella a bad feeling. She was sure she was being watched even though nothing so much as a leaf rustled around her. Still, she couldn't shake the feeling that this was a message for her.

"What are we going to do about this, Detectives?" Sheriff Darlow said. "Janet was a pillar of the community. Everyone knew her from the grocery store baggers to the Mayor himself. Do either of you want to tell me what the hell we are going to do?"

"You're going to take pictures of the body and campfire. You're going to take her in for an autopsy. And you're going to give us the file and photos once they are done and let us do our job," Stella ordered.

"I don't think you realize the severity of this, *Detective*," Sheriff Darlow hissed.

"Calm down, Sheriff," Ben said. "We've got to have pictures, forensics, and an autopsy before we can be sure of anything."

"You're covering for her," Sheriff Darlow said quietly to Ben.

"Are you requesting we leave? Because I can't speak for Detective Carrigan but I sure the hell can speak for myself and quite frankly I've had enough of this shit-kicking town. If you want the case, Sheriff, then say so. But remember, you requested *our* help. You're going to have to let us do things the way we know how," Ben said every word just above a whisper but only about six inches from the sheriff's face. There was no mistaking any word of it.

Sheriff Darlow raised his arms then let them drop to his sides. He ran his hands through his hair, looked at his team but said nothing else. Instead, he stood back as Tiffany, who was shocked to silence, took pictures. When she was finished there was no playful banter or an argument over the phone with one of her kids. She just left and Stella and Ben knew they'd have the pictures by the very next day if not sooner.

"Thanks for handling the Sheriff. I don't even know what to say anymore," Stella said as she spoke quietly to Ben like they were formulating a big plan.

"Don't mention it. I've had about enough of this place myself. I wish they'd throw us off the case," Ben said before snapping his fingers. "I've got to return a phone call. I almost forgot. I've got that information for you that we talked about last night. I thought finding out where Henry Budrene was living these days, if he was even still alive, might help you feel a little more at ease. He's probably living the life in Colorado with a wife and seven kids."

"I hope you are right about that," Stella said.

Yards of police tape had been strung up. Its neon yellow was a sharp contrast to the soothing golden color of the leaves. This flashy yellow was industrial, cold and meant that something had gone wrong, someone was hurt or in this case dead. People who had come for their morning exercise were surprised to see all the police activity but instead of turning around and going back the way they came they stayed to watch the gruesome performance of collecting evidence in the brutal murder of a local. It was morbid. Stella never understood why anyone would like to hang around a crime scene. But then she looked at the small gathering and wondered if any of them looked suspicious, like they'd been here a while and knew what they were looking at because they put it there.

Stella kept an eye out for Vietnam Victor, but he was a no-show. She couldn't give up her suspicions of him since he did have a questionable past. But she didn't see him, and she certainly wasn't going to go back to the Washington Motel to question him again.

No, his wasn't the face she was looking for. It wasn't the guy on the bike with the black helmet and blue pants either. It wasn't the guy giving a blow-by-blow description on his cell phone nor was it the older man with the bag of birdseed. The culprit had slipped by probably minutes before Stella hit the trail.

"That boy in foster care," Stella said to Ben as they watched the coroner's assistant move to bag Janet Gazak and take her to Christine for a thorough examination.

"What boy?" Ben asked.

"I'm just talking to myself," Stella said as the sing-songy "In three days, you'll be mine" kept playing. She didn't like the boy who kept saying this to her. Still, his face wouldn't come but she felt it in her gut.

"Are you riding with us to the coroner's office?" Ben asked as they walked toward the car with his phone in his hand.

"I've got to go wash up. I'm a sweaty mess. I'm going to just run back to the motel. By the time you guys back out of here, I'll already be there. I'll meet you at the coroner's office," Stella said, looking forward to a hot shower. Ben nodded and got in the car. Stella took off. She was correct. Within just a couple minutes she was already unlocking her room. Once she shut the door tight and slipped the deadbolt and chain into place, she let out a deep sigh.

"Three more days, you'll be mine. Three more days, you'll be mine. What is it?" Stella shook her head. Finally, it hit her that Janet Steeple-Gazak was dead. They'd just spoken to her yesterday and she revealed absolutely nothing. Why would anyone want to kill her?

Maybe whoever is doing this has been watching you the whole time, Stella. They watched you go from motel victim to Ms. Casio in the basement, to the park and Therese, and finally this. Mrs. Janet Steeple-Gazak. Whoever is doing this knows you talked to her. Maybe they even know you didn't care for her. This wasn't her voice. This was some annoying devilish response from the negative side of her brain that wasn't helping anything.

Quickly she got into the hot shower just as her phone started to ring.

"I'll be done in fifteen minutes," She muttered from under the hot water. "I can't imagine much more happening in fifteen minutes."

Chapter 32

When Stella arrived at the coroner's office, Christine answered the back door in a pair of goggles, a blue apron, and rubber gloves.

"Hey, Detective. You're just in time. I'm just getting started. When do you expect Detective Casey to arrive?" she asked while holding the door open for Stella to walk in.

"Ben isn't here yet?"

"Nope. Just you and me and, well, Mrs. Steeple-Gazak," Christine said with a shrug.

Stella stepped inside the building and pulled the door shut behind her. She grabbed her phone, forgetting she'd ignored the call she'd gotten earlier and quickly called Ben.

"I'll catch up with you in a second, Christine," Stella said.

"Sure. Make yourself at home, Detective. You know where to find me," Christine jerked her thumb toward her examination room and disappeared behind the door.

"I left you a message," Ben said without saying hello. "Did you get it?"

"No. I'm at the coroner's office. Where are you?" Stella asked with her hand on her hip.

"Heading back to Chicago," Ben huffed.

"What for?"

"You aren't going to believe this. Henry Budrene was placed in foster care. They searched the entire country for relatives, and it turned out he was the only Budrene left. So welcome to The System," Ben said.

"Okay. That makes sense," Stella replied as she slipped into Christine's office, sat down at her desk, took out her pad of paper, grabbed a pen, and began to take notes.

"Right. So he gets adopted by a family who was happy to take an older kid. He was about nine maybe ten years old. Now, Henry's father's name was in the papers and it's been in some books and well, the people who eventually adopted him had enough foresight that they didn't want him to carry the burden of that name throughout his life," Stella thought Ben sounded like he was reading the description of a new book he was reading. "They changed his name to Wes Tyler."

"Wes Tyler? As in the caseworker at DCFS?"

"That's the guy," Ben replied. Stella's jaw hit the floor. Her mouth went dry. What were the chances that someone she knew from the most traumatic event in her life might be able to help her solve a case that was twisting her mind into knots? He obviously didn't recognize her. How could he? He hadn't ever seen her without a blindfold. The truth was that even if her abductor was sitting right in front of her, Stella was sure she wouldn't be able to recognize him, either. Years of suppressing the memories had taken care of that. He was just a shadow she hated and was glad to think he was dead.

Suddenly her heart went out to Wes and Stella wondered if he'd suffered like she had due to his father. Part of her wondered if he'd ever like to talk about it. But that idea was quickly shut down. Stella didn't want to go back to that place. She didn't want to know things that might make her feel compassion for the man who terrified her and changed her life forever. In fact, if she never had to see Wes again that would be better. What kind of reunion would it be? What could either one of them say to each other that wouldn't be awkward and humiliating?

"Ben, don't mention anything about me," Stella said.

"I had no intention of doing such a thing," Ben reassured her. "But I have to talk to the man because he was the caseworker who dealt with Therese Foley's complaint about Joshua Molitor."

"There has got to be something there," Stella huffed. "One common thread might help us unravel the whole sweater. Ben, be careful and call me as soon as you get done with Wes. I'll keep canvasing around here. Joshua and Jimmy have mugshots on file. I'll start showing those around and see if anyone has spotted them around here. They might have alibis for the nights in question but if someone saw them around the area with someone else, we might be closing in on this case, finally."

"Sounds good. Talk to you in a couple hours," Ben said before hanging up.

Stella thought this had started out as a crap day but had turned around one-hundred-and-eighty degrees. She couldn't help but grin.

"You look like you just got the test results back and they are negative," Christine said when Stella walked in the examination room.

"What?"

"Sorry. It's just a little doctor humor. Not really all that funny I guess," Christine shrugged as she leaned over Janet's body, shining a tiny flashlight in her gray dead eyes.

"Oh, you mean I look like I got good news. I did. At least I hope I did. This case has been a wild ride. I don't mind telling you, Christine, but I'm not going to miss Vandalia once we solve this," Stella admitted.

"Country living isn't for everyone. Believe me, I understand. I've grown to love being out here because, well, I've got an important job no one else wants to do," She raised her hands and shrugged. My house is small but paid for. I do know my neighbors and they are all nice people. But don't get me wrong,

Vandalia has its share of weirdos."

"How so?" Stella asked as she pulled up a metal stool close enough to the examination table to see what Christine was doing.

"Take Mrs. Steeple-Gazak here. Now, I'm not talking ill of the deceased. But to say she was hard to get along with is like saying the ocean is wet," Christine kind of chuckled, like she was trying to feel Stella out before she told any off-color jokes.

"Did she have a lot of enemies?" Stella asked.

"I wouldn't call them enemies. It's just that Janet had a way of making certain people feel they were expendable. Okay, I'm just going to say it and if it makes me a suspect so be it. Janet was a bitch to a lot of people. I'm not saying she deserved this," Christine said as she measured some marks on the corpse's forehead and noted them in the folder that would eventually be handed over to Stella. Janet's face was bruised. She was beaten in the face and there were some defensive wounds. Not like Regina's but it looked like Janet tried to block the blows.

"People always say that. I'm not saying she or he deserved it...but," it was Stella's turn to shrug. "In the news, every victim is portrayed as just a great person who lit up the room with their smile and you just know it isn't always true. Often, I learn about that cheerful, sparkly individual and find out they were selling prescription drugs, or they bullied the person who ultimately did them in," Stella shook her head. "But you have to say they didn't deserve it because no one deserves to have their life taken from them. Take their money or their car or better yet, their power and you are really causing the pain. Kill them and their troubles are over. Maybe."

"Do you believe in heaven, Detective?" Christine asked.

Stella wanted to blurt out that she certainly believed in hell because she'd been there as a kid. So of course, there was a heaven. Instead, her old tendency to guard herself snapped into place like a steel bear trap and she just nodded confidently and said, "Yes."

"I do too. But I don't think everyone goes there," Christine said as she pried open Janet's mouth and peered inside with the flashlight. "Uh-oh."

"What is it?" Stella asked as she leaned forward.

"Her partial was knocked down her throat and it looks like there are kidney beans in there, too." Christine clicked her tongue. Stella hadn't noticed any around the scene. She had looked around the body and the smoldering campfire but would have remembered seeing them. The gurgling gut reaction was hard to forget. Even now the mere fact that there were more in Janet's throat made Stella want to heave.

"You got any coffee?" Stella asked.

Christine pointed with a pair of forceps she was using to retrieve the items from Janet's throat. There were only four kidney beans but that was enough.

After getting herself a small cup of burnt coffee Stella avoided looking at the beans Christine placed on the blue piece of paper towel on the counter. She did watch as Christine pulled out the partial that had fallen out of place obviously during the struggle.

"Did she die of strangulation or did she choke to death?" Stella asked.

"It's hard to tell. It was this pop in the mouth that knocked her partial loose," She pointed with the forceps to the huge bump on Janet's lip. As Christine continued to move down Janet's face and over her neck, she studied the marks left there.

"I'm getting really tired of seeing those," Stella muttered and took a sip of coffee.

"Me, too. These look like the ones on the other victims. But I can't say if it was strangulation or if she choked to death. Either way, the popped vessels in her eyes tell me she couldn't breathe."

Stella looked at Janet's body as Christine cut off her remaining clothes. They were dirty and torn in places. The old girl put up a fight and that was good to know. Perhaps underneath her fingernails, she'd got some DNA to confirm if it was Jimmy or Joshua Molitor she had been in contact with. Stella knew she was putting all her eggs in one basket but was hopeful Ben was going to find out something substantial back at DCFS.

"This twine was tight around her wrists. And it looks like her fingers were removed after she was already deceased. That's good to know. I don't really understand why he'd mutilate her this way. I guess we are dealing with just one person, right, Detective?" Christine asked.

"Do you think it was more than one?" Stella blinked. Good God, if it were more than one person, doing things a little differently to set themselves apart from one another it was a thought Stella hadn't dared entertain. But now that it was out there the idea made her chest tighten.

"I'm not a profiler. I'm really just thinking out loud," Christine said.

"Well, it's a good observation. But I hope you're wrong," Stella smiled. "If that turns out to be the case, I'm afraid I'll have to call Chicago for reinforcements, and I know the sheriff won't like that."

"The sheriff won't like what?" Sheriff Darlow asked as he walked into the examination room. He glared at Stella as if he just caught her trying to lift his wallet.

Stella adjusted herself on the metal stool, crossed her right leg over the left, and smirked at him. "You wouldn't like it if I had to call for reinforcements from Chicago."

"Is that what you are doing? No one clarified this with me. Detective, I think I've been more than helpful and deserve to be told when these kinds of decisions are being made. This is very unprofessional and I for one am not used to being igno..." Stella put up her right hand while she raised her left hand to take a sip of her coffee.

"See, that's what happens when you eavesdrop. You get half a story but no information. I'm not calling Chicago for anything, Sheriff." She thanked Christine for the coffee before tossing the Styrofoam cup into a metal trash bin. "Let me know when the report is done, and I'll be by to pick it up."

"I've got the press camping outside my office. The mayor is going nuts that someone like Janet Steeple-Gazak was a victim and his police department isn't any closer to catching the responsible party than we were a week ago," Sheriff Darlow huffed.

Stella wondered what the Vandalia Press consisted of. All she could picture was some middle-aged guy with a receding hairline, a steno pad, and a pen who wanted a statement before he headed off to interview the people at the post office. There was a community emergency there. People were complaining about the patrons parking in the handicapped spot because it was closest to the drop box.

"Tell them you'll have more information this evening. Ben has gone back to the city to talk to a man who might be able to link a couple of people to these incidents," Stella smoothed out her pants and sauntered past Sheriff Darlow, leaving the examination room and walking out the back door.

What she didn't know as she stepped outside was that not only did Vandalia have a halfway decent sized press corps but they had connections to several surrounding counties and they knew who she was. The news of Janet Steeple-Gazak had already spread through the grapevine. As the handful of reporters approached her Stella pulled out her phone and dialed the sheriff's number.

"What's the problem, Detective?" he sounded very pleased that he let her walk right into the lion's den.

"Do you have anything special you'd like me to tell these people?" Stella asked as the individuals quickly approached her, their cell phones and tiny pocket recorders out and pointed in her direction.

"You always seem to have a smart-ass answer. I'm sure you'll come up with something," Sheriff Darlow said with a sneer in his voice.

Stella shook her head, shut off her phone, and stuffed it in her back pocket before putting up her hands. "One at a time," she said and gave her first statement to the Vandalia press.

Chapter 33

It never ceased to amaze Stella how ignorant the press was. Even in a small town like this, there was no common sense being utilized, and if there was it wasn't shown in any of the questions they asked.

"Are you getting any closer to finding who is committing these murders?"

"Do you feel that you are partially to blame for the death of these women since you haven't got a suspect in custody?

"Is this case too much for you to handle?"

"What is your next step to ensure no one else falls victim to this maniac?"

"Are you concerned about the well-being of the population of Vandalia?"

"What a bunch of assholes," Stella muttered as she made her way back to the motel. She was surprised that they didn't follow her there. But she had obviously given them enough meat to chew on. With just a handful of facts, the police were speaking with someone today who could definitely shed some light on the topic. Stella ended, of course, with the usual plea to the public to help. If anyone saw anything or heard anything, even if they think it's unimportant please call the sheriff's office. Maybe an additional lead would come in.

Once in her motel room, Stella kicked off her shoes, spread out the files of the three previous victims, and read them simultaneously. She started with their backgrounds and scoured every detail for something she might have missed that they had in common. She moved on to their physical descriptions. Then she moved on to the wounds each victim sustained. Aside from

Regina, who the assailant did a real number on, there was nothing more to go on other than the method of strangulation. Still, Stella went over everything. And the more she read and studied the less she saw any of these women having in common.

"Please, let Ben find something," she prayed. Her eyes stung from staring at the fine print and the pictures for so long. When Stella looked up at the clock, she realized it was past noon and her stomach took the cue and instantly started to growl.

"A lock of hair. Three rosebuds fair.

Then wrap them all in twine.

Toss on the fire. Stoke my desire.

In three days, you will be mine."

Stella gasped as the words finally came to her. It was like she'd been saying them every day for years. Like a mantra or a prayer, they came rushing back to her, spilling out like someone offering their name, rank, and serial number. She sat on the edge of the bed and put her hand to her heart. It was pounding madly.

"Three days you'll be mine," she said again out loud. The words all together were too scary for her to repeat. She didn't know why but she didn't like them. They made her feel sick and dirty just like those fucking kidney beans did. Something told her she had to calm down and think. Why did this suddenly come back to her? Why now? What had she been reading? She looked at the files, but everything seemed to blend one into the other. There was nothing she could see that would have triggered this memory. Except that it had been swimming its way to the surface of her mind since she remembered part of it this morning.

"Three days. Three days..." She stood up and began to pace the room. "Three days is Saturday. It's October 29. The last day of the Harvest Festival. It's almost Halloween. Three days." She tapped her head with a closed fist. What did it mean? Did it mean anything? Maybe this was just a strange recollection that went with everything else that was strange about this case. Yes, something was connected to her. But this poem, this strange lullaby was something only she would know.

"Regina's lock of hair. There were rosebuds in Barbara's hair. Each woman had their hands bound with ornamental twine. Toss on the fire..." Bile rose up in Stella's throat. She dashed toward the bathroom and heaved nothing but a mouthful of the bitter stuff into the toilet before gasping for air.

"I didn't look at the fire. I didn't look at it. Forensics did but they might have missed something. It was meant for me. I didn't look at the fire. I didn't even look at the fucking fire!" She grabbed her shoes and within seconds was out the door on her way back to the coroner's office where she'd last seen the sheriff.

"He already left, Stella," Christine apologized when she answered Stella's frantic banging on the back door. "Did you call him? I'd check the station. I'll bet he's there."

"I got no answer on his cell. He is probably ignoring my calls. I thought he might have still been here. If you see him tell him to call me asap," Stella said.

"Sure will, Detective," Christine said before waving a file in front of Stella. "Here is Janet's report. Tiffany dropped off the pictures. The whole file is as complete as it's going to be."

"Great. Thanks, Christine," Stella said as she tucked the file under her arm and headed across the lot toward the police station. She peeked at Janet's file and saw the pictures of the crime scene. There weren't any of the small fire that had been smoldering just a few yards away from the body.

"None?" Stella stopped and flipped back through the file again but sure enough not one single picture of the campfire. She was beside herself. She thought back and was sure forensics saw it still smoldering. They would have asked had they not known if it was part of the crime scene or not.

"What am I saying? Of course, it was part of the crime scene. It was just a few yards away," Stella scolded the air in front of her. "What the hell kind of Podunk town am I dealing with? Jeez, what the hell else have I missed because the forensics team didn't take a minute to look around?"

When she walked into the police station the woman behind the receptionist desk wearing olive green eyeshadow to match her ensemble looked at her with worry. Immediately, Stella calmed down. This woman who Stella had seen several times was just doing her job.

"Hello, Detective. Are you all right?"

Stella let out a deep breath. "I'm sorry. You know, I've been really rude. I've never even asked what your name is," she said with a frown on her face.

"I'm Rosemary Nardi. But you can call me Rose," Rose said as she tilted her head to the left.

"Hi, Rose. Is the sheriff in?"

"He is. Go ahead in," Rose replied kindly.

"Thanks," Stella said and walked into the bullpen after Rose hit the buzzer to unlock the door. As usual, every eye was on Stella like a leper had just snuck past security and infiltrated their sterile environment.

"Detective Carrigan, what can I do for you?" Deputy Winger said, hurrying to cut her off from the sheriff's office.

"Rose said the sheriff is in. I need to talk to him," she said attempting to side-step him.

He was quick and without hesitating got in front of her again. "If there is anything you need to tell him, you can tell me," he grouched.

"Okay, for starters, why aren't there any photos of the campfire that was still smoldering at the crime scene where Janet was found? I know for a fact that I mentioned it to him. Tiffany should have been informed. And if she didn't take pictures, I know there isn't anything in the file about the fire, either," Stella said, her voice loud and her eyes narrow as she stared down Clarence.

"All right, calm down. I know things can easily make you emotional but..."

"What did you just say to me, Deputy?" Stella's demeanor instantly changed, and she lowered her voice. The look on Deputy Clarence Winger's face was the expression of a man who just realized he went one step too far but was too pigheaded to apologize quickly.

"Come on, don't act like you don't know what I'm talking about," Deputy Winger urged.

"You're going to have to clarify for me, Deputy. What things are you referring to? The fact that the crime scene wasn't completely evaluated? Is that what's making me emotional? Or could it be that the photos didn't include the smoldering fire that was a couple of yards from the body? You showed up at the crime scene. You didn't check out the fire, did you? I mentioned it to the sheriff which is what I'm here to talk to him about. Did the sheriff tell you to check out the campfire?" Stella rattled off.

"I didn't see any campfire," Clarence said.

"You didn't? You were standing right there when Ben told the Sheriff about it. Obviously, you didn't evaluate the scene that well, either. If you need confirmation, which I'm sure both you boys do, you can call Ben, *my* assistant on this case. He'll confirm it was there, still hot to the touch, just a couple yards from the body," Stella lectured. "He'll also tell you we needed pictures of it and for forensics to gather it up."

Just then the door to the sheriff's office opened up. Sheriff

Darlow stepped out looking as if someone had just reported a UFO landed in the parking lot.

"What the hell is going on out here?" Sheriff Darlow barked.

"Go on, Deputy. Tell him. Tell him why I'm getting *emotional*," Stella demanded. She turned and looked at the bullpen. The few officers who were on duty were looking at her again as if she were wearing sandals on sacred ground. "And what the hell are all of you looking at? I'm sure there are crimes that need to be solved in this town."

"That's enough, Detective," Sheriff Barlow said. "If you'll come in my office, we can talk this out."

"That's not what I'm here for. What I'm here for is to tell you that I have a hunch something is going to happen at the festival this weekend." Stella didn't dare say it was because of a lullaby she heard in foster care. Instead, when the sheriff asked where she was getting her information, she gave the only answer she could.

"I just have a feeling, Sheriff. Look, what harm would there be in putting a couple dozen more uniforms out on the street just for the festival? Doesn't someone in top brass from another county owe you a favor? They've got to know by now what's going on here in Vandalia."

"Maybe that's how you do things in Chicago but we don't collect on debts that way," Deputy Winger replied and cleared his throat as he put his hands on his hips.

"Oh, for God's sake, this isn't Mayor Daley politics. I'm talking about getting a couple of uniforms from the next town to pitch in. Hardly unheard of and not really a scandal," Stella chuckled at Clarence with the intent of making him look ignorant. It worked.

"We don't have that in the budget," Sheriff Darlow let out a long sigh. "Besides, isn't that why you're here? To make sure nothing more goes wrong? Isn't that why we were sent a big city detective?"

"You were sent a big city detective because you would obviously fuck up a one-man funeral," Stella snapped. "I'll be doing your job checking out the campfire which has probably already been contaminated a hundred times over. This will most definitely be in my report, gentleman. Just like the phone call to Captain Briggs about some crazy idea I snuck into the home of a suspect early on."

Stella stared at Deputy Winger who looked at Sheriff Darlow nervously.

"Come again?" Sheriff Barlow asked.

"Tell him, Clarence. I've got work to do," Stella turned and stomped out of the police station not before politely saying good-bye to Rose.

"Detective?" Rose called before Stella could reach the door.

"Yes, Rose?" Stella replied, trying to keep her annoyance of the whole station out of her voice. She'd been rude enough to Rose and for no good reason.

"It's about time someone put that Clarence Winger in his place," she winked, and casually started to file some folders in the desk drawer to her right.

Stella smirked. And then she smiled and chuckled a bit. While she was dealing with the sheriff and deputy Stella was about to explode. But Rose's comment made her feel like the air was being let out of a balloon. Calmness overcame her and she nodded before walking out into the cool fall air. She'd have to hurry to the hiking path. Maybe, by some chance of a miracle, the remains of the campfire would have been missed by everyone else in Vandalia, too.

Chapter 34

The biking and jogging trail was alive with people as the news of the gruesome story hit the general population in Vandalia. Stella had enjoyed running the path because there were very few people. But now there were families with strollers, couples walking hand in hand, groups of teenagers all meandering around to catch a glimpse of where Janet Steeple-Gazak was found dead. It was just human nature. Stella was annoyed because it meant that the crime scene was already contaminated.

Sure enough, when she reached that point of the curve in the path she saw the police tape was torn already and flapping in the breeze. There were people taking pictures, whispering as they walked by, some gawking openly, others shivering as they peeked and hurried past the spot like somehow the murder might be catchy.

Stella took out her badge and flashed it around. "Alright, let's move along. Just move along. There isn't anything more to see here."

The small crowd that had gathered took a look at her and her badge, some lowered their eyes while others looked at her like she might suddenly start arresting people. Within seconds she was alone at the scene. She crossed the grass and went to the place where the campfire had been. She was right; it had been kicked and stomped on with nothing of value left for her to inspect. For all she knew the culprit had come and destroyed whatever he'd burned in the fire. Stella's gut told her that there had been something in there.

Stella picked up a stick and poked in the ashes. That was all that was left. Just gray powdery ashes filled the circle of stones. They were as cold as the breeze that was starting to stir as the afternoon gave way to evening and the sun started to set.

Her blood boiled when she thought of Deputy Winger and Sheriff Darlow and their callous behavior regarding this case. They had the nerve to demand answers when they may have just, single-handedly, delayed the progress of this case. And worse, they had reported her to Captain Briggs for investigating Vietnam Victor's home in the Washington Motel. Sure, she snuck in and the guy had every right to complain but she was trying to find the man who had killed a woman. Stella was no longer surprised that there wasn't very good cooperation among the locals. It was frustrating but not surprising. If only she had a couple of stoolies like she did in the city she might have been able to find out more that was going on here. Of course, that might be a can of worms she didn't want to open. Small towns always had their own skeletons and sometimes they were more bizarre than the craziest thing happening in the nearest big city.

Without anything else she could do, with no evidence being available, Stella headed back to the motel. After stopping at the liquor store and picking up some Coke along with a bag of pork rinds Stella threw the report on the bed with the other files, locked the door, kicked off her shoes, and took off her clothes before going into the bathroom to throw some cold water on her face. It had been a long day.

At first, Stella was going to throw herself back into the files, read Janet's file, and compare it with the others but her heart just wasn't in it. She needed a break. She turned the television on, but nothing could hold her interest.

As much as she was reluctant to give Ben's relaxation CD another try Stella needed to unwind. So, she cracked open a Coke, tore open the bag of pork rinds, and sat back in the bed. The man's voice was as soothing as it had been during the first chapter of the CD.

Before she knew it, Stella was stretched out comfortably on the bed, no longer interested in the pork rinds, her Coke on the nightstand within arms-length. She sank into the mattress and pillows and felt warm and light as she drifted off to sleep. But in her dreams, Stella wasn't warm. She was freezing.

Chapter 35

It was so long ago. How the memories even lasted this long was a testament to the ability of the human mind to cling to the things that hurt most. They will rise to the surface when their surroundings are disturbed and will be raw, ugly, and rotten. It was something Stella didn't want to see. But her mind would have none of that.

It was a country fair. The sound of clanking metal rides and blasting rock and roll music filled the air along with the delighted screams of people being spun in circles or dropped from high places. The smell of popcorn and cotton candy filled the air. Even though there were dozens of booths with steaming ears of corn, deep-fried Oreos and pickles, greasy burgers, charbroiled hot dogs, and more of the unhealthiest foods ever created, it was the popcorn and cotton candy that smelled strongest.

Stella remembered walking with a group past the food booths and toward the games, face painting, and craft displays. She liked to look at the jewelry. Even though she was only eight and had no money, she liked to see the shiny chains and earrings people made. So did one her foster sister. She was the daughter of the family that had taken Stella in just a few months ago. They were nice people. They weren't what Stella would consider loving. They didn't hug her or read her any stories before bed. But they were nice. They made sure she had food and clothes. They checked her homework and let her have her own things on her side of the room that she shared with her foster sister.

It had been a good day. A trip in the car to the country where there was a fair with animals, rides, and all kinds of things to see that Stella never saw in the city. It was like visiting another country. There were pumpkin carvings, hayrides, and a maze in a cornfield that Stella was told to stay away from.

"You get lost really easy and it takes forever to find your way out," her foster mother warned. "We don't want to spend the whole night looking for you."

So, Stella walked in a wide arc away from the corn maze entrance when they passed it. She watched tractors pulling long trailers of people in and out of an apple orchard and pumpkin patch and passed by booths selling hot cider that smelled sweet and warm.

"Stella, keep up," her foster sister said, holding her hand out for Stella to take hold. But when she reached for her hand, it pulled away. She watched her foster sister turn and run to catch up with her mother, leaving Stella behind. Something strange was happening. Stella tried to keep up, but her legs were so heavy like someone had wrapped chains around them. All she wanted to do was lie down and take a rest.

"Don't worry, honey. We'll meet your family in the parking lot," a man said against her neck. The smell of his breath was like licorice. Stella didn't like it. It was a sickly smell that she'd learn later in life was the smell of someone who had been drinking. The words he said echoed through her head. No, she didn't want to go to the parking lot. She was told if she ever got lost to stand still and look for a woman with children or a cop.

"They are mad enough you are making them wait. We have to hurry," he said.

Stella didn't want her foster family to be mad at her. She'd promised not to get lost in the corn stalk maze. So, she let him guide her through the clusters of people, seeing so many mothers with their own children... she could ask any of them for help. She didn't know the man behind her. She was afraid to look at him and see that his face matched the terrible smell of his breath.

Her heart began to race as they got further and further away from the fair. The cars were parked on a huge gravel lot. Every aisle looked the same. Stella had no idea where her foster family had parked. How could she ever go to their car and let them know she was sorry for being late?

As if reading her mind, the man with the bad breath sensed Stella was about to run and grabbed her by her arm. "Don't try to run. They gave you to me. I'm your new family now. And you'll do exactly as I say," Stella looked up to see a man who could have been a teacher, a doctor, a grocery store manager. He looked like any normal man in town except for his red-rimmed and glazed eyes. Had they really given her away? Was this man going to make sure she was fed and had enough blankets at night? He threw her in the back seat of his car.

Stella's eyes popped open, wild with terror and the urge to scream. Now it was clear. Twenty-five years ago, she had been abducted at a fair just like the Harvest Fair. There were pumpkins and rides and lots of people not paying attention to the things going on around them. He lied to her. He told her that *they* gave her to him. He made her believe she'd done something wrong at the age of eight that made her foster mother and father give her away. She hadn't remembered that until this moment. Her heart broke with renewed terror and relief that it was over. Tears of remembrance ran down her cheeks and Stella sobbed openly while stroking her right arm with the left hand in an attempt to comfort herself.

Why was all of this coming back? Why couldn't she keep it buried? There was no use digging all this up, exhuming the corpse of the man who took her. He was dead. But someone knew the details about what had happened, and they were skulking around Vandalia killing women and...

"He's going to strike again at the fair. It would be easy. Just like it had been when I was taken," Stella said to the empty room. She felt helpless. Aside from an all-out cancellation of the event, there was no way Stella could prevent it from happening.

She picked up her phone and called the sheriff. Not surprisingly it went to his voicemail with an excruciatingly long message stating he was unable to answer his phone and if this were a real emergency the caller should dial 9-1-1. Finally, the beep came. But when it did Stella didn't know what to say. She chewed her lip as she looked at her phone, the line still open. Instead, she hung up. There was no use in telling him she woke up from a dream and was certain beyond all reasonable doubt that there was going to be some kind of kidnapping attempt at the fair. He'd immediately be on the phone with Briggs telling him Stella had a breakdown and was not safe to carry a badge or gun or even her purse. She just knew it.

What was worse was that Sheriff Darlow had acted relieved that she and Ben were there when they first arrived. Now, it was like pulling teeth to get him to help. It was a pissing contest she didn't want to participate in.

Stella hadn't even realized she was off the bed and pacing back and forth like a lion in a cage before a thunderstorm. Ben's relaxation CD did the complete opposite of relaxing her. Now she was wide awake with a premonition in her head that no one was willing to believe.

Chapter 36

The next morning, Stella got up after a heavy sleep that left her with a headache. She picked up Janet's file, the wrong thing to do immediately before even getting out of bed. She read what Christine had basically talked her through while she was at the coroner's yesterday. The one thing that stuck out was that Janet had been dead almost two days when she found her according to Christine's assessment. That horrifying lullaby replayed in Stella's mind as if it had never not been there.

"In three days, you'll be mine," she muttered. The words tasted worse than her morning breath. Three days...three days from Janet's death? Three days of the fair? Three days of the weekend? What three days is this asshole talking about?" she growled as she looked through the file. Something told her the answer had been in the campfire but none of that mattered now.

The last day of the Vandalia Harvest Festival was packed. The streets down the center of town were blocked off for food vendors and pumpkin carving contests. The fair spread to a huge field not far from the jogging trail where a huge Ferris wheel was positioned in the middle, surrounded by rides that had only sprung up two days ago. The smell of grease came from rides that had names like The Zipper or The Octopus. There were inflatable bouncy houses for the little kids whose parents held their hands and watched them closely.

The teenagers walked in packs, not interested in getting separated from their cliques or talking to any "old people," that is anyone over the age of thirty. It was the jailbait Stella watched for.

Thankfully, the police had posted several signs around the grounds to gently remind families to stick together, keep an eye on wallets and purses, and make sure they knew where their children were at all times.

"It isn't the kids that have to worry. It's the old farts," said a long-haired teenager who flicked his cigarette at the poster making his long-haired friends chuckle.

"Did you hear Janet Steeple-Gazak had her head nearly sawed off?" one of them asked.

"Yeah, I heard she was raped, too. Who would want to rape that old bitch?" another replied. Stella stared at them as she watched them blend into the crowd. Teenagers believed they were invincible.

After her revelation last night in her motel room, Stella was having a hard time not letting her anger get the best of her. Everyone looked so relaxed, so calm like there hadn't been four murders in this town over the past several days. What was wrong with all of them?

There are murders every day in Chicago but that doesn't stop you from going to dinner with a stranger at a Mexican restaurant, her conscience taunted. She was a hypocrite, criticizing these people when she was no different. But the nervousness still wouldn't leave her. She kept waiting to hear the scream of some woman who suddenly realized her child was missing. But all she heard were the screams of the people on the rides. It was enough to almost drive her crazy. It felt like her bones were trying to climb out of her skin. A tingling, uncomfortable itch nagged at her until finally, she had to get away from the area with the rides and go where things were calmer. As she strolled down the main drag, she looked at the officers who were spread out, two to every couple of blocks.

Unlike when she was a young girl, parking for this festival was street parking as well as several government facilities like the Post Office, the library, City Hall, which allowed people to park for free. There were cameras in all those locations, and it would have been a lot more difficult to coax a child under the watchful eye of "Big Brother".

"At least there is that," Stella muttered. While she walked, she swept her eyes back and forth among the people focusing on any men who were walking alone. There weren't many. This was a family affair. There was a family running the petting zoo that had a farm on the edge of town. The kiosk in front of the animal pen stated they had been providing a farm experience for the children of Vandalia and the surrounding counties for the past three generations.

There were also families working several of the food vending booths. More families walked hand in hand, pushing strollers with babies and walking their dogs as they said hi to neighbors and friends.

Stella felt a pang in her heart as she walked along and wondered how people could let their children walk ahead of them or lag behind them. She thought the idea of having children was just too scary. Worry all the time; it would never end. Not even once they reach the age of eighteen because if they've made it that far then they will be looking for a spouse. How many girls with happily-ever-after on their minds marry a man only to have him turn out to be abusive? Yet, God or the universe put the desire in us to want a family, to want that happily-ever-after.

Stella shook her head. She saw a stand selling hot cider and thought that sounded just right. The storm cloud of negativity following her around was just too much. But it was nothing the sweet, hot liquid couldn't soothe.

"One small," she said pulling her money from the pocket of her coat revealing her shoulder holster for just a moment. The young lady behind the counter saw it and her eyes bulged for a second. Stella didn't say anything as the young lady turned and told the man she assumed was her father. He looked at Stella suspiciously, so she quickly flashed her badge. He didn't smile but nodded and she saw his lips mouth the words 'she's a cop.' The girl turned around with a look of relief on her face as she handed Stella her change and a Styrofoam cup that smelled wonderful and warmed her fingers and hands. It was just what the doctor ordered and with the sweet elixir, Stella's mood lightened.

Suddenly, she heard a young child crying. She stopped and blocked out all the other sounds as best she could and followed it. Her heart began to race as she heard it getting closer and closer. Where was he? Finally, she zeroed in on it. Her body tensed as she put her hand on her weapon. Between two booths, out of sight from the preoccupied festival-goers Stella heard the mad sobbing. But when she peeked around the corner, careful not to scare the child or give any perpetrator a chance to run, she couldn't help but gasp.

A mother, quietly changing the diaper of one baby, had standing next to her a red-faced boy about six years old who had a big mad on his face.

Stella quickly recovered. "Everything okay back here, ma'am?"

"Yes," she huffed. "See what you did. All your wailing made that poor woman wonder *what the heck is wrong with that kid*." Stella let out a deep breath and grinned at the mother before she looked at the little boy again. "It's nap time and we dropped our cotton candy and well, you know the trials of life."

"I do," Stella had to chuckle. Then, the woman scooped up her young baby, an adorably round bundle of pink, and slipped her back into a stroller. The trio then wished Stella a good time at the festival and went about their merry way, the boy holding tightly to his mama's hand before turning around and looking at her, his blue eyes wide with interest. She waved to him and got the sweetest grin in return.

A scene from the movie *Jaws* flashed into Stella's mind. Roy Scheider is the town sheriff. He's trying to keep an eye on every single person at a crowded beach because he knows there's a hungry killer shark out there in the water. He hears a woman screaming and is about to freak out when he sees it's just some beach bunny cavorting in the water with her boyfriend.

So, what did Chief Brody do in the movie? Stella asked herself, as she walked still searching for the monster that had murdered four women. In the movie, it turned out the shark wasn't anywhere near the beach. It was off somewhere where the action wasn't so hectic. It was still attracted to the movement but the animal was smart enough to feed where the bodies weren't so crowded. The pickings were just as easy where there were fewer people.

Stella's brain seized. She wasn't going to find a human version of that shark here in the mix of all these people having a good time. This person would be slinking around under the cloak of darkness. A seedy motel. A divorce's basement. The corner of the park. And then the only victim displayed for everyone to see, the only one to put up any kind of real fight was killed somewhere else and brought to the running path.

"Killed somewhere else," Stella thought. As she walked, she thought of her interview with Ben at Janet Steeple-Gazak's home. Janet was a big, robust woman. It would not have been easy to carry her anywhere. Plus, she lived in an affluent neighborhood and according to everyone was heavily involved with the community. So, a stranger showing up at her door would probably draw some attention.

"And if the person who killed her wanted to do it alone, in private, where in this tiny town would they go?" Stella stood still. People crisscrossed in front of her. They paid no attention to her as they enjoyed the festival. She, on the other hand, for the first time felt like she was seeing everyone, all at once. The row of attractions led to the park just a stone's throw from the jogging path. And off the jogging path, off in the distance, were the abandoned cabins that had been used for business retreats, summer camps, vacations. Without hesitation, Stella strolled in that direction. There might be something there.

Chapter 37

As Stella walked down the path in the direction of the rotted-out cabins, she remembered Ben was back in Chicago. Had there been anything to report she was sure he would have called her by now. Of course, if he stopped back at the station for anything Briggs would have cornered him, asking where Stella was and grilled him for anything that might indicate she'd cracked under pressure.

Not yet, she thought. A thick row of dark clouds was advancing across the sky from the west. It was a cool day, but it was going to get downright cold without the sun shining.

She pulled out her cellphone to make sure that she hadn't somehow missed Ben's call. An impossibility since it was in her pocket and set to vibrate. More often than not in meetings or while driving she'd jump thinking a detached hand was trying to cop a feel on her backside only to realize it was just her phone doing its job. No, Ben hadn't called. There had been no activity for a long while which is why she hadn't realized the little red bar indicated she was out of juice.

"Shit," she muttered. Quickly, before the thing died altogether, she texted the words *old rotten cabins* and hit the send button just as the screen went blank. This was not an unusual position for her to be in. Stella was forgetful when it came to the most basic things like charging her phone or computer. The thought of that made her wonder how much juice was left on her laptop at the motel. She was sure she'd hear from Ben about it once he was back in town. He was a stickler for those minor details. His phone was always charged, his computer was always at 100%, he always had an umbrella in his car, and a battery charger in his trunk along with a bag of salt for Chicago winters. Of course, he had to think that way now that he was a proud papa. Stella knew how long they'd been waiting to have a child; trying the old-fashioned way since he became her partner and then reaching out to adoption agencies when that wasn't working. It actually turned around fast. Surprisingly fast, as Stella recalled. But a Chicago cop and a stay at home mom with lots of family close by was an adoption agencies' dream come true. Of course, they'd quickly place a baby there.

Stella hoped he got to spend some time with his family before he came back to Vandalia. He'd not be as angry about her being out of reach if he did. But she would prepare herself for a lecture. How could she be a cop with her reputation for solving cases fast and sinking her teeth into the bad guys when she couldn't remember to keep her phone charged? The thought made her smile.

As Stella made her way past the carnival rides and the sound of the people and music began to fade she became acutely aware of her own footsteps, her breathing, the change in the smell of the air from the hot cinnamon smell of the fair to the cool, clean scent of the trees, the tall grass, and a cool breeze.

The path was empty. There was no one running or walking or riding their bike. Stella's shoes made a lonely pat-pat-pat-pat as she walked along the concrete. Everything still looked pretty with the leaves giving their last display before the rain and wind of this upcoming shower would probably blow most of them away.

There was no path leading to the cabins. If there had been one it was long grown over by now. Stella looked around for the easiest way up the side of the hill, but it all looked the same. The cabins had all fallen into a sad state. But imagining them even after they were first built, Stella thought they lent themselves more to a scene from a horror movie than to a place where a group of professionals learned teamwork skills. Still, they had to be checked out.

Thinking like her killer, Stella wondered if he would have chosen one of the nearby cabins to bring or lure Janet to or if it would have been one of the cabins higher up on the hill. There were too many for her to inspect on her own so she had to imagine herself in his shoes. It was a horrifying but necessary part of the job. Trying to consider what an insane man would do led her down some very dark paths.

The last case she'd solved was a significant child porn and extortion ring going on that required she consider the point of view of the pervert harassing the girls involved. His motivation and the desire of his "clients" were enough to make her want to puke. But Stella's desire to catch them, as many as possible, was greater than her disgust. And slapping the cuffs on him while whispering in his ear what the inmates at Leavenworth Prison were going to do to him was just the icing on the cake.

Maybe Stella had a sadistic side as well. At this point, she didn't care. Her cop's intuition was starting to stir and as she got closer to the cabins something told her she was on the right path.

With each step, she stretched her legs and pushed herself along the uneven ground. Finally, she saw what was left of a gravel path, invaded and nearly overrun with weeds, and what looked like poison ivy. Careful not to let it touch her skin, Stella got to the old path. At the midway point of the hill, it branched into three directions. There were two small cabins that flanked a bigger one in the middle. She remembered Deputy Winger telling her about the fire. It was obvious by the black around the windows and door and the gaping hole in the roof that looked like the space where a rotten tooth might have been extracted but it wasn't completely destroyed. In fact, the integrity of the walls looked halfway decent for a place that had been on fire. However, since no one had tended to it after the fire the rodents and bugs and not to mention Mother Nature's four distinct seasons had done the damage the fire didn't.

The cabin to her right was missing the front door. Stella walked to that one first. Her hip-hugger pouch also held her flashlight specially designed in a flat shape but that sent a beam of LED light bright enough to blind someone temporarily. It had one of those strobe functions. For a brief second, Stella thought of setting it off just to see the terrifying effect on the ramshackle old structure. But her professional demeanor took over and she just shined the light inside.

It didn't shock or surprise Stella that there were six-pointed stars and the numbers 666 spray-painted on the walls. The old mattress in the corner was pretty gross and had become more of a home for mice and vermin than a romantic getaway. A couple of newspapers were strewn about. It was apparent to Stella that a fair share of transients and teenagers had passed over this threshold. Tinfoil circles used for ashtrays or cooking heroin over the heat of a lighter were also on the floor. It was probably how the fire in the other building started. Why the town wouldn't demolish this was a mystery in itself.

There had been a kitchenette that looked to have been robbed of its copper piping. The cabinet below the sink lay open, black with grime and mold as the water that pooled there never really dried. Instead, it became a breeding ground for wet, slithery things that Stella didn't care to explore.

A warped doorframe led to a bathroom. The toilet had been cracked and left on the ground. The plastic floor tile was bent at the corners and had curled up on itself. The pipes from here had also been removed. There was a walk-in shower that had nothing but a raised ceramic lip on the floor and an arched shower curtain rod that still had the plastic rings on it. The tile in there was chipped and sinister-looking like the pictures of old sanitariums that had long been shut down, but the stories of the mental patients abused and tortured still circulated. Every broken, cracked, or chipped piece of porcelain told another horrible story.

Spiderwebs were as thick as wool in the corners of the ceiling and dangling from the skeletal light fixtures.

This cabin had not been visited in some time. Once she stepped outside the sound of the festival could be heard and Stella was grateful. It grounded her, reminding her that there were

people not far away and that she could get to help quickly if she
needed to.

"Why would you even think that?" she muttered, even her
quiet, singular voice cutting through the silence of the area like a
sneeze in the middle of an empty church.

The other small cabin on the other side had its front door
still intact and locked. The windows were busted out like all the
rest of the cabins. When Stella peeked inside, she saw the same
telltale signs that someone had stolen the piping from under the
sink and in the bathroom. But there was no mattress or satanic
symbols on the walls. It was just a sad little structure that should
have been put out of its misery long ago. There were bird's nests
poking from the beams across the ceiling. Along the floor was
enough raccoon and mouse shit to fertilize a five-acre farm. Tufts
of fur and feathers showed there had been signs of a struggle but
not what Stella was looking for. The flooring looked rotten and
Stella doubted it could support anything heavier than a squirrel.
She didn't bother to go inside.

Tenderly, she stepped around the snaking vines of poison
ivy and looked around for any signs that someone may have been
at the cabin recently. The sky had gone from blue to overcast
slowly as if it was giving Stella just enough time to search these
cabins. The dark clouds were still off in the distance. Stella looked
at her watch and then pulled out her cellphone. It was completely
dead. Not even a flicker of life to it. That was of no real matter.
She'd charge it as soon as she got back to the motel and she'd be
heading there right after she searched this last cabin. It was the
'big' cabin in that it looked like it had at least two bedrooms
judging by the number of windows.

Stella stood at the base of the dilapidated and rotten steps
and looked at the ground around the entrance. Her heart jumped
as she saw footprints in the dirt and dust. After swallowing hard,
the smell of moss and rotten wood, not totally unpleasant filled
her nose. There had been someone here not long ago. A shiver

raced over Stella's shoulders as if a spider had scurried across there. Carefully, she ascended the three front porch steps. They groaned painfully. High up in the trees Stella heard the rusty call of a blue jay.

The marks in the dirt on the porch looked like two sets of prints. Boots that she guessed where those of a man and maybe her perpetrator. The others were considerably smaller and looked to be made by a female. If Stella remembered right from Janet's file, she was wearing those comfortable older lady slip-on shoes with flat bottoms.

Careful not to mess up the prints, Stella went to the door. It was open and the dirt and grime on the doorknob had also been disturbed. Stella didn't touch any of it and instead used the flashlight to push it open far enough for her to tiptoe inside.

This space was much bigger with what looked like a sitting area and an island in what had been the kitchen. The cabinets were either missing the doors or they dangled by the hinges. There were two doorways on either side that looked like small bedrooms, still bigger than the sleeping quarters of the other cabins.

Although the other cabins were creepy, Stella felt something strange as soon as she crossed over into this cabin. A shaft of gloomy, gray light came in from the hole in the ceiling. Animal nests that had been tended by animals for years bloomed out of the radiator vents. The LED light made the place look like a scene from a black and white movie. She listened but the only thing she could hear was her own breath and her blood pumping in her ears. She didn't know what it was but there was a familiar odor in the air. It triggered the fight or flight feeling inside Stella except when she looked around, she saw no reason why this should be happening. She was alone. There wasn't anyone, anywhere. She'd have heard them, if not seen them by now. However, her gut was screaming for her to leave. Not just leave but run.

"No," she mumbled as she shined her light around. Melted

candles that had dripped and hardened into tumorous globs welding old bottles and cheap glass plates to the ground indicating someone had been here recently.

Stella wasn't sure what had raised the hair on her neck. She held her breath and listened as she shined the light around. In one sweep she was about to dismiss her fears as silly and paranoid until she caught a brief flicker in the beam of light. She took two steps forward before she gasped. There, in the corner of the room was a fork on the floor between two empty cans of kidney beans.

The urge to throw up violently seized her. She felt like she'd stepped into a pit of spiders and snakes. The revulsion was overwhelming and as she spun around to dash out the front door a shadow stepped in front of it. Before Stella could raise the beam of her flashlight there was a crack, then another, and a loud snap. The floor beneath her feet was no longer there.

For a brief second, she was suspended in the air before gravity did its job. In that brief second, Stella saw the silhouette of a man. In that split second, she thought it was Ben. But as she fell, swallowed up by the darkness below the decayed floorboards her mind exploded in terror. It was the shadow of the man who had abducted her all those years ago.

Chapter 38

The minute Ben walked into the DCFS office on Friday morning he was already in a bad mood. He'd arrived early enough the previous day but was not given any information by Tammy at the front desk as to why he couldn't talk to Wes or why no other information could be given.

"You'll have to come back tomorrow when Joyce is back in the office," Tammy had said. A person didn't have to be a seasoned cop like Ben was to realize that Tammy had a lot to say but under no circumstances was she going to whisper a word. She might have hated her job, but no one willingly gave up a government job in the city of Chicago. Hell, Ben knew the only way to get fired from the city dole was to get the boss in hot water. You could be a grade-A screw-up who gave foster children homes with alcoholic prostitutes in condemned housing projects but so long as you didn't drag your boss into it, you'd get to keep your job. However, assisting a police officer without your boss's okay, grounds for termination. And Tammy wasn't budging.

The next day Ben arrived before the DCFS office officially opened. He saw Joyce walk in and followed right behind her.

"Ms. Keyes," he shouted and waved as he jogged to catch up with her. "Officer Casey, remember me?"

"Oh, uh, vaguely. I'm sorry, officer. We don't open for another ten minutes," Joyce said with that same simpering look on her face.

"This really can't wait," Ben insisted.

Joyce looked at the small line of people that had formed outside the DCFS office. It wasn't unlike the DMV. People knew they were going to be in for a long wait, so it was worth standing out in the elements, rain or shine if it meant getting a place at the head of the line.

"Well, as you can see, there are people who are here ahead of you and..." Joyce started to say before Ben stopped her.

"I'm not here for a check or to meet some court requirement. Why don't we just cut the shit and talk in your office? Otherwise, we can go downtown to *my* office," Ben said.

Joyce pinched her lips together and hurried toward the front door where she said good morning to all the people and that they'd be opening shortly. No one was even phased by Ben going in with her. They all knew he was a cop. He had the cheap suit and tie and the badge off to the side on his belt.

Once inside Ben said good morning to Tammy who only mumbled a quick hello for fear that Joyce might think she had something to do with the detective arriving so early. Joyce hurried to her office, ignoring anyone saying good morning. Ben could see she was nervous, and he wasn't sure what for but once they were behind the conference room door he asked.

"I'm not nervous about anything. But I am rather annoyed," Joyce confessed as she took a seat at the head of the table. "Detective, this kind of interruption in my day is unacceptable."

"Ms. Keyes, I need to speak with Wes Tyler. Is he in yet?" Ben said without sitting down.

"What is this in regard to?"

"It's a police matter. And it is timely. Can you please get Wes for me?" Ben said as politely as he could.

Joyce pursed her lips as she had done over and over again during their first meeting. Ben wouldn't be surprised if the woman didn't wipe her own ass without asking permission first. It was this kind of bureaucracy that made every government institution a plague upon the people.

After several seconds of trying to stare Ben down, Joyce finally cleared her throat, adjusted her blazer, and rolled her eyes.

"Ms. Keyes, what is the problem here? I'm here because I'm trying to solve a murder. Do you understand that? Now I am trying to be patient but unless there needs to be an investigation on this branch of the DCFS, and in particular you and the people you answer to, I suggest you get Wes in here and stop wasting my time," Ben snapped.

"I can't do that!" Joyce shouted. "Wes is no longer with the Department. He quit."

"What? Why didn't you just say that instead of wasting my time?" Ben was beyond annoyed. If Joyce had been a man, he would have grabbed him by the collar and shoved him against the wall, demanding to know how such an idiot could be in charge of an entire office.

"I'm not at liberty to discuss the employment status with anyone outside the department," Joyce said, folding her arms across her chest.

"By your own admission, he is no longer employed here. What happened?" Ben demanded.

"I'll need to clarify with my superiors that it is okay to divulge this information to you. That may take an hour, it may take a day. It might even take a week," Joyce replied.

"Ms. Keyes, I need you to stand up for me," Ben said, removing his handcuffs from the back of his belt. "Please put your hands behind your back."

"Are you serious?" she squawked.

"Obstructing an investigation is an arrestable offense. Now stand up and put your hands behind your back," Ben insisted. "Unless you plan on helping me. I have no use for you, and you are doing nothing to help solve the murder of one of your employees!"

"Fine!" Joyce barked back as she stood from her seat and stomped past Ben to open the conference room door. "But I want it known that I am doing this under duress!"

By this time every head was above its cubicle looking in their direction. It was a rare occurrence at any job to see the boss get an ass-chewing and Ben could tell by the wide-eyed stares it was no different here at DCFS. Some people looked downright scared. But the rest betrayed themselves by watching with subtle smirks on their lips.

"Did you already clear out Wes's desk?" he asked.

"I told one of the girls to do it but whether or not she did..." Joyce said as Ben walked in the direction of Wes's desk. It looked neatly prepared as if someone had cleaned it at the end of the day so all the work would be ready to tackle in a specific order first thing the following day. He picked up the files on children in the foster care system and flipped through them.

"Those are private," Joyce hissed as she stood almost on top of him.

"Then why are they left on the desk of an employee who no longer works here?" Ben replied and handed the files to Joyce before sitting down in Wes's seat. He pulled open the desk drawers and at first found nothing but pens and Post-Its. Four of each. Four pens. Four pads. Four tacks in his corkboard. Four giant paperclips binding together four yellow pads of paper. Ben found that odd but he knew people at the precinct who kept their desks in a bizarre order, reflecting some level of obsessive-compulsive disorder.

"Tammy? Tammy! Didn't I tell you to clean out Wes's desk?" Joyce yelled at Tammy as she passed by with her coffee cup in her hand.

"I told you I wasn't able to get to it yesterday. Remember, you had me making those files for you and I didn't get around to it," Tammy replied nervously feeling the heat from Joyce's stare.

Ben listened but said nothing as he pulled open the next drawer. For a moment he paused and stared.

"Joyce, can you tell me why Wes would have this in his desk?" Ben asked. The weight of the situation was slowly seeping into his bones.

"What is it?" she asked, suddenly very curious.

Ben reached in and pulled out dead rosebuds on a vine and twine that looked nauseatingly familiar to him.

"I don't know," Joyce replied. Sometimes the girls get flowers from the foster families, but Wes never placed any children with any families."

"Ever?" ben asked.

"Not since I've been here and I've worked here just a little over two years," Joyce replied as if what she was saying was normal.

"You mean to tell me that Wes Tyler worked here for all this time and never once placed a child with a foster family, yet he was kept on the payroll? How does that work? I mean, seriously, how does a man whose job is to put foster children with foster families get away with not placing a single child with a family for the entire time he is employed by the DCFS? Can you answer that question? Because I'd sure the fuck like to know!" Ben hollered. He couldn't help think about the hoops he had to jump through to get his baby and here was a man who was supposed to be helping these kids collecting a paycheck just for showing up.

"Well, I d-don't know. I don't have the..." Joyce stammered.

"You have reviews in this place, don't you?" Ben demanded.

"Unfortunately, yes!" Someone from the cubicles piped up.

"Then please explain to me how a man can work in this office and not do his job for years and manage to *quit* and not get fired? Ms. Keyes, do you have that answer for me?" Ben was on a tirade and he stared at Joyce who looked at him with contempt but didn't say a word.

"I want to see Wes's personnel file," Ben announced. Joyce shook her head and marched to her office with Ben close on her heels. There was a huge oak desk with very little paperwork on it. The calendar across her desktop was filled in with meetings and more meetings and seminars and workshops. All the things middle management gets off on doing while doing very little actual work. There was a lot of Chicago Cubs paraphernalia which was another reason Ben didn't like her. He was a southside White Sox fan.

She pulled the file out and practically threw it at Ben before stomping around her desk and taking a seat. She picked up her phone and dialed a number she probably called for every issue throughout the day.

"It's Joyce. I need to speak to Faye. It's an emergency," she pinched her lips together but refused to look at Ben. Ben didn't care. He took a seat in one of the chairs in front of her desk and reviewed Wes's file. There were reviews in it stating he'd done a satisfactory job, that he was always punctual, was familiar with procedures and protocols, had an intimate knowledge of their computer programs and the database they were continually updating with the status of kids entering or leaving the DCFS system. Basically, Wes Tyler knew how to work the system himself in order to get a paycheck for doing nothing.

Still, it wasn't what Ben was there to talk to him about. He needed to ask him about Joshua Molitor, Jimmy Molitor's son who had made an appearance on the radar all the way in Vandalia.

Ben took out his pad and took a pen from the cup of them on Joyce's desk. He quickly wrote down Wes's current address as he'd need to track him down and ask him about the Molitor's and what the story was regarding Therese Foley getting so scared she moved. Just as he was about to thank Joyce for her cooperation, Ben read something troubling.

In fact, it was so bad he wasn't sure he'd read it at all. But when he looked, he saw that he did indeed see the town listed as Vandalia, Illinois.

"Wes Tyler previously lived in Vandalia, Illinois?" Ben looked at Joyce.

"If that's what it says," she snapped as she waited on hold for whoever Faye was.

Ben scribbled the address down and stared at it for a couple minutes. Wes, whose birth name was Henry Budrene, the son of the man who abducted Stella when she was a child, had a place in Vandalia where four murders had taken place over the past several days.

"Only he'd know what Stella went through," Ben muttered. "All this time she said it was personal and I didn't believe her." Without wasting a second Ben pulled out his cell phone and tried to call Stella. There was no answer. Worse, it went right to voicemail without ringing. It was out of juice. His stomach sank as he remembered warning her to charge her phone and that he'd be calling. Switching gears quickly, Ben hung up and called down to the Vandalia Police Department.

"I'm sorry, Detective but Detective Carrigan had requested the Sheriff put extra uniforms out at the fair. So, he's out there too. I can try and reach him and give him a message," Rose said since she was also the non-emergency phone operator.

"Please, tell him that we are looking for a man by the name of Wes Tyler. I can fax you a picture of him and his home address," Ben rattle it off quickly and begged Rose to call him back as soon as she spoke with the sheriff. She promised to do so but her reassurance didn't make Ben feel any better.

There was still the Chicago address Ben had to investigate. Maybe, just maybe there would be a miracle and he'd still be here in the city. With all the information he had, Ben called Captain Briggs and told him Stella might be in trouble.

Chapter 39

Stella's eyes popped open. The first thing she noticed was that she was in the dark. Her heart started to race as unfamiliar things began to come into focus. And for one terrifying moment she wondered if she wasn't a child again. Had her whole adult life just been some kind of dream to replace the horror of her reality? Was she still there in the cellar of the man who had kidnapped her at the fair? It smelled different. Like there was some kind of cleanser mixed with a dirt floor. Slowly, Stella moved her fingers and felt the damp, crumbly ground she was laying on. As she raised herself to her elbows, Stella felt a throbbing start in her head and her wrists and shoulders ached.

From the fall, she reassured herself. From the fall. However, when she went to move, she couldn't. At first, a rush of terror raced through her body, and for a moment she thought she was paralyzed. The fall through the floor had snapped her spinal cord and she should have been screaming in pain, but all feeling was gone. The ability to move was lost forever. Only when she remembered she'd moved her fingers did she realize she wasn't paralyzed. But she wasn't able to move freely, either.

"Oh, God," she muttered. The sound of her own voice assured her she wasn't still a little girl. She'd grown up but was in a world of trouble.

Stella felt a raw tingling feeling starting in her wrists and spreading all the way up to her shoulders. When she tried to move them, she realized they were bound behind her back. She tugged only to feel the plastic tighten painfully as blood tried to circulate. A zip-tie held them together.

Without wasting any more time, Stella painfully rolled herself up to a sitting position. The dirt floor was freezing. An idea came to her and although she'd never done it before in her life there was a first time for everything. She laid back down and pulled her bound hands around her butt as far down the back of her thighs as possible. The move made her grunt, hold her breath and struggle but she managed to get one leg folded in tight enough to slip it through the circle her bound arms made. Now she was stuck hunched over with just one more leg to go. She took a couple of breaths and knew that she had to hurry. He could show up any minute and catch her half-in-half-out of trying to escape. She bent her leg, folding it tightly against her chest. She was sure her pants were going to rip. Sweat coated her forehead and her hands and she thought wouldn't it be funny if she got so sweaty her hands just slipped out of their restraints.

"Yes, it would," she muttered, before holding her breath. Finally, after rolling around grunting and stuttering and bending her body in ways it wasn't meant to go Stella let out a great gasp. Her hands were still bound but they were in front of her now.

The adrenaline combined with the pounding behind her eyes almost blinded her. With a shaking hand, she felt the back of her head tenderly. There was a goose egg and her hair had become wet and matted. Either there was water on the floor, or she was bleeding. With slow, deliberate movements, Stella moved to her knees. She blinked and tried to focus on any bit of light. It was nearly impossible for her to open her eyes wide as even the tiniest glow made her head pound. However, to her right, there was a shift in the darkness. Things were slowly coming into view and just as Stella was sure she was looking at a pillow on the floor next to a chair, it moved.

"What the hell!" Stella shouted. Her body shook, almost convulsed with fear. Whatever it was on the floor was not far from her. Too close, in fact. Terror filled her eyes in the form of tears and her bottom lip began to tremble. Hadn't she gotten over this? Hadn't she learned not to be afraid in situations like this?

When she tried to swallow her mouth was completely dry. She felt for her gun, but it was gone. The entire holster was gone.

So was her jacket and her hip hugger. She might as well have been stark naked. As Stella slowly inched back to get away from the thing in the middle of the floor the sequence of events began to come back to her. She'd been at the big cabin. The one with the burnt-out roof. There had been footprints and evidence of people being there. Janet Steeple-Gazak had been there. Stella knew it in her heart. But what happened?

She had fallen through the floor. The rotten wood of the floor, after having been disturbed by the murderer and Janet, had decided it didn't want any more visitors. Stella fell right through the aged, termite-eaten floor the very moment that she saw *him*. He *was* still alive. And now he was coiled up like a snake in the middle of the floor in the dark. He was going to slither up to her and choke the life out of her like a boa constrictor. Beneath her hand was her flashlight. Quietly, she wrapped her fingers around it, pressed the little button, and aimed for the mass on the floor.

The bright LED light was like a needle through her eye directly to her brain making Stella wince and grit her teeth. There was no amount of time that would get her eyes to adjust and the pain to subside. She had hit her head and probably had a concussion. If she thought of those things, real issues, real concerns, then maybe she could tap down the urge to scream that was welling up like a tidal wave inside her.

The light shook madly as Stella's fear betrayed her. The thing that moved wasn't a person with a ghoulish face and lust in his eyes. It couldn't be. That was stuff they did in Hollywood but it didn't happen in real life. Still, the childish fear held her fast. There was an old, familiar-looking blanket covering something. What kind of game was *he* playing? Was *he* under there? Stella didn't want to know. She wanted to slip back into the darkness where her head didn't hurt. But then she heard the noise. It was a voice. The whimper of a little girl.

"Oh, no," Stella whispered. Was she watching herself? Had she died and gone to hell and this was her eternal existence watching herself being terrified by the man who abducted her? But there it was, underneath that blanket that looked rough and itchy and nothing like the blankets she had in her apartment that were soft and smelled clean.

"I won't do it again," the little girl said. Had Stella had her gun she would have shot at the blanket and then turned the gun on herself if she wasn't dead already.

"No. This isn't real. This is a breakdown. I fell through the floor and this is a break..." Stella gasped. She'd fallen through the floor yet there was no light from the ceiling. When she shined the flashlight up quickly, she saw a regular ceiling of an old building with copper pipes and electrical cords crossing back and forth. Before it could move Stella flipped the light back on the blanket.

"I won't do it again," the blanket whimpered. Stella took a deep breath. She wasn't in the cabin anymore. She had no idea where she was, but she wasn't alone.

"Do what?" she snapped, not completely sure she wasn't having a conversation with herself and this was just some kind of hallucination. "Do what again? Huh? What aren't you going to do again?" Stella felt tears fill her eyes.

"I won't wet myself again," the little voice said.

Suddenly, Stella froze. It wasn't herself under that blanket. She wasn't seeing a hellish vision or being tricked by a shape-shifting monster. There was a child under there, hiding the only way she knew how. Thinking that the monster won't get her if she's under the blankets.

Chapter 40

The address for Wes Tyler in Chicago was an apartment building in Andersonville on Chicago's north side. Just in case he was home Ben didn't want to alert him. He and a backup squad car had to race to the scene with the flow of traffic. He prayed that

Wes would be there, maybe packing. Maybe getting ready to make a break for Vandalia tonight or tomorrow and Ben would catch up with him *just in time*. Stranger things had happened, right? It wasn't beyond the realm of possibility that he'd caught up with him before he could hurt anyone else. Before he could hurt Stella

But something in Ben's gut told him not to get his hopes up. As he pulled up to 6000 N. Ashland Avenue which butted the corner of Peterson Avenue all he had to do was look down three buildings on the north side of the street to see the one he was looking for.

It was a classic brownstone complex with a courtyard and was home to maybe a total of twelve to sixteen units. Ben pulled up in front of the place and had radioed the squad car to go around back to cover the fire escape and back exit.

"It's a good chance our guy might be armed and he is definitely dangerous. I want him alive, but we don't always get what we want. You guys be careful back there," Ben said before he got out of his car and walked up to the front door. As he approached two women were exiting the building and he stopped them, holding up his badge. He asked if either one of them knew Wes Tyler.

"Uh, yeah," One of the women with a long scarf wrapped around her neck half a dozen times replied as she jerked her thumb toward her friend who wore huge hoop earrings. "I do. She doesn't live here but she knows about him too."

"What can you tell me?" Ben asked making sure to keep the door to the building open.

"Just that he's a jerk. One time I was coming in with my arms full of groceries and yelled for him to hold the door, please. I even said please," the scarf girl said. "Not only did he not hold the door, but he pulled it shut just as I got up to it and laughed.

"Yeah, and remember that time he was sitting on the

stairwell?" Hoop earrings added.

"Right. One time I was taking the stairs instead of the elevator because it's usually quicker and he's on the stairs, sitting there crying and he won't get out of the way. I tried to go around him, and he just moved to block the way so I ended up taking the elevator to the second floor."

"Has he acted like this to anyone else?" Ben asked.

"I don't know. I don't really mingle with anyone because I'm afraid I'll find out they're all weirdoes like him. I might be the only normal one out of the bunch," Scarf girl chuckled.

"And that would be bad in itself," hoop earrings teased her friend making them both chuckle before Ben thanked them for their time.

"Has he done something?" Scarf girl asked.

"I'm not sure," Ben replied honestly as he walked into the lobby then hurried up the stairs to the fourth floor. Wes was in apartment 404. As he walked down the carpeted hallway, he listened for any noises coming from any other apartments. A television murmured from one at the end and there were quiet voices from another. But other than that, it was calm. Once he reached 404 Ben put his hand over the peephole and pressed his ear against the door. He strained to hear the sound of shuffling feet, of moving boxes, of anything to indicate there was a person on the other side of this door and that he'd gotten there in time. But there was nothing. A tomb made more racket than that apartment.

Ben knocked loudly. He called out Wes's name and announced he was police. When he still heard nothing, he jiggled the doorknob but of course, it was locked. Taking a step back, Ben took a deep breath, and with all his might kicked the door. The simple apartment locks flew apart as the door jamb shattered and the door fell open. A tingling sensation ran up his leg. Ben was sure he was going to feel it tomorrow and might be walking with a limp. With his weapon drawn in one hand and his flashlight in the other Ben walked into the apartment.

He wasn't sure what he'd expected to see. Maybe satanic symbols all over the place. Garbage and bottles of human waste maybe. But he didn't. After he snapped on the lights, he realized the place was scarcely furnished. The man who lived here obviously wasn't planning on staying forever. There was a plastic patio chair next to a card table. There was no television but there was a battery-operated radio on the floor by the window. *You get better reception that way,* Ben thought.

The kitchen had an unused package of paper plates on the counter and a couple of empty cans of kidney beans. Of course, there were. Stella would be retching right now if she'd seen those along the counter. Just then, Ben's radio went off making him jump. He pulled it from his belt and spoke.

"Looks like we missed him," he said into the small black box. "Come on up. I'll need forensics."

"Roger. Over and out," came the uniformed officer's reply. Ben put the radio back on his hip and continued to look through the apartment. The living room and kitchen held nothing of importance except things only Ben and Stella would understand. There was twine that matched the stuff in Wes' desk as well as what was on the victims. And the guy's obsession with rosebuds spread to his home as well as a few were scattered about randomly.

When Ben stepped into the bedroom, he found the nightmare he was looking for. There was no door on the hinges. It was wide open. Ben found the light switch and the first thing he saw when the room brightened was the picture of Stella on the wall. It had been taken outside. She wasn't posing or smiling for the camera. Her image had been snapped without her permission.

If there had just been one picture Ben would have felt a

little better. Or at least as better as he could feel in this situation. But there wasn't. There were pictures of Stella everywhere. And not just pictures of her in snapshots. They were attached to things. There were a dozen little dolls with her face taped onto them. Those horrible, oversexed dolls they make for little girls where they are painted up like whores and wear slutty clothes, those kinds of dolls had Stella's face attached to them. They were posed obscenely along the floor in front of an air mattress.

Again, Ben jumped when he saw the mattress as it was covered with several blankets and looked to have someone still in it. Cocking his gun and holding it toward the mass Ben kicked the mattress with his foot. It didn't feel heavy. Wouldn't it feel heavy if there was a body in it? Ben kicked it again and it slid a couple of inches across the floor. Carefully, he grabbed hold of the blanket and mustering up his strength and courage, bracing himself for whatever he might see, he gave the blankets a yank.

Chapter 41

For a minute, Stella was afraid to approach the girl. What if it was a trap? But then her police instincts took over. Stella pushed the pain in the back of her head aside and crawled over to the mass under the blanket. When she put her hand on it, the little girl winced and began to sob.

"Hey, it's okay," Stella whispered as she patted the blanket and felt the girl tremble underneath. "It's okay. I'm here to help. I'm a police officer."

Those words gave Stella courage. She was a police officer and already she'd gotten her hands in front of her. Already she'd assessed the area. Yes, she was a police officer. But damn the memories of when she was here the first time and had prayed and prayed for someone to help her.

And they did, she heard the words inside and outside of her head like they were whispered to her by a Guardian Angel. Maybe it was just her conscience. Maybe God had sent an angel or two to help them in this hell. Stella didn't care. Somehow the police got to her and now she was here for this child.

The girl let out a whimper as Stella slowly pulled the blanket away. When she looked down at the little girl's face, Stella had to hold back her tears. He'd beaten her.

"What's your name, honey?" Stella asked quietly.

"Marie," she whispered.

"Okay, Marie. You've been brave. I can tell. I'm going to need you to keep being brave, okay? We're going to get out of here together," Stella whispered as she tried to assess the girl's injuries by the light of the flashlight.

Marie nodded her head, her brown hair falling in her face. When she raised her hand to wipe the dirty strands from her eyes Stella saw her knuckles were bloodied and dirty. She'd been banging on something, maybe a car trunk, maybe the door to this place.

"Do you know where you live?" Stella asked quietly and received a nod in reply. "Do you know what it looks like upstairs?" Stella continued but the girl shook her head.

Stella shined the light around and it was apparent they were in a basement. They were nowhere near the cabin she'd been in and that gave Stella hope that maybe someone had seen *him* taking her unconscious body and putting it into or taking it out of a car. The realistic part of her that knew she couldn't sit around waiting for a maybe.

She was startled when a heater kicked on making a rumbling hum and a blue flame burst to life becoming orange and yellow but it chased some of the chill out of the room. Stella looked around the room and saw a water heater, crusted with flaking calcium around the emergency valve. Across from those, tucked in a corner was the water softener and the circuit-breaker box. Stella wondered if disabling the lights might do something.

As she continued to shine the light around, she saw stacks of blankets in a box. Useless. A metal shelf stood proudly against the wall with a couple of paint cans on it. Also, useless. A folded wheelchair was leaning against it. Who that belonged to Stella couldn't imagine and didn't care. At the bottom of the stairs were over a dozen cans of kidney beans. It didn't make Stella nauseous this time. It made her mad. If he thought he was going to spoon-feed her that crap he had another thing coming.

Still, this wasn't a regular basement. It had the four walls, the exposed water and electric pipes but he had this place set up just like it had been when Stella was in it all those years ago. No washer and dryer. No extra freezer like many people keep in order to stock up when a bad snap of cold weather hits the Midwest in

January. But there was a mattress in the corner. Stella's stomach folded over on itself. What if he'd done more than beat Marie? She was only about nine years old. He was reliving what he'd almost done to Stella.

But he *was dead! Shot by police at the scene! That happened! That was real!* Stella was screaming in her head as she looked around for a way out of their prison cell. There was nothing. No windows, the walls were cinder block. There was only one way in or out and that was up the stairs.

As soon as Stella shined the light on them, she saw a ghoulish familiar face grinning down at her. Wes Tyler. Also known as Henry Budrene! The son of John Budrene! The man who had abducted Stella when she was a little girl.

He gripped the wooden banister and pushed his head through it in a grotesque maneuver that made his neck look elongated as his shoulders bunched up around his ears. He began to laugh quietly like he was amused at the scene playing out. Two girls thinking they could get away from him. Isn't that cute? Isn't that just what silly girls would think? Then he stopped laughing and Stella didn't have to be close to him to see what was burning behind his eyes. He flicked his tongue in and out like a snake. Stella was afraid.

She remembered back when she was a rookie, to a bust she made of a man who had diddled the best friend of his ten-year-old daughter. When he was sitting at the station in the holding tank, she watched him as she filled out her paperwork. Within minutes he was whispering to another person about what he'd done and how it wasn't his fault. His newfound pal was completely sympathetic telling him girls can't be trusted. They all want it. When he saw Stella staring at them, listening to the conversation with a look of disgust on her face, the father who had been busted made that same gesture with his tongue.

"Save your stories, gentlemen," Stella remembered saying to hide the fact that obscene gesture made her uneasy. "You know the big guys where you are going just love kiddie-diddlers."

That comment sobered them up for a while. But Stella knew they were just like the rest of the pervs she was going to encounter with a future in Vice. And now here she was in a basement, without a set of bars keeping her safe, without a dozen random uniformed officers ready to jump in, without her weapon. She was alone except for a little girl who was relying on her to get her home safe.

"You like when I do that, don't you?" Henry asked as he continued his obscene performance. Stella knew right there she wasn't just dealing with a killer. There was something much more wrong with Henry Budrene.

Chapter 42

Ben stood over the inflatable mattress, staring with disgust at what was under the covers. A cheap, plastic blow-up doll with a satin ribbon sash that read Bride across its body and a picture of Stella taped to its face stared back at him. When the two other policemen came into the room, they had the same reaction.

"If I hear any wisecracks about this in the bullpen or anywhere, I'll personally make sure you'll be pounding the beat in West Englewood," Ben said.

Both officers nodded and they knew better than to test Ben's patience. Everyone knew he stuck up for Stella and everyone wished they had a partner on the job like him. He was a good cop. But right now, underneath his calm, controlled anger he was flipping out. Stella wasn't answering her phone. The sheriff of the town of Vandalia wasn't answering his phone. What kind of police chief did that? The whole thing had Ben in knots.

One of the officers, a good cop by the name of Orwell cleared his throat loudly and said, "Detective, did you see this?"

"What is it, Orwell?" Ben said before covering up the blow-up doll and turning around. The closet door was open. The door itself, the interior walls were covered with pornographic pictures that each had a picture of Stella's face taped or glued on. But, as if that wasn't bad enough, there were also gruesome pictures of dead bodies. They looked to Ben to be from horror magazines. Bloody female bodies each of them with Stella's face taped to them.

Was this what he wanted to do to her? Was this his goal? Ben ordered Orwell to get forensics up here.

"I want fingerprints. Check the bathroom for hair samples. I'm sure that mattress has enough DNA on it to clone the man. We need to get all this collected, bagged and tagged." Ben said. He took out his phone and tried Stella one more time. As soon as her voicemail kicked in his stomach sank even lower. What was he going to do if she didn't get out of this? How was he going to explain it to...who? Cole? Stella's funny neighbor with the cat he'd heard so much about over the years? Ben was the only family Stella had and right now he felt the real pain that comes with being worried about family. He always knew Rochelle and the baby were safe when he was gone. Always. Family was always with her. He never worried about her. But now, like a father whose daughter wasn't home when she was supposed to be, each minute Stella couldn't be reached dug into him like a thorn and his concern quickly turned to fear.

The more they searched around Wes Tyler/Henry Budrene's apartment the more apparent his obsession with Stella became. Aside from the pictures and the doll, there were notebooks in the bathroom of letters he'd never sent to her. He had pictures of her coming out of her apartment. He knew where she lived.

"Why the big production?" Ben muttered. "What was all the fanfare for?"

And then, as if to answer that question, Ben was handed a notebook that read "Honeymoon Destination."

"This guy was really off his rocker," another uniformed officer said as he handed the notebook to Ben.

"Yeah, love will do that to a guy," Ben replied and took the notebook. It was Henry's playbook. In it, he described the time he spent cultivating the friendship with Regina Phelps at the DCFS office. She was really the key to it all. The way Henry would eventually get Stella in Vandalia where he wanted her, alone and away from the city.

There were crude drawings of Regina, nothing more than a stick figure with long hair and a smiley face. He'd written her name above and wrote his method of luring her to the Washington

Motel.

"He told us Regina had never mentioned any new boyfriend. That's because he invited her to Vandalia. He wooed her. Got her to trust him at work. Dammit, when we were questioning him, he knew exactly who we were and why we were there," Ben scowled as his officers went about their job of collecting everything from the apartment. "Regina's murder would tie Stella to the case. He knew it was our jurisdiction. He knew he'd get her down there and that's exactly what he did. Here, he jokes about how violent he had to be in order to make it an interesting case for her. He wanted Stella to be really, really interested. The other murders, were just...fluff."

Ben kept reading Henry's descriptions. The writings of this madman had the entire scene planned long before the first body was even found. The women he killed were just unlucky. They were the canvases on which Henry Budrene depicted his love and dedication to Stella. They were unfortunate women in the wrong places at the wrong time. Sadly, only Regina Phelps was intentionally manipulated and led to her death in search of a possible relationship. The others were victims of opportunity.

There was no use waiting any longer. The scene at the apartment would be handled by the book. Ben called Captain Briggs and gave him a quick synopsis of the situation. Then came the hard part.

"She's not answering her phone," Ben said.

There was silence on the other end of the line. Ben prayed Briggs wasn't contemplating taking him off the case and sending someone else down there to clean up the mess. The fact that once again Stella had been correct when she suspected that this whole thing had been orchestrated with her in mind was a hard pill to swallow. Hell, it was downright unreal. What kind of lunatic goes off on this kind of quest to get a girl?

"I'll call the State PD down there. They'll arrive sooner than you will. Get going, Ben. She'll need to see a familiar face when all this is finished. How long does it take to get down there?" Briggs asked.

"About five hours under normal circumstances," Ben replied.

"Then get an escort. Make it two. Bring her back, Ben," Captain Briggs said. Before he'd even hung up, Ben was in his car. Three units would get him to Joliet and Interstate 80 with lights flashing and sirens blaring. From there, state troopers would take over and finish the rest of the journey to Vandalia. With his light on the dash and a State Trooper in front of him, he raced through the red lights, stopping traffic, honking his horn all in an attempt to get one foot closer to his destination that much faster.

Along the way, Ben made one last call. It was Stella's last best hope.

Chapter 43

"Wes. Or is it Henry? I think you'd prefer to be known as Henry. You are your father's son." Stella between clenched teeth. Without thinking Stella pushed Marie behind her and got to her feet. She hoped it would stop her voice from shaking.

He didn't reply but continued to grin at her as he flipped a light switch that gave the stairs a sickly yellow glow then slowly moved down the stairs like a spider delicately maneuvering its web.

Maria grabbed the blanket and ran to a corner of the room hiding as best she could. Stella was not going to let her get hurt. And she wasn't going to get hurt herself either. She had to just focus, remember her training, and try to outsmart the man who had her bested for the past several days.

"I think you were trying to get my attention, right?" Stella said. "You don't have to talk. I know that all this was for me. The twine. The rosebuds. The *beans*. You were letting me know you were out there.

"You haven't changed," he said, staring at Stella like a man dying of thirst might look at a glass of water.

"No? Why don't we talk about it?" Stella took a slow step closer.

"You'd like to talk? To me?" Henry asked, his face never dropping the grimace even when he spoke. There was something strange about his voice. It sounded greasy like it was coming from far down his throat as if maybe there was something else there making him talk. Of course, it was only Henry. The child of the monster who had kidnapped Stella when she was young. But as she reminded herself of this fact, as if she could ever forget, the terrifying thought that he was his father's son gripped her heart.

The apples don't fall far from the tree, she supposed.

"Yeah. I want to know what made you go through all this trouble," she replied as calmly as possible.

"Wasn't any trouble. No trouble at all," Henry kept coming down the stairs. When he got to the bottom, he stood up straight. Stella hadn't realized when she first saw him sitting in his chair at the DCFS office that he was so tall. He had to be at least a foot maybe even eighteen inches taller than her. Without her gun or the element of surprise, she was in a tight pickle.

"So why don't we let Marie go. You did all this for me and I'm dying to know why. We don't need her here, do we?" Stella didn't move. She stared into Henry's eyes and saw a beast staring back at her. He was starting to sweat, his cheeks as flushed as the rest of him was pale. As if he hadn't slept in days, his eyes peeked out from dark caverns made all the more menacing by the lighting in this dungeon. His clothes, black cargo pants with a gray button-down shirt were wrinkled. His boots looked like they were military issue and added at least two inches to his stature.

"She can't go. She's for my father. You don't really remember me, do you? You don't really remember what happened between us," Henry hissed, then licked his lips.

What the hell did he mean Marie was for his father? Stella looked nervously around the room. There was no one else here was there? Could it be his decomposed corpse had somehow managed to claw and scrape its way out of hell and out of his grave to nestle between the rafters or inside the insulation only to emerge at a time like this? *No, Stella! He was dead. How many times do you have to go over this?*

"Your father is dead, Henry. He was killed by police on the night I was rescued. Shot over five times. It was in the papers and on the news," Stella said.

"Oh, no. He's here," Henry nodded.

Stella stared at him. "Where is he?" she asked with her voice coming out as barely a whisper. She'd lost her ability to speak, to think, to reason when Henry said his father was there. Had she been lied to all this time?

"He'll show up. He told me I could have my fun with you first," Henry took a step closer to Stella and began sniffing the air. "You smell so good. You don't have to pretend anymore, Stella. I know you had to play your game, to make sure I noticed you. I'd been searching for you for a long time. But I never lost hope."

"Well, nothing is going to happen with *us* until you let Marie go," Stella snapped.

The sadistic grin fell from Henry's face. "I can't do that," he growled.

"Sure you can. Just step aside and let her go. She'll find her way somewhere," Stella said casually as if it was the easiest thing in the world to do. If she didn't get riled up maybe Henry would stay calm too. But it didn't appear to be working.

"I can't do that because she's for my father," Henry said almost bashfully.

"What?"

"He doesn't like girls your age. See, and that's fine. That's why this is so perfect. See, you and I, we've already solidified our relationship. He doesn't want you anymore. You're all mine. You don't have to worry about my dad like last time," Henry said as if all this made perfect sense.

"Worry about your dad doing what?" Stella prodded.

Henry shifted from one foot to the other. He looked Stella up and down like this discussion was doing nothing but getting in the way, yet he had to answer. He had to make things clear and Stella was sure that if she could keep him talking, she could get Marie out of there.

"He promised you were for me. Not like those other little girls. He took them for himself. But you were for me. He promised. He told me that you and I could be together forever, and he'd never touch you. That's a pretty big sacrifice for a man to make to his son," Henry beamed. But there was an anger there, too, and it was starting to bubble up. "So, the least I could do was give him his own play-thing."

"P-play thing?" Stella stuttered.

Henry pointed behind her at Marie who was under the blankets again, dreaming of her own room, her own toys, warm in her own bed with her mother and father just a shout away. Stella knew that's what Marie was thinking because she'd been there in that exact spot. Stella especially remembered wanting a slice of chocolate cake. No more beans. Never again.

"Yeah, so he won't touch you. You're mine. My bride-to-be. We are to be one, Stella. And if you don't want to, if you are feeling like a headache is coming on, then I'll have to make do with her. I thought she looked like you did when you were her age. That's why I picked her. It would be like traveling back in time to our special place in the foster home." Henry smiled.

"So, if that's all this is about, why did four women have to die?" Stella asked. She was looking at the face of insanity. There was nothing she could say or do that Henry was going to understand as real or helpful or true. He was as nutty as his father. The apples *don't* fall far from the tree.

"Did you like that?" Henry asked.

"No. No, I didn't." Stella replied. But it didn't seem to bother Henry that she wasn't impressed by his decision to commit murder for her. "Typical guy overshooting his load on the first try. But I'll tell you what, you can make it up to me by letting the little girl go. That's very fair and then you and I can get down to business."

271

"She can't go because she's for my dad. And he'll be home soon, so you and I need to move things along," Henry took two long strides, but Stella backed up and put her hands up. "Dammit, Stella! Don't you remember what we are here to do?"

"Sure, I do. But I don't want to talk about it with a child in the room. Let Marie go at least upstairs to watch television. She's really just in the way," Stella hoped the child understood what she was trying to do. She didn't want to turn around and give Henry any kind of hint that she cared more about Marie than anything else. So, she didn't look at the poor girl. She couldn't.

"No. You don't remember. Oh my God," Henry panted. "It will be like the first time all over again." He rubbed his thighs like he was getting ready to pounce on her right there. Those words made Stella's heart turn into a block of ice in her chest. Was there something deep in her past that she'd pushed so far down it hadn't come out with the other memories? Something so disgusting and vile that she refused to dig it up. What would happen if she remembered?

"What are you talking about?" Stella asked, breathy and nervous.

"Us. You and me. Stella, I knew once you saw me again, you'd remember. My father had picked you out for me and he'd be so happy to know that we found each other after all this time. Now we can pick up where we left off," Henry took a step closer as his gaze groped over Stella's body.

"Where did we leave off?" Stella was afraid to know.

"At the foster home. Remember now? I was placed in the same home as you for a short time. We talked. You told me you wanted to be with me. That nothing could keep us apart. Don't you remember what we did in the spare room? Alone?" Henry's eyes danced sadistically, and she couldn't be sure because of the lighting but something made a long thin line from the bottom of his lip to the floor. It looked like drool.

Stella was breathing as if she was walking uphill. She searched her memory and there was nothing there. She did remember being in foster care and a new boy being brought in for just a few days before he was transferred. Like her own thoughts were going to back her against a wall Stella waited for the horrific memory Henry was talking about to surface. But it didn't.

"What did we do?" Stella was afraid to ask.

"The same thing you told me you wanted to do when I saw you walking down the street two weeks ago," Henry replied confidently. "I was walking behind you and you were with your partner, teasing me, talking about going on some date to try and make me jealous."

Stella's mouth fell open as she listened.

"I knew it was a game. It wasn't a very nice game, but I knew you were just playing. Especially when you flipped your hair back. You know, your signal that you know I'm there and that you are just teasing me. Oh, but the time for teasing is over," Henry took a step closer. He was standing just three long strides from her.

Stella began to tremble. There was no memory, repressed or otherwise, of her ever doing anything with Henry. But that didn't matter. In his mind, they were intimately involved and no amount of arguing or pleading was going to convince him otherwise.

"Let Maria go. Please?" Stella asked. "You don't have any need for her."

"She's here for my father," Henry repeated as he took another step closer, rubbed his hands together, and cracked his knuckles. It made Stella's stomach churn.

"Your father is dead," she snapped.

"I'm tired of waiting. We're together and if we don't hurry

Dad is going to come home and then we'll have to wait," Henry said like he was telling her the timer was about to go off on a ticking bomb. "You've been promising! You can't go back on your promises!"

"Promising?" Stella was trying to make sense of insanity. Nothing Henry was saying was in this reality. Sooner or later arguing wasn't going to mean anything and Stella was going to have to fight, not just for her life but for Marie's as well.

"No! No! See, now you've done it! Now you wasted too much time and he's home!" Henry winced and for a minute Stella thought he was going to cry. "Maybe it's better this way. He has a way with women. He certainly had every one of them eating out of the palm of his hand before he killed them. He'll convince you, too. You'll just have to wait until he's done with her." Henry jerked his thumb toward Marie in the corner before he turned and headed back upstairs. Then she heard the door lock from the outside. For the first time, Stella was afraid she wasn't going to make it out of this. But If she could get Marie out, or at least give her a chance, she'd stay and take her licks.

"Marie, honey," Stella dashed to the little girl who was cowering beneath the blankets. "Okay, time to be really brave. I want you to go hide underneath the stairs. When the bad man comes down, I'll distract him, you run up the stairs and find a way out. Okay?"

"I'm scared," she cried.

"It's okay to be scared. It means you're smart, too. So, when you run up those stairs, be smart, and find a way out, okay?" Stella hated the plan. It was paper-thin at best. If Henry had some dude parading around like his father, messing with his head while making him an accomplice to all this murder, it was going to be twice as hard to get anything past them. But Marie nodded and even if Stella thought it was a shitty plan, it was better than nothing. Quickly, Marie scurried behind the stairwell. Stella grabbed some of the blankets and covered them with the blanket

Marie had been under. It looked like she hadn't moved.

"Good enough," Stella mumbled. But before she could give Marie any more words of encouragement, the door leading upstairs opened. As Stella watched something in her mind wouldn't click into place. Henry's dad was dead. So, who the fuck was this coming down here to rape a little girl? Who was Stella supposed to be so afraid of? Then she saw him and realized she was in bigger trouble than she ever imagined.

Chapter 44

"So, you're the little girl who got away," the man said as he came down the steps. Stella didn't want to see his face. She didn't want to see that it was decomposing and rotten with worms in his eye sockets and his skin peeling away. John Budrene was dead. He had seven bullet holes in his chest. Who the fuck was this? He pounded down the steps, and each one made the entire house shake. In the horrible yellow light over the stairs, Stella saw the same pair of black cargo pants and boots descending the steps that she'd seen before. Did they dress alike? Another symptom of the crazy that had been passed from father to son?

Of course, they aren't dressing alike, Stella. Because they are the same person. The voice in her head was so crystal clear that Stella almost wanted to laugh. But it was true. Henry appeared at the bottom of the steps and although his expression had changed, everything else about him was the same. He was much more confident, or maybe the word was cocky. He looked Stella up and down and wrinkled his nose as if the sight of her disgusted him. She preferred it to his previous ogling.

"You're what has my son all torqued up. Yeah, I guess I can see it," Henry said in a deeper more sinister voice. "But you ain't my type. Where is she?"

"What are you talking about?" Stella had to play this game, to make believe that she was really talking with two people when the insane reality was there were two occupying Henry's mind and neither one of them deserved any sympathy or kindness. They were both monsters.

The ghost of John Budrene occupying Henry's body marched up to Stella and slapped her so hard across the face she fell to the floor. Her entire body was shaking, and her teeth felt like they were rattling in her head. All sound was muffled for a few minutes but came back with John shouting at her.

"You know what I'm talking about. My boy got me a tasty little morsel and after a hard day staying scarce and away from the police I deserve to treat myself," He grabbed Stella by the hair, raising her to her feet, he hands still bound in front of her, a fact that had escaped Henry and John. "Now, where is she?"

Stella didn't say a word but looked nervously toward the pile of blankets in the corner. John grinned through Henry's face as he dropped Stella again where she crumpled to the ground. Quickly, she looked with eyes wide and desperate toward the stairs. Marie had done what she was told. Just as John yanked the covers back Marie ran up the stairs undetected. Stella let out a sigh of relief just as John turned and grabbed her by the scruff of the neck, yanking her to her feet.

"You tell me where she went or I'll make an example out of you," John hissed, his face just inches from hers. Stella did nothing. The thought of spitting in his face did cross her mind but the reality was she was in a pretty tight spot. No use making it worse. And although she was terrified, she felt a satisfaction that Marie had gotten away. Help might be on its way.

"What else can you do to me? Kill me? I'd welcome the vacation," Stella said. And in a scary way, she felt she was saying the truth. How long was she supposed to carry around the events of her past? They were heavy. She hadn't realized how heavy until this case stacked them all up in front of her. Hell, she'd had a good run and accomplished more to better the world than some people would ever do living to eighty-years-old. So, no she didn't want to die. But if she had to, she was ready.

"Oh, no. I won't kill you. Do you have any idea what my son wants to do to you?" the words cut into Stella's grand idea of dying with dignity. It wasn't going to happen. "You don't, do you. Typical cock-tease. Well, you'll be almost as good as new to him once I'm finished with you." With those last words, John shoved Stella with such force she fell face-first onto the old mattress on the floor. It barely cushioned her fall and she banged her nose on the dirt floor underneath it. Quickly, she rolled over onto her back just in time to see John diving for her.

Her hands, still bound by the zip-tie were easy for him to grab and hold over her head, out of the way.

"Dinner bell is ringing, boy! Come and get her!" John shouted. Stella stared up at him as if he began to melt or contort into something else. And in a way he did. John's face shifted. His cruel and heartless expression changed to the eager, sadistic grimace of Henry who was suddenly looking down at Stella like she'd just popped out of a cake for him.

"You'll see, Stella..." He pressed his lips to hers as she tried to pull away. But where could she go? Her head couldn't turn all the way around. She was disgusted and what was worse was that she was sure she could taste those wretched kidney beans on his breath. If she were to vomit, she'd choke on it.

"That's my girl," he panted as reached down to unbuckle his pants with one hand. "You won't fight every time. You'll get used to it."

Just as he was about to rip Stella's clothes right off her body while muttering obscenities he jerked and froze. At first, Stella wasn't sure what had happened but then she saw it. A can of kidney beans was rolling across the floor after it cracked into the side of Henry's head. Stella looked over him to see Marie standing on the bottom step with another can in her hands. What was she doing? Why hadn't she run out of the house!

"Marie! Run! Run!" Stella screamed only to be slapped again across the face. Her hearing went out again making everything sound like it was underwater. Henry tried to get up but was woozy from his head injury. Stella knew quite well how that felt. But when he turned and lumbered toward the girl, Stella jumped up. With her head swimming and her hands still bound she pushed him from behind but it did very little good, only making him angrier. Henry whirled around. Stella turned to get away from him but he grabbed her from behind, squeezing her so tightly she couldn't breathe. One of her ribs was going to break for sure as Henry held her tightly, taking her back to the mattress.

With the thought of her concussion, the pain in her wrists, and the inability to breathe, Stella leaned her head forward and with all her strength threw her head back right into Henry's nose. She heard a snap and then a howl. He dropped Stella with a thud to the floor where she tried to crawl away, but he was on top of her in a split second. She could feel the warm drops of blood from his nose hitting her back as he ripped her shirt.

Stella was not going to make it out of this. By the time Marie got any help and they made it back to the house, she'd be long dead. Her head was aching as she was sure she'd clobbered him right on the goose egg she'd gotten falling through the floor. Her hands were purple from lack of circulation. And now her clothes were being torn off her body. Where was that sweet blackness she'd been in after she fell through the floor? She wanted it again. Henry flipped her over onto her back. With one punch, he gave her the blackness she was hoping for.

Chapter 45

"It's all right, Stella. I've got you," Stella heard a male voice. But it wasn't Ben. Where was she? What had happened? "Don't worry, about a thing. You're going to be just fine. You just hang on to me now and I'll get you out of here. Boy, you city women are trouble."

She could only open her left eye and when she did everything was a blur. Blinking didn't help and instead caused her right eye to throb in pain. But when she felt the strong arms of someone scooping her up off the ground, she felt a strange sense of déjà vu.

"Gangway, fellas! Is the ambulance here?" the man shouted, his voice going over her head as it rested against his chest.

"It's just pulling up, Clarence!" Another officer shouted.

"Ok, Stella. The ambulance is here. You're going to be just fine. You hang on and I'll make sure they get you taken care of." It was Deputy Clarence Winger. He was the man carrying Stella upstairs out of the basement and through a house she didn't recognize. How embarrassing to have her clothes torn and her face bloodied. But once they were out of the house she felt the cool, fall evening air on her face, cooling the heat radiating from her eye. She was underneath a soft blanket, and no one saw the terrible state she'd been in.

"All right, guys. This is Detective Stella Carrigan. She's a cop from Chicago. She's been through a lot so please take care of her," Clarence instructed as he gently placed her on a stretcher that the EMTs had ready and waiting. Before he could leave Stella grabbed Clarence by the hand.

"Marie?" she croaked.

"The little girl?" Clarence stopped and looked down at Stella. His eyes had softened, and Stella was more than a little impressed with his bedside manner. He held her hand tightly and smiled as he leaned over. "She's fine. A little banged up. Like you. But no other damage," he winked letting Stella know she hadn't been raped by Henry.

"Deputy," Stella muttered. It felt like her lips were the side of semi-truck tires and her head was pounding even worse as the lights of the cop cars and ambulance swirled around and around. "Thank you." They were the only words she could get out before tears filled her eyes. She wasn't even sure why she was crying except that she'd almost been raped and was on her way to being tortured by a lunatic who thought they were meant to be together after an abduction when she was a child. Once the tears started Stella couldn't stop herself. She sniffled and then sobbed.

"Would you like me to ride with you to the hospital?" Clarence asked softly. Stella wasn't sure why, but at this moment there was no one she trusted more. She nodded her head yes. He yelled to another officer he was riding to the hospital. In just a few minutes the ambulance was speeding down the road, siren on and lights flashing.

"It won't take any time to get you to the hospital. You know, one time I got into a brawl at the Glass Tap with some drifter. Well, I wasn't on duty, mind you, and he'd had quite a bit more than me to drink. Cracked a beer bottle and tried to stab me with it. Well, I was able to step out of the way, but when he fell and dropped the bottle, I stepped on it, slipped, and ended up getting cut by that fucking thing. Except, I couldn't blame him for it," Clarence rambled on talking softly in between the questions from the EMTs and the keeping out of their way as they patched Stella up until she could get to the hospital for x-rays and such. All the while Clarence held Stella's hand, talking to her. He was almost as good a partner at this moment as Ben had been their whole time together. She hoped he was okay.

As if reading her mind Clarence squeezed her hand for a second. "Ben called me. He gave us the address of where he thought we could find you. He was right. He said quite a few things about the Department of Child and Family Services, too. Not very flattering things. But he's okay and he'll meet you at the hospital."

Stella nodded her head. The EMTs might have given her a shot of adrenaline or something because she was starting to shake the groggy feeling she'd had before. Still, she wasn't able to pry the other eye open, she blinked her good eye and was able to focus. Every word Clarence said made sense. Before she knew it, they were at the hospital.

"Okay, Stella. I'm going to leave you here. You're in good hands, okay? They'll fix you right up," Clarence said. Stella nodded her head and with puffy, painful lips thanked him and squeezed his hand tightly.

Stella had only been in an ambulance once before. When she was a kid and had been rescued from John Budrene by a gentle cop. It was like the procedure for rescues hadn't changed at all. She was okay with that. But one thing Stella didn't know was where Henry was. Had they apprehended him? Was he at the Vandalia police station? Clarence didn't mention him at all. When he'd picked her up Stella didn't even remember hearing anything that sounded like Henry or Miranda rights or anything.

Who knows how long you were out? They could have dusted the entire premises by the time you came around. Her thoughts were clear and rather rude. As Stella lay on the table in the emergency room under bright lights with a throbbing head, she was happy to be feeling more and more alert. Speaking of alert, she wiggled her fingers and moved her hands. There was an ache around her wrists, but she was free of the zip-ties. There was no immediate memory of them being removed but she was thankful they were.

Someone came in and asked Stella her full name, her

address, date of birth, and who the President of the United States was. They also wanted to know the date and how many fingers they were holding up. There was crazy talk about x-rays for a concussion and therapy for PTSD. But other than that Stella was to just stay in bed in the private room they'd assigned until the doctor gave her the all-clear to leave. She wasn't going anywhere tonight.

Later that night at around one in the morning, Stella was wide awake. She turned on the television keeping the volume barely above a murmur and settled on some crazy house hunting show for a couple of nuts who had over half a million to spend to find a house in Greece.

Her stomach growled and Stella realized she hadn't eaten all day. She rang for the nurse and within minutes a chubby lady who reminded Stella of Rose at the police station showed up.

"How are we doing, honey?" the woman in white pants and a navy blue scrub shirt asked as she looked at Stella's chart.

"I'm hungry. Any way I can get something to eat here at this hour?" Stella asked, hoping for a miracle but the nurse's pinched lips and slowly shaking head told her it was out of the question.

"The kitchen closes at seven. They are just cleaning up and will be getting ready for breakfast in just a couple hours," she replied. "There's a vending machine down at the end of the hall."

"Oh, great. I don't have my wallet, but I know my piece is around here somewhere maybe I can use bullets to get a Kit-Kat bar," Stella mumbled.

"I'm sorry but you aren't allowed in here with a weapon. Deputy Winger should have told you that and taken your weapon for you," the no-nonsense nurse said.

"Hey, the little girl that came in with me. Do you know how she is?" Stella asked.

"I don't know but I can check for you. What was her name?"

"Marie," Stella said.

"Do you have a last name?" This nurse was a real stickler for the details.

"No. But I can't imagine many little girls named Marie were brought to the emergency room after being abducted and suffering mental torture the past few days. Could you check for me?" Stella didn't mean to come across rude. She was just stating a fact. But the nurse's expression looked like her patience with Stella was running thin.

"And could you tell me if Henry Budrene is a patient?" Stella asked. The nurse let out a long sigh and shook her head.

"Now that you mention it, I won't be able to sleep all night. I have no idea where my gun is," Stella shrugged, swallowed, and smiled. "Do you know when I can get out of here?"

"Not tonight. The doctor will be in tomorrow and let you know. Would you like something to help you sleep?" the nurse asked. Stella shook her head. She didn't want to sleep. Not because she was afraid to but because she just wasn't tired. Plain and simple. In fact, she wanted to talk to someone, but the nurse was already out the door when she realized it was just a case of hungry and no emergency.

A strange feeling settled over Stella. She couldn't name it but something had shifted in the air and the light. Like she'd been putting off cleaning out a closet or a junk drawer and it was getting more and more intrusive and annoying until finally, she'd had enough. She dumped everything out, without sorting or analyzing a single element there but was just happy to be rid of it.

Dear God, had she somehow been waiting for Henry Budrene, too? Had she known somewhere deep inside that he was going to come looking for her?

"I don't think so," she soothed herself. The guy was a nut case and would probably end up in the Tinley Park Mental Facility for those deemed a threat to society. The signs all read don't pick up hitchhikers around that area.

She thought about Marie. What a little firecracker, that girl was. Coming back to chuck a can of beans at the bad guy.

"My sentiments exactly," Stella thought and smiled. But would Marie go through the same trauma, the same trials Stella had all those years ago? The nightmares she never told anyone about? The fear of being in a basement? Of course, the story behind the kidney beans was out of the bag now so no need to worry about explaining that one. The thought made her chuckle a little.

It took a little effort and struggling to find where all of her wires were connected but finally, Stella figured out what was attached to what and that nothing prevented her from getting out of bed. She flipped the covers back and gasped. She had bruises on her knees and thighs. But she wiggled her toes and could feel the cool air. She needed to shave her legs. How embarrassing.

With a few aches and pains, she slung her legs over the edge of the bed and stood up. The tile was cool beneath her feet. Her body smarted as if she overdid a workout.

"Didn't you?" she teased as she shuffled over to the window dragging behind her an IV drip like a skeleton with a water balloon head. With one yank she pulled the curtains open. Outside it was pitch dark except for the hospital parking lot. It was well lit and there were dozens of cars in the parking lot. People were pulling in and out. This was like the police station. It was never completely quiet. Even at nighttime.

Stella stood there for a long time feeling what she could only call a confusing state of relief. She wanted to be home in her own bed. The hospital was no place to recuperate. After a few minutes, she started to feel a chill and was about to head back to the bed when the no-nonsense nurse came back in.

"Why are you out of bed?"

"I just wanted to stretch my legs. I can't sleep. I don't want any pills. I'd really like a Big Mac with fries. You aren't going out for lunch, are you? I don't have any money on me, and my gun is missing but I can still provide a hearty handshake if you'd pick me up a meal deal," Stella asked but the nurse just shook her head. Stella shrugged.

"The girl you were asking about, Marie Bennet. She was released to her parents a couple of hours ago.

"That's good," Stella smiled. "That's good. Nothing was wrong with her?"
"I can't give out that information," the nurse replied.

"Yeah, yeah, sure. What about Henry Budrene?" Stella asked carefully as if the words might turn around and bite her.

"There was no one admitted by that name."

"What about a John Budrene? Sometimes he went by that name."

"Nope. There was no one admitted tonight the name Budrene," the nurse replied. "Now, how about you get back in the bed."

"I guess so. But I'm not tired and I'm going to be up all night. Hey, do you play cards? Maybe we could play a cut-throat game of go fish," Stella suggested.

"Come on, Stella. Let's get back into the bed. You'll be asleep before you know it," the nurse said. And she was right. Stella got back in the bed and caught another glimpse of the bruises on her legs. She was sure they'd gotten bigger and darker in the few minutes she was walking around. But once her head hit the pillow and the nurse had walked out of the room, she looked at the open curtain and saw the lights of an airplane fly across blinking red, white and green. She was asleep before it was out of view.

Chapter 46

"YOU? I thought you were the doctor," Stella barked at Ben who came into the room with a bouquet of flowers, a six-pack of beer, and a bag of McDonald's.

"I can take all this stuff and leave," Ben said.

"No! Get over here," Stella said, her hands stretched out like a little kid with her arms stretched out finally getting a present on Christmas morning. She took the McDonald's bag and groaned with happiness. Although she noticed Ben staring at her face, she made no mention of it. She hadn't even gone to a mirror yet to see the damage that had been done. Her eye was open a little more than it had been yesterday. Her lip still hurt but only if she bit down on it. Her head was a lumpy mess and she was sure when Henry yanked her by her hair, he gave a slight case of whiplash because her shoulders ached something terrible. But she wasn't going to let anyone know. What good would it do?

"I haven't even had breakfast yet. They are so slow in this hotel. The Open Plaines Motel had better service than this," She pulled out a couple of fries and shoved them in her mouth.

"The flowers are from Rochelle. She says get well soon," Ben said as he sat down on the bed, pulled the rolling table up to the side, grabbed one beer, and cracked it open for Stella then did the same for himself.

"Cheers," Stella said with a mouthful of fries. They both took a drink and let out long, satisfied sighs.

"So, once again you were right," Ben said with his head down looking at the top of his beer can before taking another sip.

"Right about what?" Stella asked.

"Right that this case had more to do with you than anything else," Ben said. "I'm sorry about this. I'm sorry I didn't believe it was what you said it was."

"Don't be sorry, Ben," Stella said after swallowing a mouthful. "It was that one in a million case where it was so farfetched it just couldn't be true. But it was. Look, I was trying to convince myself it wasn't about me too. For once, I was trying to say it wasn't about me."

They both chuckled. Stella took a sip of beer and groaned again. The salty bitter taste was perfect.

"I met the little girl, Marie," Ben said. "I had to take her statement. What a kid. She said that she watched true crime shows with her brother and that she learned if someone was trying to touch her private parts, she was to pee on herself. So she did."

Stella gaped with her mouth full. "She's 100% right."

"I know. She's one smart kid. She said you distracted Henry so she could get away," Ben said and helped himself to a couple of fries.

"That was the plan, but she came back," Stella shrugged.

"She ran upstairs when you told her to, and she was about to run out the door when she realized there was a phone. She called 9-1-1, told them there was a crazy man in the house, and let dispatch do the rest. She knew the cops would be coming so she opened the front door so the officers could get right in, left the phone off the hook so dispatch could trace it, and decided to get one good lick in for good measure. I'd just gotten off the phone with Deputy Winger. You can imagine his surprise when dispatch had just gotten a call about the same address." Ben shook his head. "It's like the stars all lined up in order last night."

"I wish I'd seen her chuck that can at Henry's head. She was dead on," Stella smiled.

"Yeah, she's the pitcher for the Vandalia Mavericks. Has been playing little league since she was five."

"Ha!" Stella shook her head and laughed. "Hell, Ben. Did I rescue her, or did she rescue me? I think Chicago PD ought to hire her on the spot."

They sat in silence for a few minutes. Stella happily ate her Big Mac and fries and sipped her beer totally planning on having another once this one was finished.

"He's dead, Stella. Gone for good," Ben said. "Deputy Winger was the first on the scene. He saw him over you on the ground. Told him to freeze. Henry charged him. Two shots were fired. One in the shoulder and one between the eyes."

Stella swallowed hard and took a sip of her beer with trembling lips. When she put it down the tears surfaced in her eyes and she couldn't stop them. She looked at Ben who took her hands in his and held them as she cried. She was relieved. That was what it was. She wasn't scared or sad. It was a wave of liberation that somehow she'd been waiting for even if she didn't know it.

"It was a mess down there, Ben. The two of them wrapped in one person," Stella sobbed. "We're lucky, Marie and I. Lucky we made it. But look at all the destruction he left behind."

"Stella, I'm not a preachy man, but let the dead bury the dead. You've got more important things to tend to," Ben said as he reached in his pocket and pulled out his note pad and a pen. "I'll need a statement. But take your time. We've got two more beers a piece to get through."

Stella sniffled and nodded her head while she finished her food. She started at the beginning with the cabins and just let the words fall out. She wanted the story out of her so it could be put to rest. She was done with John and Henry Budrene. The world was done with them.

Chapter 47

Once Stella was out in the cold air, she took a deep breath. The sound of the city was music to her ears. The smell of exhaust fumes, the sound of horns honking, the busy street on a Friday night, the taste of a dry martini, and anchovy olive still on the tip of her tongue.

"Would you like me to hail you a cab?" Cole asked.

"It's such a beautiful fall night. Would you like to walk with me a little? I don't feel like going home yet," Stella said.

"That would be nice," Cole replied.

"I'm so stuffed. I should have never had that cannoli for dessert," She rubbed her stomach. Tonight, she wore a casual pair of slacks with a tight sweater and a denim jacket out on her date with Cole. She'd called him about two days after she'd gotten back from Vandalia with a clean bill of health from the doctor at the hospital. Cole had been a real gentleman the entire night. He asked her a little bit about what had happened especially since she still had a shiner around her temple and her lip was still a little bruised.

"One time I got into a fight in high school. Those were the days when a fight in high school leveled the playing field and didn't result in lawsuits and therapy," Cole joked to which Stella smiled and nodded. "Anyway, when I got home, I told my dad. His suggestion to me was that if anyone was to ask what happened, answer with 'You should see the other guy'."

Stella laughed. She put her hand on Cole's hand and leaned in close to him

"That is so funny. I hate to tell you what happened to my other guy," Stella replied shaking her head. It wasn't that she thought Henry Budrene's death was funny. His death happened way back in that basement the first time around. All that had been walking the city was an empty shell, fixated on one thing. Poor Henry wasn't living. He was dreaming every day of something that consumed him and made him something else.

"Well, you can tell me about it when you feel like it. I'm just glad you're home safe," Cole said.

"You are?"

"Yeah. I've been waiting and I was sure that I was going to have to chase you down. I never suspected that you'd be the one calling me," he teased.

"It's not a big deal," Stella said.

"Sure it is. Do you know how envious the guys at work are that I've got the prettiest female cop in Chicago calling me to go out?" Cole lifted his chin and began to strut, making Stella chuckle.

"Prettiest female cop? Do you know any male cops that are prettier than me?" Stella teased back.

"Nope. No, I don't," Cole said slipping his hand around Stella's. Normally, she would have pulled her hand away and run it through her hair or fidgeted with her purse. This time she didn't. She liked Cole. He was funny and he was really handsome.

"You know we're coming up on the Twelve-to-Twelve gym," Stella said.

"What? You want to go in for a quick workout? I'm not really dressed and if you are going to try and run in those heels I don't think..." Cole started.

"No. I live just down the block from there. Would you walk me home?" Stella asked.

"Of course, I will."

At the door to her apartment, Stella told Cole what a good time she had. She was glad that Ben had convinced her to call him.

"So, how long are you on vacation?" Cole asked.

"I've got almost three months saved up but I'm just taking one more week after this," Stella said. "So, I'm off the weekend of course, and then all next week."

"Well, maybe you'd like to meet for breakfast tomorrow? I know a nice greasy spoon that has the best coffee in the city," Cole asked, still holding Stella's hand.

"Yeah. Okay," Before she could slip away from him and into her apartment building, Cole gently pulled Stella to him and kissed her tenderly on the lips.

"Did I hurt you?" he asked and pointed to the tender bruise still on her lip.

"No, Cole. You didn't hurt me at all," Stella replied with a smile.

THE END

Dear reader,

you are AWESOME! I hope you already knew that, but if not, know you do. And I mean this very seriously, because to me, you are exactly that: AWESOME.

Without passionate readers like you, who give indie authors a chance, it wouldn't be possible for us indies to do what we love doing most – writing. So thank you, thank you, thank you!

I really hope that you've liked my first full length novel. If you did – great! There's a lot more to come. I'm in the process of writing the sequel to his one and I'm having an absolute blast!

I will send a notification as soon the book is done. If you are interested in becoming a beta reader, you will definitely get the chance!

If you want to reach out to me for feedback, inquiries or any other kind of message, just send a mail to: lisakentbooks@gmail.com

I promise to reply to each mail personally.

Thanks again for being you!

With love,

Lisa

Made in the USA
Coppell, TX
14 October 2021